Waiting for
Al Gore

Bob Katz

Flexible Press
Minneapolis, Minnesota, 2024

Print ISBN: 979-8-9887213-2-1
eBook ISBN: 979-8-9887213-3-8

Flexible Press LLC
Minneapolis, Minnesota
www.flexiblepub.com
Editors William E Burleson
Vicki Adang, Mark My Words Editorial Services, LLC

Waiting for
Al Gore

Bob Katz

Prologue

THE BEST WAY to observe the enigmatic Oswald's thrush in the days when it winged freely across Northern Hemisphere skies was to act like, and truly *feel like*, you hardly cared whether it showed itself or not. The bird, so it was said, had a nearly telepathic capacity to intuit the desire among human beings to ogle its elegant cobalt blue and burnt orange feathering. The comparison often made—until neofeminist values rerouted such points of reference—was to the acute sixth sense many women have for detecting the leering stares of horny men, even when those men are hidden from view or pretending to look the other way. The Oswald's radar system was, according to legend, so finely calibrated that it could detect even a single curious hiker casually scanning the treetops, let alone a whole pack of dedicated birders. Then, literally in the blink of an eye, the creature would be gone.

If one wished to observe the bird in its natural habitat, the green valleys of central Vermont during the milder months or various eastern Caribbean islands in the winter, it was recommended that one assume a pose that conveyed utter disinterest. In the bird-watching literature of the period during which Oswald's thrush was most popular—that is, when sightings were coveted yet not impossibly rare—the analogy embraced by bird aficionados was to the deft gamesmanship involved in applying to a bank for a small-business loan: The applicant must appear to be so prosperous and financially secure that the loan hardly seemed needed.

Upon becoming designated officially extinct in the mid-1990s, the Oswald's thrush began a second career as myth and pop culture artifact. It launched with the peppy, lilting, Calypso-inflected radio tune that soared to number four on the Billboard Hot 100 chart, "Two Birds, One Stone." Whoosh, the Rastafarian albino singer-songwriter behind the hit, explained that the repetitive three-note structure of the tune was inspired by the thrush's mating call, which he'd been privileged to hear in the highlands of his native St. Lucia. Whoosh reputedly donated a portion of his royalties to a short-lived, failed campaign to preserve the bird's nesting grounds.

The bird lived on in the form of a phenomenally successful poster and best-selling T-shirt. Illustrator Maxfield Chung created the iconic depiction of the gallant thrush perched in the hazy uppermost branches of a cloud forest, posed like Washington at Valley Forge. The image's aesthetic style was a kind of tongue-in-cheek photo-realism, conveying bombast while slyly winking at it. Like Whoosh's jingle, this image was deviously catchy and wildly popular.

Cute, quirky, free-spirited, pure of heart, noble of purpose, bizarrely telepathic, and, yes, sadly gone. That, in a nutshell, is the story of the Oswald's thrush.

But our story doesn't end there. It might not have ended yet.

<h1>One</h1>

IT HAD BEEN a dry spell for Lenny Beibel, freelance journalist and environmental blogger, yet he still harbored hopes of Pulitzer-worthy investigative reports and blockbuster book deals. Increasingly, these hopes needed to be jump-started with either a stiff belt (current preference Cuervo Especial, eighty proof) or a few lung-bursting tokes. Then, just maybe, he'd be able to push on despite all the unpleasantness about a shrinking media market and the dwindling suitability of his skill set.

Beibel's father, a tax attorney, had begged him to go to law school and berated him for his refusal to consider it. Law school, then and now, struck Lenny as a near-death proposition, and a legal career, at least the kind of career he'd wind up with, loomed as a gloomy purgatory. That's how the young and headstrong Lenny Beibel, infatuated with Tom Wolfe and Joan Didion and the expansive ambitions of the so-called New Journalism, once viewed the practical pursuit of conventional vocational opportunities. He was older now, if not yet technically old.

So it was with a decidedly downsized set of aspirations that Beibel found himself driving northward one fine morning. His 2002 Corolla had nearly 200,000 miles and was showing its age. A spiffy white when he bought it new, the car was now the color of curdled milk, save for the rust pocks speckling the dented hood. Still, it was capable of hitting sixty, or sixty-five on the downhill. From Somerville, Massachusetts, to central Vermont, depending on traffic, it should be no more than three hours. Beibel definitely had three hours to spare. Or three weeks. Or three months, if he was honest with himself.

His assignment was to write a series of web posts that ideally might be expanded to article length about the notoriously quirky environmental group, EarthKare. They were headquartered in a remote valley of the Green Mountains and would soon be hosting an international conference of global eco-activists. Depending on the caliber of experts presenting and the specifics of the action agenda that grew from the conference, it could be the sort of gathering that coughs up a few catchy sidebars and, with any luck, a worthy idea or two for future development. A rumor was circulating that no less a personage than Al Gore, former vice president and international environmental hero, was to deliver the conference keynote speech. That alone would guarantee a degree of newsworthiness.

EarthKare was not well known, and it was easy to guess why. Some of their positions, as gleaned from their website, struck Beibel as pretty loopy. And they had a reputation for picking ideological fights. They'd accused the esteemed Sierra Club of "recklessly overwatering" the concept of "green." They'd posted a controversial position paper contending that anyone advocating "sustainability" was, in effect, guilty of endorsing the status quo when radical change was the only viable course. They'd made a campaign of protesting shareholder meetings of financial service companies by handing out family variety packs of Johnson & Johnson Band-Aids to make their point about the pointlessness of eco-friendly investment funds. Beibel found it odd that Gore would be associated with such a group, although he allowed that a Nobel Laureate might have a superior grasp of the struggle ahead.

Beibel's strategy was to blog for several websites that claimed to respect his work. He'd get his gas mileage and food covered by a kindly family foundation that encouraged environmental reporting. Conference lodging was apparently cabins and tents at no charge. And if nothing else developed, if no news service picked up his dispatches, if no magazine editor gave him the go-ahead to write something more substantial, if no public radio outlet bit on his proposal to file colorful three-minute reports, if no podcast producer bought into the idea of tape-recording lengthy interviews with conference organizers, if no freak occurrence delivered the golden opportunity he continued to believe was just around the corner, he would at least break even financially. And perhaps get to pal around with Gore and his well-connected staff. There was consulting work to be had, so he'd heard, within the Gore network. White papers, speech writing, Twitter contributions. Not the kind of gigs that would do much to boost his brand, but paid gigs nonetheless.

Beibel's plan was to arrive in Vermont several days before the main event to conduct preconvention interviews and, more important, spend time hanging around the communards and encouraging the illusion they were getting to know him. The idea was to establish himself as the sort of reporter who really cared, even if he didn't. That's how the cunning Tom Wolfe allegedly operated.

Having phoned ahead to solidify his plans, Beibel was relieved to find EarthKare so receptive. He understood there was a pecking order when it came to news access and that he ranked somewhere near the bottom. Why would a group like EarthKare with its lofty ambitions open up to a Lenny Beibel? Sadly, he was fairly certain of the answer: High-status media outlets either ignored EarthKare altogether or, worse, were so clearly predisposed to scornful mockery that it would be an act of masochism for EarthKare to invite them in. He was, comparatively, better than nothing.

Beibel already knew what questions he'd pose to EarthKare: What did they hope to achieve? How did they assess the political landscape around their core concerns? Where did they see activism heading? And, of course, was there any hope? He understood this might be a paint-by-numbers exercise. So what? It was honest work. At least he'd not succumbed to becoming a lawyer.

The EarthKare staffer in charge of media relations was Frederick Wolfram. Gruff and dissembling, he enjoyed renown in radical eco-circles for being the co-author—with Rachel Seagrave, EarthKare's highly respected founder and public face—of the seminal book, *Pity the Trees*. That tome, initially developed as a University of Wisconsin graduate school thesis, was widely credited with launching the renegade faction of the environmental movement devoted to Spartan self-denial as an organizing tool.

Before heading to Vermont, Beibel had made a point of leafing through the heralded tree book. He'd found it provocative, succinct, well argued. In short, everything a manifesto should be. It was amazing to him that such strident writing, and thinking, could survive the bludgeoning meatgrinder process of graduate school. Then again, maybe it didn't. On the book jacket and in their EarthKare literature, neither Rachel nor Wolfram touted academic credentials.

According to his preliminary research, mostly Wikipedia, Wolfram had been a grad student colleague of Rachel's in the Department of Evolutionary Botany at Wisconsin. His subsequent rise to quasi-prominence was mostly attributed to a fortuitous coattail ride. Yet something about Wolfram's demeanor on the phone—grumpy, suspicious, verging on hostile—made Beibel wonder if there could be more to their relationship.

Meeting up in White River Junction, Vermont, had been Wolfram's idea. This arrangement struck Beibel as needlessly complicated when first proposed in a phone call. Wouldn't it be simpler to drive directly to EarthKare headquarters and meet there? But wary of starting off on the wrong foot, Beibel elected to go with the flow. If Wolfram wanted it complicated, complicated it would be.

Wolfram's instruction was for Beibel to arrive in White River by 2 p.m. At that hour, Rachel Seagrave herself, the queen bee, was due to arrive by bus from Montreal. It would be Beibel's task to transport her back to the EarthKare compound. Wherever that was located. Beibel still had not been told.

"Two birds with one stone" was how Wolfram had characterized the merits of this nimble piece of administrative wizardry, only to swiftly correct himself. "Actually three. I'll be there too. I won't have a car, so you'll be the one to drive us all back home."

Before Beibel could digest the byzantine logic of these machinations, Wolfram corrected himself again with a farm animal snort. "That birds-and-stones remark? It was meant ironically. And was entirely off the record. We love birds. Stones, well, they're not ever to be used for violence."

Early September was an exquisite season in the Green Mountains. Beibel, while not so crafty as to have planned the expedition to explicitly bask in the golden glow, was pleased to swap the cluttered gray city for this grand annual display. During the drive up, all three hours, he amused himself by singing to himself. No gloomy NPR newscasts. No ranting talk shows. No vintage rock or classical stations. The CD player in his rickety Corolla had recently been repaired, and he had several disc selections—Arcade Fire, Nora Jones, Wilco—wedged in the driver's door side pouch. But as he navigated the traffic, out through the tangled Somerville streets, then up I-93 toward New Hampshire, as the stress and snarls receded and a cruise control sensation (his Corolla did not actually contain this upscale feature) settled over him, as the sun beamed down and the landscape became rolling and thickly wooded, he found himself belting out a mental mixtape of tunes he knew the lyrics to, spanning eras. "Someone Like You." "California Stars." "House of the Rising Sun."

It was not like him to sing aloud for the duration of a long car ride, especially with no discernible reason to be happy. Then again, maybe he did have a reason to be happy and just didn't know it yet.

The reporting he envisioned around EarthKare would pose an interesting challenge. He'd have to pretend more concern for their cause than he possessed and feign affinity for an alarmist worldview that he did not share. He would have to spend hour upon hour engaged in conversations, observing planning sessions and, at the grand finale convention itself, listening to speeches that lamented the sorry fate of planet Earth. And all the while he would have to hold his tongue and refrain from disclosing what he truly believed. Which was: There's not a frigging thing mankind can do at this late stage to forestall the wretched consequences of what we have wrought. Like many a hard-nosed journalist, Beibel recognized that the world faced a monumental accumulation of dire threats, and the only reason humankind retained any hope for a turnaround was that we cannot face the mortifying truth.

On a wide range of hot button issues, including the environment, Beibel was agnostic. Was global population growth worth addressing? Was social media, for all the rancor created, best left unregulated? Should we ditch the Electoral College? The hotly debated bill pending in the Congressional Committee on Natural Resources to open up selected national forest areas to logging and mineral extraction was, to Beibel's way of thinking, a classic he-said, she-said debate. Who was he to impose his sketchy grasp of what the experts alleged? Ideological dexterity was how he preferred to frame this agnosticism. He firmly believed that's the way reporters should be, ideologically nimble and politically nomadic. Noncommittal was a virtue.

What Beibel had in mind for the blog postings he'd contracted to deliver to nature and wildlife outlets, and the spin-off features he hoped to pen for donor-friendly publications devoted to these causes, were breezy, fact-filled, three hundred-word missives. These would not exactly whitewash the extremism of these activists but would forego the temptation to caricature them as deluded dreamers with little more than a child's grasp of realpolitik. Of course, there was a healthy market for exactly that type of scorn—reactionary websites, free enterprise broadsheets, logging industry newsletters, etc. Maybe later, after the conference, he could explore such options.

Two

SERENADING HIMSELF, BEIBEL nearly missed the sign for White River Junction. At the last second, he executed a hair-raising two-wheel turn at 65 mph onto the sloped exit ramp. Whew! Disaster averted. A positive omen.

As stipulated by Wolfram, he pulled the Corolla onto the gravel skirt of the strip mall just up the ramp. He'd made good time. The sun was bright. The air was brilliantly clear. Beibel was pleased to have a few extra minutes to linger and bask and continue softly singing. "You can hear the whistle blow, five hundred miles . . ."

The Greyhound depot was little more than a rain shelter tucked among shabby storefronts that were what you'd find anyplace where short-term capital joined forces with short-term vision. On one side was House of Beijing, identifiable by a knobby red miniature pagoda on the roof. On the other side was a discount shoe outlet specializing in knock-off Nikes in rainbow colors. Beside that was Green Mountain Adult Entertainment with a hand-printed "For Rent" sign taped to its smudged plate-glass window.

Beibel marched across the lot to stretch his legs and to distance himself from the cloying stench of garlic and fried MSG. Did the Communist Chinese, so Spartan and frugal, actually dine on such gaudy confections? He doubted it.

Wolfram had been quite specific as to where in White River to meet, but he'd not told Beibel how to recognize him. On the book jacket for *Pity the Trees,* the only author photo was of Rachel Seagrave, although Wolfram was fully credited as co-author on the cover. The headshot of Rachel, sullen and expressionless in black and white, resembled a

Grapes of Wrath Dust Bowl widow, severe of gaze, void of mirth, all life's zest drained from her by the hardships she'd endured. If indeed that was the effect the publisher's marketing department was after, Beibel could not imagine why.

To Beibel, she looked like a woman who needed some color in her cheeks, some joy in her life. That was not part of this assignment, but he could still toy with the thought.

A burly, slope-shouldered man, as large as an NFL lineman, had his face pressed to the video store window, back turned to the parking lot, peering inside. Could this be his guy? Beibel sauntered over, still humming with song. "Lord I'm one, Lord I'm two, Lord I'm . . ." He could not remember the last time he'd been this relaxed. The tune was like a thick pour of maple syrup sweetening his mood.

On the far wall inside the video store, bathed in a sharp slant of sunlight, was a lurid poster of a buxom redhead in a halter top, bent at the waist to allow the viewer a clear view of her fulsome breasts.

The hulking figure peering in the window was oblivious to Beibel's approach.

"Are you . . ."

Frederick Wolfram spun as if slapped across the cheek.

"Hand in the cookie jar?" Beibel asked.

This was not the introduction to a member of the fourth estate that Wolfram would have wished, and Beibel made a mental note of the possible advantage he'd gained.

Bringing it back to the prosaic, he asked, "Bus from Montreal usually on time?"

"Time," Wolfram remarked spookily, gazing at the distant green hills, "is relative. Always has been."

Beibel flipped open his pocketsize spiral notepad and busily jotted.

"What's that you're writing?"

"Poetry."

"Poetry?" Wolfram spat, and the gob nearly hit the worn toe of his own lime green Nike knockoff. "Really?"

"Not really."

"So that's a joke?"

"A bad one."

"I'll say."

The very concept of poetry, Beibel sensed, stirred sour feelings in the big fellow. And possibly jokes did as well.

The navy blue Greyhound bus with sleek silver lettering squealed and crunched to a halt on the gravel. Two young boys in matching yellow Life is Good T-shirts hopped off, followed by an elderly woman—Grandma?—in a beige raincoat that did not fit the day or the season. Next, a young dude with long, straight hair, clutching a guitar case plastered with colorful decals.

Rachel Seagrave followed. An overstuffed purple knapsack caused her to tilt, as if she had a spinal deformity. Beibel's first impression was that the weight of her belongings was the least of this woman's burdens. What he meant by this observation was her looks. The book jacket photo was clearly dated. As most publicity photos are. In that shot, she'd appeared somber, sincere, humble yet handsome in a rustic, homespun way. Now she looked like a woman who'd altogether given up.

Her evident disregard for the fine points of primping— unruly auburn hair, sallow un-rouged cheeks, dry lips, drooping mouth, pale blue smock that could have been a modified hospital Johnny—all but announced her as a woman who'd opted out of the quest for male attention. Whether this was because she was likely to fail or because, like so many women (and men), she'd once upon a time made a determined run at real romance only to be disappointed, Beibel could not tell. It had to be one or the other.

As Rachel came down off the bus, Wolfram stepped forward to greet her. They said not a word to each other, although she did allow him with a nod of thanks to lift the hefty backpack from her shoulders.

Beibel lingered back a few steps. Rachel stared at him blank faced, as if to say, who are you? Then she said it aloud. "Who are you?"

Wolfram got the cue. "Remember Lenny Beibel?"

It was clear that she did not.

"The journalist? I sent you an email. He's giving us a lift back to camp."

Beibel waited for Rachel to make some remark or at least acknowledge his existence. But she appeared too weary, or uninterested, for any of that. So he turned and began walking to his parking spot beside House of Beijing. The thick odor of garlic was making him hungry. He knew better than to ask if anyone wanted to grab a bite.

To make space in the Corolla's passenger seat, he scooped up the pile of old newspapers, including the detested *New York Times* (not once had they even bothered to answer his queries), and tossed them in back. Then, chauffeur-like, he graciously opened the dented door for whichever of the pair wanted to sit in front.

Happily, it was Rachel.

Three

THE COROLLA SLOWLY climbed the access ramp back onto I-89. Acceleration was not the car's strong suit. They crossed the Connecticut River, heading north. There was a fairy-tale beauty to the swooping valleys, all green and gold, capped by a blue blue sky.

For the next several miles, nobody spoke. Beibel was itching to ask why Wolfram was even along for the ride. In hindsight, it would have been simple enough to fetch Rachel in White River on his route north and ferry her to the mountain compound without third-party assistance. Beibel did, however, have a guess. But only a guess. Wolfram the drone was leery of allowing unmediated access to his queen.

Finally, Wolfram broke the silence, blurting to Rachel, apropos of nothing, "Meet anyone?" His tone aimed for casualness but fell far short.

"Like a man?"

"Well . . . uh, sure."

"You really want me to go into it?"

"Uh, I guess."

It took Beibel several seconds to grasp where this was coming from. Then he recalled that Rachel was in fact the author of two books. There was the seminal work of environmental consciousness-raising, coauthored with Wolfram, and another, on prodding from her publisher, that had an entirely different focus and appealed to a different demographic. Beibel had bought a used copy on Amazon.

It was a memoir chronicling a solo trip through the hinterland jungle waterways of Ecuador and Peru Rachel had taken in her mid-twenties during a year off from grad school.

Titled *Alone in the Wild*, the book drew sharp contrast between the relative safety of her experiences trekking through remote jungles teeming with animal predators and the more disturbing perils of being hit on by men every time she checked into a population center for R&R. As part of his research, Beibel had skimmed this book also. Surprisingly, Rachel's author photo on the second book jacket told a very different story. In that one she was bright eyed and beaming. Her lips glistened. Her cheeks glistened. Her hair was a lighter shade and feathered outward, windblown without seeming wild. Marketing departments knew what they were doing and why. Still, Beibel was curious how a woman could appear so profoundly different when wearing a smile.

The dramatic highlight of that second book was an episode in which Rachel found herself camped with a small group of international adventurers on the banks of a tributary to the Amazon, where, astonishingly, she met her soulmate, a freelance nature photographer from Arkansas. They spent three miracle days together, exploring the jungle, exploring each other, making gymnastic love in a hammock. It was Rachel's suggestion, one she would dearly regret, to go for a moonlight dip in the dark eddies of the muddy river. The photographer did not disclose that he barely knew how to swim. The book was dedicated to Adam's memory. Self-deprecatingly, Rachel wrote that she was "nobody's Eve."

"Actually I did meet someone," Rachel answered after a lengthy pause. "Curious?"

Beibel was, although no one was asking him.

"The afternoon before the fundraiser I was hiking near the city, in the Bois-de-Liesse woods." Rachel's easy pronunciation of this Quebecois tongue twister caught Beibel's attention.

"I'd taken off my blouse. It was pretty warm. I mean, I was alone. Who cares, except for some insects? So out of nowhere—scratch that—out of the creek comes this man. He'd been bathing. Butt naked. So there we are, me topless, him naked, nothing but forest and undergrowth and a gurgling stream. I could scream. I could run. I could nod and keep going. Or I could communicate, depending on his native language."

Beibel realized he'd accelerated beyond the speed limit, pushing the aged Corolla to its engine-shaking max. He eased off the pedal.

Wolfram tried to sound chipper. "Cut to the chase."

"Interesting choice of words."

"Planning to see this letch again?"

"Geez, Wolfram, you're so old-fashioned. Just because you live in a log cabin doesn't mean you have to live in the seventeenth century."

Rachel made a show of shooting Beibel a wink, perhaps to let him know she was teasing. It was Beibel's first indication she might think he was worth heeding.

"No, I won't see him again."

"Well, if it was me . . ." Beibel jumped in to lighten the mood and perhaps, though he wasn't sure why, to test her response.

She cut him off. "Just kidding. Never happened. I did go for a walk in the woods, but I didn't encounter anyone. Not there, nor anywhere else." She fell silent, and for a few miles nobody else knew what to say. Or, in Beibel's case, realized it shouldn't be said.

Finally, Rachel spoke again. "So what's up with the conference?"

Wolfram clicked off the basics with a crisp down-the-checklist efficiency.

Progress was being made in several infrastructure areas, like transportation, lodging, waste disposal, food, security, and foul weather contingencies. The one exception was the keynote speaker.

Wolfram recapped, mostly for Beibel's benefit, why the keynote speaker mattered and why securing the right one was problematic. The pool of personalities who conformed to EarthKare criteria was smaller than one would think. It needed to be a man or woman with name recognition, someone skilled as an orator, sympathetic to the cause, and comfortable with, or at least unafraid of, EarthKare's reputation. Lastly, this rare species of human had to be available on September 26–27, a mere six days away.

"Any word yet from Al Gore?" Rachel asked.

"Nothing conclusive."

"Meaning?"

"It's being considered."

"And you know this for certain?"

"From his agent, yes. She assures me."

"That he'll come?"

"The agent needs to speak with you. I told her you'd call as soon as you got back."

"Why does she need to speak with me?"

"Apparently Team Gore is very systematic. They have a committee that makes recommendations to the CEO." Wolfram sounded touchy about being cross-examined. "Maybe she thinks we operate that way."

This information seemed to fatigue Rachel. She leaned her head heavily against the Corolla window. Puffy white clouds were amassing in the eastern sky. Lumpy shadows crawled across the hills.

"There is," Wolfram briskly added in a determined stab at a brightness, "some good news."

Rachel's head remained pressed morosely against the window.

"You know, the bird? Oswald's thrush? Guess what? It's been spotted, first time in thirty years, over by Randolph. Bow-and-arrow hunter." He waited for Rachel to perk up, but didn't wait too long. "Okay, so the guy might've been drunk. Still could be an omen."

"You don't believe in omens."

"That's not my point."

"What exactly is your point?"

"We need to stay positive."

"Because?"

Wolfram jerked his head in Beibel's direction. He did not want to say it out loud. A member of the news media was listening.

19

Four

LENNY BEIBEL HAD no knowledge of what the EarthKare compound would look like. Subconsciously, and this probably said something about his fascination with certain types of cataclysmic news events, he had in mind something akin to a New Age Jonestown—a remote enclave reachable only by footpath hacked through thick undergrowth, inhabited by outcasts from Western civilization emulating the holistic lifestyle of aboriginal tribes.

It was a mental framework that Beibel was not inclined to discard for it was the type of setting that just might tempt a publisher or movie producer. And should this conference miraculously culminate in a cataclysm triggered by the rash acts of a power-mad megalomaniac (he already knew a person who might step into this role), well, the rest would be history, and he would be an eyewitness to it.

With Rachel reclining in the passenger seat, eyes determinedly closed, Wolfram issued Beibel instructions on where to exit the interstate and what to do after that. Cross the river via an old covered bridge, hug the paved two-lane for a mile past a quarry, then straight uphill along an unmarked dirt road.

The Corolla groaned. At the peak of a long incline with panoramic views of a valley, they came to a deteriorating clapboard structure with peeling reddish paint. A former one-room schoolhouse, Wolfram informed him.

“Norman Rockwell country,” Beibel gushed. As soon as he said it, he realized that was an image, although fetching, he’d have to put aside. Jonestown was where the action was.

Past the schoolhouse, there was no road, only a wide, grassy meadow. Wolfram instructed him to keep driving. Tall weeds and prickly berry bushes lashed the low undercarriage. Beibel steered with utmost caution. Getting stuck up here without a functioning car for a quick getaway was not how he saw this story unfolding.

Eventually they came to a stone wall constructed of large irregular rocks, mossy and gray. This was also Robert Frost country.

"Stop," Wolfram blurted. "From here we walk."

A directive every bit as authoritative, Beibel mused, as the Rev. Jones himself might have used to command his beleaguered flock.

They exited the car. The silence, the peace, the serenity, was palpable. Beibel instantly relaxed, as if submitting to a skilled massage. A nap would feel about right. Instead, with Rachel taking the lead, they entered the woods. Stepping deftly over gnarled roots and rotting logs, they moved single file beneath a dense canopy of maple limbs.

Without warning, Rachel lit into a sprint. She had a powerful stride. Who'd a thought it? This newfound pep burst from her like a puppy's urge to romp. Soon she was out of sight, hefty backpack and all.

Wolfram made no effort to quicken his own plodding pace, and Beibel got the vibe that it would be bad form to do anything but hang behind with him.

Yet something in Beibel hankered to catch up. It was an unexpected sensation. It was a sensation worth tucking away. Rachel's bounding energy, like a deer in the wild, would be nice to latch onto, journalistically and otherwise.

"Not much farther," Wolfram wheezed.

"She's in good shape," Beibel remarked. Immediately he recognized the potential misunderstanding. "Not what I meant," he felt obliged to add, though why he felt obliged he could not say.

On one level, Wolfram's posture toward Rachel seemed protective, even paternal. On another level, it could be proprietary and jealous. And it seemed possible that Wolf-ram himself was not certain of the difference.

For the remaining ten-minute walk—probably five at Ra-chel's peppy pace—the path was discernible only as a tram-pled swath with fewer ferns and a thicker bed of dead leaves.

The path rimmed an oval clearing where the grass was flattened in patches, perhaps from reclining deer. They came to a gurgling stream and picked their way cautiously over slick stones. Circumventing a bog teeming with blue-tailed flies, they doubled back to higher ground. The earth here was moist and pocked with footprints, human and non.

Beibel's dirty secret as an environmental writer was that he was not especially knowledgeable about nature. His de-gree was in journalism, not biology or botany or geology or ecology. With each assignment, he generally managed to learn what he needed to know. He was a quick study, but not a scholar. He'd already spotted numerous small wonders along this trail that prompted him to ponder: What kind of stone shimmers in the shade? What's with the white birches preferring tight clusterings? And what's with all those irides-cent orange newts creeping about?

But Wolfram was the only person he could ask, and the problem was twofold. It would be wrong to admit such igno-rance, and Wolfram's answer would not be succinct.

Beibel mused aloud, "Nice day."

"All days," Wolfram sternly corrected, "are nice."

They came to a long meadow, about the length of a foot-ball field. A row of small cabins flanked the meadow on each side. At the far end was a larger, barn-like structure. Nearing the compound, it became clear that this was not a barn but a simple two-story house. EarthKare, Beibel would learn, kept no farm animals and had deep philosophical problems with the concept of domesticated livestock. They did not, however, publicly condemn the practice. Don't ask, don't tell was the strategy that allowed them to peaceably coexist with their agrarian neighbors.

The EarthKare compound contained a cluster of crude, modest cabins and several prefab yurts, courtesy of a grant from the one of the board members who was a principal investor in an Oregon company that manufactured them. Most of these were planted at the far edge of the main clearing, looking out on a descending sequence of green-gold hills. The compound resembled a Hobbit village. Beibel half-expected to find Bilbo Baggins in the doorway, his pudgy hand shielding his eyes as he tracked a butterfly flitting among the dandelions.

On the wide front porch of the main structure was an assortment of benches and rocking chairs. Several men and women, casually dressed in T-shirts and jeans, were relaxing in the sun. The entire setup had the quaint coziness of a cut-rate summer camp. Which, as Beibel would learn, was what the property originally had been designed for.

Wolfram was sweating profusely. "Where's Rachel?" were Wolfram's first words on catching his breath.

A cherubic woman in pigtails and cutoff jeans jerked her thumb, indicating upstairs. "The office," she reported. "The big call."

"Gore?"

"I think so."

Beibel did what reporters do. "Mind if I tag along?"

"We mind," Wolfram grumped.

"I'll be a fly on wall. Not one peep."

Wolfram shook his head. "Flies," he grumbled, "don't peep."

It was a setback to have been denied permission to go upstairs and sit in on the "big call." Such access could furnish the sort of banal detail that readers go for. But Beibel got it. A critical level of trust had to be established first. He'd worm his way in there eventually.

Beibel couldn't help but notice that the pig-tailed woman would not stop staring at him. Speaking of flies, could it be that his was open? She didn't seem to be the kind of lady who'd care one way or the other.

"Is this him?" The pigtailed lady nodded toward Beibel.

"Yep, the journalist," Wolfram grunted before trudging up the unvarnished stairs to join Rachel.

The pigtailed woman had long tan legs. "Celeste," she announced, introducing herself by tapping her ample chest and more or less forcing Beibel to glance in that direction. "We think it's great, absolutely great, what you're doing."

Her enthusiasm caught him by surprise, so much so that he muttered a line he thought would never cross his lips. "Just doin' my job," he allowed with the contrived modesty of an all-star athlete sloughing off effusive praise. It was all he could do to restrain himself from adding, with a tip of his imaginary Stetson, "Shucks."

Celeste had full hips and large eyeballs that seemed to bulge outward. There was a quiet samba sway about her, as though beckoning a phantom dance partner. A prominent nose that was not entirely centered kept her from being classically gorgeous.

Beibel would later learn that Celeste had spent but one semester at college. A trip to Puerto Rico had introduced her to a band of fun-loving idealists who were trying to establish a latter-day Eden near the jungle hot springs that Ponce de Leon had grandiosely claimed as the actual Fountain of Youth. It didn't work out, not for de Leon or Celeste. She would try again with EarthKare.

Her snug T-shirt was bright white, a nice contrast to the copper-pink of her tan. In the middle of her chest, where anyone's gaze would naturally alight, was a full-color artist's rendering of the Oswald's thrush, wings stretched as though in full flight.

"Cute," Beibel nodded toward the image. "But sad."

Celeste glanced downward. "Oh, this. You know the story?"

He did not.

Oswald's thrush, she explained, had once flourished in this very region, in these very hills. It was considered a cherished sighting for birders owing to its plumage, particularly the burnt orange trailing feathers on its wings, and its cheerful song. Part of the bird's renown, and key to its cult-like status, was its preternatural ability to elude being captured on camera. It had not been convincingly photographed in more than seventy-five years. There were several grainy, ambiguous black-and-whites from the 1940s, and nothing since.

"Like Big Foot," Beibel offered, eager to demonstrate he was listening and not just staring at her.

Celeste ignored this, and Beibel was thankful. Actually it was the Loch Ness monster he'd been thinking of.

"Bottom line, Oswald's gone." Celeste's tone dipped, then brightened. "But not forgotten."

And thanks to your alluring T-shirt, Beibel was tempted to note, I too will remember it forever. "The struggle continues," he flatly concurred.

Celeste poked out a comradely fist bump. "Can I get you something to drink? Juice? Something cold?"

"No thanks, ma'am."

She giggled. "Call me Celeste."

"Call me," he rejoindered, imaginary Stetson tipped back to show respect for the fairer sex, "Lenny."

"Hungry?"

"Now that you mention it."

"Follow me. Kitchen's back this way."

The interior of the main cabin emitted a vague oatmeal scent. The easy sashay of Celeste's hips struck Beibel as a rudimentary metronome, keeping time the EarthKare way. He jotted a note to this effect. Small epiphanies were now popping every step of the way.

"We're excited about you being here," she said without turning around. "Most of us, anyways."

"Hope I can handle the pressure." False modesty was not a pose he'd had much practice with.

To reach the kitchen, they had to traverse the long dining hall. It was a simple utilitarian space, long wooden tables with long benches. The hall was vacant. The tables were cleared and spotless. There was a hodge-podge of disparate aromas that Beibel could not quite identify. Peanut butter and tuna fish mixed with garlic was his guess, but he could not imagine anyone, even these characters, dining on that.

What Beibel was in the mood for was a cheeseburger, slathered in catsup, crisp salty fries on the side, washed down with a frosty, fructose-sweetened carbonated beverage. There were occasions when his body screamed so loudly for protein slathered with grease and a mega-dose of calories that it would constitute an act of masochism to deny it. Sadly, he knew that veggies and sprouts and nuts and fruit were the likely offerings. Washed down with room temperature tap water.

The kitchen was a bit of a surprise, with a high ceiling and tall cabinets built into the walls. There was a butcher block island in the middle with half a dozen barstools surrounding it.

"Dinner's not for another hour," Celeste informed him. "How about a snack?"

Celeste swung open the Amana's stainless steel door to allow Beibel to survey the choices. The contents were chilling to behold: great slabs of tofu, a ceramic bowl containing globs of a pale yogurt-like substance, another bowl containing a moist, greenish-gray lump that could be animal or vegetable or neither, bins stuffed with carrots and beans and onions and gnarly roots fit for beaver teeth, a platter piled with spinach leaves.

Celeste leaned close, her lips nearly grazing the back of his neck. "Anything you like?"

What a day this had been already. First, the unexpected exhilaration of merrily singing to himself the entire drive up, as if he were a legitimately free-spirited fellow, a man letting loose. Then his encounter with Wolfram and Rachel and the growing realization that he'd stumbled on personalities who were quirky and driven and complex, and therefore perfect for journalistic purposes. And now this, a tantalizing *pas de deux* with an eco-hippie femme fatale. If a juicy cheeseburger were added to this day's menu, he might well become overstimulated to the point of paralysis.

"Anything to eat, that is," Celeste added with a giggle.

Beibel flinched. He'd not been aware that his attraction to Celeste was so transparent. From an oversized wooden bowl on the center island, he grabbed a darkening banana and hurriedly peeled it.

With catlike grace, Celeste hopped to the opposite side of the island. "I just think it's wonderful that you're going to get our story out."

Beibel wolfed down the bruised banana, plucked a Golden Delicious apple, and ravenously chomped away, down to its core.

"I mean," Celeste continued, "the timing could not be better. You're like, I don't know, sent to us from central casting."

A Cheshire grin swept over Celeste's lovely face. Beibel didn't have a clue what flaky thought had just crossed her mind. He grabbed another apple, this one suspiciously mushy. He would like to believe that a demonstrably rotted piece of fruit would have been tossed, but who knew the true habits of EarthKare or the theories behind them? He took a cautious bite.

Celeste's sleek and reflexive manner reminded him of a kind of animal, but he wasn't sure which. His knowledge of nature's mammals drew almost exclusively from urban zoos and Discovery channel specials. A lemur? A coyote? A howler monkey? He knew better than to give voice to such inexpert musings, but it prompted him to ponder where on the animal-analogy chart he would place himself: of middling size, imperfectly coordinated, slow of foot, dependent for survival on cunning rather than physical prowess? He himself was a kind of endangered species.

"Wolfram says you're also working on a book?"

Was he? Beibel had turned it over in his own mind, but he was always turning half-baked fantasies over in his mind. What, after all, were minds for?

"Perhaps, down the road, depending . . ."

"Like Tracy Kidder, the one about Haiti?"

A Kidder-size publishing deal would be outstanding. "That's one direction, sure."

"Research intensive?"

"I am a reporter at heart."

"Third person? Is that what you're thinking?"

He wished she'd quit with the interrogation; sooner or later he was bound to trip himself up. "Frankly, Celeste, those decisions come much later in the editorial process. Writing's a lot like building a house. First you need to gather the building materials. Then you . . ."

"I can also see first person working. You have that kind of, I don't know, panache."

"Perhaps." Beibel switched the soggy apple core to his other hand, looking for a genteel place to discard it.

"Ever read Hunter S. Thompson?"

"The dope fiend?"

"A tremendous writer. Thing is with first person, the reporter gets involved. You know, becomes part of the story. You might consider it."

An awful gaseous gurgling was gathering force in his lower abdomen. The culprit, he suspected, was the damn banana. It dawned on him that indoor plumbing might not be among the compound's amenities, and his mounting intestinal pressure was instantly made worse by this realization. Fat beads of perspiration sprang from his reddening cheeks.

Celeste, the gracious host, intuited the problem. "Also, if you would like to use it, the outhouse is . . . follow me."

"Just tell me!" Beibel blurted. "Tell me where!"

He was bolting out of the kitchen as she shouted the directions: back through the dining hall the way they'd come, down the porch steps, then left all the way to the edge of the clearing.

Five

THE SPASTIC BUZZING of an irksome housefly was far from Rachel's only irritation as she settled into the office. But it was the one annoyance she felt she could most effectively address.

EarthKare's office was located directly above the dining hall in a semi-finished attic with a slanted ceiling. The office had knotty pine walls true to the rustic pioneer values of the camp masters. There were two unvarnished desks and two small windows facing the nearby forest. Back in the day, the cramped enclosure functioned as a clubhouse for the summer camp counselors who, once the younger kids were safely put to bed, were allowed to be their irresponsible teenage selves up there.

Rachel had to duck her head to fully access the window, which was already propped halfway open. With some fumbling, she managed to yank away the ill-fitting portable screen. Her strategy was to shoo the fly into escaping by vigorously fanning a yellow legal pad to create an air current that swept straight out the window. But the fly was too stupid to know what was good for it, and she wasn't in the mood to hunt it down and swat it.

The conference would begin in six days. Whereas Gore had not formally agreed to appear, EarthKare had been led to believe or, more accurately, slipped into believing a decent chance remained that the former VP would accept their invitation. The fact that Wolfram, nobody's optimist, continued to characterize Gore as "still interested" was taken as a promising indicator.

Rachel was skeptical. Wolfram's ability to accurately hear or lucidly interpret any message that displeased him was suspect. And EarthKare's group dynamics were never better than muddled. It would take intensive therapy to figure out how, through some combination of delusion and desperation, they had mangled the sketchy noncommittal response from Gore's agent into a conviction that, Messiah-like, he would majestically appear. Alas, they had no budget for group therapy, nor time for it, although the need was indisputable. The closest thing to an actual yes that they'd managed to elicit from Gore's representative was a droll, "We'll get back to you soon." Well, soon was now.

Her narrow desk was a cluttered territory with an older model Mac, a hanging file brimming with color-coded folders, and a black Panasonic phone console, relic of an earlier age. She was jabbing in the phone number when Wolfram entered. It was just like him to magically appear at her side when she most wanted to be left alone. With her free hand, she put a finger to her lips. Wolfram obediently kept quiet, yet lingered like a storm cloud hovering at her shoulder.

"Global Talent, how may we help you?" The woman's voice on the other end was artificially cheery with the flawless diction of a stage actress.

"Eva Rasmussen?"

"Please hold."

Rachel had no recourse but to suffer the smarmy switchboard Muzak. You'd think an influential talent agency known for the eminence of its superstar clients would figure out a classier audio experience for incoming callers. Unless, it occurred to Rachel, discontent was what they hoped to incite. It was at moments like this, rankled and impatient, that she most wished her oddball confederates—Wolfram and the rest—had some knowledge of her happy Midwestern girlhood. Then they'd understand why she became so irked at minor degradations like being forced to endure a bouncy vibraphone rendition of "Let It Be."

It would be helpful, for example, if her colleagues knew she was neither by instinct nor upbringing inclined toward the political-cultural fringe. Far from it. In high school, she'd been outgoing, perky, co-editor of the yearbook, weekend volunteer at the VA clinic. Her junior year, until spraining her knee in a nasty tumble from an ill-conceived five-person pyramid, she'd been a cheerleader. Her conventional upbringing was not something she'd ever renounced, or would. She was well aware that Wolfram preferred to characterize her as a highly principled defector from the cushy benefits of a middle-class lifestyle. This was not exactly the case. The way Rachel saw it, she was simply a conscientious citizen determined to confront the plain truth about the fragile Earth that was terrifyingly impossible to ignore.

The conference had not been her idea. She was of the opinion, then and now, that staging a conference, international or otherwise, was a colossal mistake. But they'd gone too far in the planning and had announced their intentions too loudly to too many to turn back. A debacle was looming, and it gave her little solace that the historical record, if such a thing existed, might exonerate her.

"Global Talent." The receptionist was back on the line. "How can we help you?"

"I'm holding for Eva . . ."

"Oh, that's right. Will you hold?" Rachel was now listening to a cheerful piano rendition of "Light My Fire," followed by "My Way," rendered with plucked cello over the light brushing of a drum kit.

The receptionist, slightly less dismissive, was on the line again. "Where are you calling from?"

Oh, how Rachel yearned to put this officious beast in her place. "This regards Al Gore. I'm calling from EarthKare. She'll know what it's about." And to drive the point home,

Rachel added a detail, though false. "She's expecting my call."

Wolfram scowled. He had an irksome habit—nearly all of his habits were irksome—of displaying displeasure by emitting a weird guttural tsking noise with his tongue.

The importance of Al Gore could not be overstated. An appearance by the Nobel Prize winner would signal to the community of opinion makers, i.e. the loathsome mass media, that the EarthKare approach must not be dismissed as the eccentric pastime of luddites and social outcasts. Most significantly, Gore's participation would underscore a central yet persistently overlooked feature of EarthKare's contention: namely, that the old order needed to change, and that a collection of earnest nobodies far from the marble halls of power and unaffiliated with other public interest groups, even ones roughly considered to be allies, like Sierra Club and Defenders of Wildlife, was emerging to lead the movement to the next level.

Absent Gore, EarthKare would be forced to hunker down for the long, slow slog of recruiting converts one by one by one, waging a long-shot campaign with time itself. The core problem was this: The incremental approach to building a movement to transform civilization's relationship to the natural world, which in essence is what they aspired to, would be very hard to sustain long enough to succeed. Already their membership was declining. In the past year, they'd lost three key people to burnout. One, Wiley Forester, who was valued for his fundraising skills and the karmic magic of his name, quit to pursue an MBA at Wharton. That one stung. Acceleration was needed. Gore was the accelerant.

"Eva Rasmussen," sighed the exhausted voice on the other end.

"Hi, Eva. You may recall we were given your name by Dr. Rautenberg . . ."

Eva perked up instantly. "How is the old goat? I could tell you some stories. He may look like a . . . Just be careful. That's all I have to say."

Rachel was not sure what conversation this was or would be. She tried to imagine the office Eva inhabited: Midtown Manhattan, elegant furniture, modern art on the walls, a plate glass window looking down on the antlike creatures scurrying along the sidewalks below.

Rachel had promised herself to refrain from pleading. "Can we," she nonetheless pleaded, "move on?"

"You're calling about Vice President Gore, is that right?"

Rachel would have preferred to merely nod. "Yes, and we've invited him to deliver the keynote speech to our . . ."

"And that takes place when?"

Rachel was certain this woman knew the answer. "September 26 through 27."

"Wow, that *is* soon. Remind me: Do you know him?"

"Well, not personally."

Eva let loose with a wicked giggle. "You mean you admire his work and have seen his movie. So tell me, honey, whatcha thinking?"

Rachel gave a succinct summary, just the facts, intended to emphasize the unique benefits the event would provide Al Gore without wasting time attempting to connect the dots between Gore's participation and the overall fate of planet Earth. Eva, Rachel suspected, had heard that one before.

"This is a way for Mr. Gore to grow his constituency," Rachel asserted. "We're the activist base, we're the ones poised to take it to the next level. He's won the letters-to-the-editor types. He's won the eco crowd and all the well-meaning citizens who lobby their senator by hitting the Send button. He needs to win over grassroots activists like us. Speaking at our convention'll send a message." Rachel thought she detected the shrill grating of an emery board; better wrap this up soon. "This is a chance to reinvent himself."

"Do what?" The rasping sound ceased.

To avoid eye contact with Wolfram and his smoldering disapproval, Rachel bent forward over her desk, a snail pulling into its shell. "Yes, he's been a senator, a vice president, a Nobel winner. But is that all there is?"

Something told Rachel she was failing to close this deal.

"Remind me again, honey. What's your budget?"

"Budget?"

"For his speaking fee?"

This had been fully explained to Eva in prior emails. Rachel wondered what kind of sadist would force her to repeat it aloud. "Pro bono."

"Latin, eh?"

Under normal circumstances, Rachel would marshal her self-respect and tell this haughty prick (yes, women in certain situations were deserving of that title) where to shove it.

"We can't offer a monetary fee, but we do offer the chance to . . ."

"Make a better world? That sort of thing?"

Wolfram had turned his face to the wall and looked to be shadowboxing, throwing vicious jabs at an imaginary foe.

"Yes, the saving-the-planet sort of thing. Can you at least tell me if his calendar is free?"

Now the tap-tap-tap of Eva pecking at her keyboard. Again, Rachel tried to envision Eva's chic office high above New York's hyperactive bustle. How different the world must seem from up there compared to the stuffy, low-ceiling space of a former camp counselor clubhouse nestled in a forest.

Eva spoke as if she were thinking. "Well, he's in Aspen that weekend and needs to be in Rio late Sunday, plus there's a hold for a potential . . . you get the picture. If you want to push your event back to November . . . no, make that December . . ."

It was evident this woman did not give a shit. Whether that was an attitude shared by Al Gore was something Rachel wasn't likely to learn. She had little recourse but to plead one more time, "Can you at least make certain he understands the importance?"

"Just to be sure I have all the info. Date is, what, a week away? Location is rural Vermont. You're interested in booking Al Gore, one of the premier public figures in the world, to deliver the keynote address. You offer no fee. Am I missing anything?"

"Well, no."

"Let me be candid."

Rachel waited glumly for Eva to be candid, although it struck her that she'd been nothing but.

"If I were you, I'd be giving serious consideration to alternatives." Suddenly Eva's voice grew bizarrely eager. "Hold it, hold it! Wait a sec, looking at the calendar, yes, guess what?"

It irritated Rachel, she of the happy girlhood, she of the heralded environmental cult bestseller, she of a hundred better things to do, to be subjected, maliciously, it seemed, to this infuriating interaction. "OK, what?"

"I'm scrolling through as we've been talking, and you know who looks to be available? And a superb match, if you want my opinion?" Another annoying pause.

"Who?"

"Henry Marks."

"Who?"

"Never heard of him?" Eva feigned incredulity. "Gosh, you people really do cut yourself off from civilization, don't you? He's quite popular with convention audiences throughout North America. Very lively, very contemporary."

Rachel had been doing her best to ignore Wolfram's nervous antics, but it was no longer possible. He held his meaty forefinger in front of her face, pointing at the receiver. He wanted to speak.

Rachel snarled and turned her back, then asked Eva with as much casualness as she could muster, "What exactly does he have to say, this Henry person?"

"His main theme, which he can easily adapt to the particular interests of your audience, is jogging. Jogging as a metaphor, that is. Life is not a sprint, that kind of thing."

Rachel was dumbfounded.

"His audiotapes are hotcakes," Eva clucked. "Plus, although I really shouldn't be telling you this, we have strong interest in a cable show."

Wolfram, desperate to get Rachel's attention, moved to the window ledge. One swift kick of the old foot, Rachel thought, and he'd be sent flying backward.

"Fascinating. Could you, ah, tell me a little more about what it is he actually has to say?"

"He tailors his message."

The very concept repulsed Rachel. "Doesn't that sort of imply, I don't know, a lack of something? Conviction maybe?"

"Tell you what." Eva's voice softened, perhaps from empathy. Or disinterest. She promised to explore options regarding Gore but stressed that his appearance remained highly problematic and that it would be several days, or longer, until the situation could be clarified. With the comforting tones of a pastor making a condolence call, she explained that "Al would feel awful if you were left in the lurch. What do you say I pencil in Henry Marks? You know, as backup. He's beefing up his pro bono portfolio. Could be win-win."

Rachel was aware that she should express gratitude and show a willingness to play along. But it wasn't easy. "Understood. Okay, But jogging, is it really relevant to environmental issues?"

"Sure."

Rachel waited for further elucidation. But all she got was the sandpaper scratching of the emery board, followed by the brusque bleat of a dial tone. Eva Rasmussen had hung up.

Six

THE OUTHOUSES—THERE were three of them—were situated fifty yards from the main cabin on the edge of a large groomed patch that served as an organic vegetable garden, far enough away to avoid unpleasantness, near enough to get there in short order. Lenny Beibel made good time, using a stiff-legged European race-walk stride that was less disruptive to his tender innards than a flat-out sprint.

Compared to his prior experiences at state park campgrounds and a two-week stay as a high school exchange student in the Honduran highlands, the EarthKare privies were not just decent but downright lovely. There was a convex skylight made of hard translucent plastic and a strip of screen mesh beneath the roof soffit for ventilation. The walls were blond pine and decorated, at least in his case, with a large Sierra Club poster of a double rainbow above an alpine valley. It would be a stretch to call the atmosphere fragrant, but something had seemingly been done—scented candles, untreated wall boards, perhaps the contour and depth of the crap hole itself—to mitigate stench. And the toilet seat itself was made of smooth oak, lovingly sanded, pleasing to the eye. Beibel would not want to linger here longer than necessary. Nor, however, did he feel rushed to get out.

Above the toilet paper roll—he was relieved to discover EarthKare had not renounced that aspect of civilized living—was a rack of reading material, four vertical tiers, like you'd find in a doctor's waiting room. Once settled in, he began perusing the offerings, mostly paperbacks and outdated nature-friendly periodicals from Audubon and World Wildlife. Reminded of the infamous repurposing of the Sears catalog from generations prior, he had to chuckle. From the rack Beibel plucked a worn copy of *Anna Karenina*. It seemed thinner than he remembered.

"Happy families are all alike. Every . . ."

The outhouse was oddly peaceful. The temperature, which he could easily imagine becoming unbearable in terms of heat or cold, was today congenial. And the sounds, the rustling of leaves and the chirping of neighborhood birds, were music to his citified ears.

It tickled him that Celeste, a bright and reasonable woman, believed him to be a dedicated journalist committed to telling "their story." No harm in playing along. With the exception of Wolfram, EarthKare seemed to be decent folk, a bit nutty but high-minded. The fact that Celeste apparently believed that the project Beibel was developing might rise to the lofty literary standards of Tracy Kidder or Hunter S. Thompson, drug addled or not, was nothing to sniff at. Writers were ultimately performers completely capable of playing up to, or down to, as the case might be, their audience's expectation. That he was a floundering, third-rate nobody without a platform or even a steady gig meant simply that he had no audience. Not yet.

These contemplations were interrupted by the thumping of footsteps, the attenuated squeak of a wood door wedging open, then shut, followed by a gross barnyard blast, and then, amazingly, the melodious song of a female voice, high pitched and on key.

The tune was familiar. He'd heard it quite recently.

"Go tell my baby sister" sang the woman next door, "Never do like I have done . . ." No doubt she believed herself alone. Or maybe not. Who could fathom the social habits of this crowd? It would, Beibel reflected, take a trained field biologist to truly make sense of it.

By the time his neighbor's singing came around to the haunting refrain, it seemed as natural as anything, as natural, really, as the dump he was taking, to give voice to the tuneful surge in his own complicated heart. "That house in New Orleans," Beibel wailed.

Suddenly there was silence next door. Then the woman resumed, like a mourning dove in mating season. "Sewed these new blue jeans . . ."

Beibel quickly wiped his butt and hitched up his trousers. Fun while it lasted, but there was work to be done. He was, after all, a professional journalist. And participatory first person was probably not his thing.

Beibel's original game plan was to spend only a day or two at the Vermont encampment, get passingly familiar with the setting and the leading players, then return later in the week to cover the convention. But he really had nothing else to do, and this seemed a congenial place to hang out. It was easy to imagine this gentle green valley with its sweet, crisp air as the setting for a high-end health spa, like the Alpine retreat for consumptives in *The Magic Mountain*. The food was decent, if odd. The people were pleasant with one exception. Plus, his accommodations were more interesting than he'd expected.

The cramped cabin he'd been assigned was at the far end of the long pasture, last in the row of six. His cabin mates were to be Celeste—he had to feign nonchalance upon learning this—and a lanky, laid-back, slightly squirrely goofball named Slim. The whole setup—a laconic bunkmate named Slim in a rustic cabin with loose plank floorboards and plywood shutters—held echoes of a cowpoke western. Beibel even thought he could hear the lonesome sagebrush whine of an ill-tuned harmonica, but it turned out to be another staffer running a battery-operated toothbrush out back by the water basin.

There was shelving beside the bunk to stash his belongings. Here too were signs of the summer camp that had once occupied these verdant grounds. Crude cave dweller-like depictions, snakes and footballs and female breasts, were ineptly carved into the various side panels.

Slim asked him if he needed help unpacking his Samsonite suitcase. Beibel declined.

"Mind if I scoot?" Slim asked.

"No problem."

"Got work to do," Slim explained.

"The conference?"

"It's gonna be huge. I mean, if all goes . . ."

"If you guys get it together, you mean?"

"Oh, we will, brother, we will. Got no choice."

From the open window, he watched as Slim briskly traversed the clearing with loping strides. He would later learn that Slim had been a high school basketball star in the Denver metro area and had spent two years in a remote Himalayan monastery where nobody ever spoke a word. How Slim wound up *here*, doing *this*, trying to save the planet, was certainly a line of inquiry to pursue. But for the time being, what interested him most was the fact that he might at some point find himself alone in the cabin with Celeste, as darkness descended and the forest closed in and the temperature dipped.

She seemed the sort of woman, comfortable in her silken skin and confident of her place in this strange oasis, who would take the initiative when she was good and ready. No need for him to risk rejection or embarrassment. If invited into her bunk, he would have no choice but to comply. Already he was feverishly conjuring delicious scenarios. Burrowed into their respective L.L. Bean sleeping bags, she might whisper, "Are you asleep?" There would be longing in her tone, a yearning.

"Not asleep," he imagined himself replying, "but I do believe I'm dreaming."

It turned out he was dreaming. Celeste elected to switch cabins, moving in temporarily with Rachel, who had a place to herself on the other side of the pasture. The reason Celeste gave was that Beibel, as an honored guest, deserved to reside in less crowded conditions. Crowding, Beibel wanted to protest, would not be a problem. But the role of reporter compelled him to keep his mouth shut and accept the switch.

Seven

GETTING SETTLED IN his cabin, even without Celeste as a bunkmate, reinforced Beibel's belief that he'd been granted unofficial acceptance. Although he'd been rebuffed in his quest to listen in on the talent agent phone call, he felt encouraged that, in time, he'd be able to wheedle his way into their trust. In all likelihood, he could stay at Camp EarthKare for the duration of the conference. The fact was, he kind of liked it here, far from the maddening traffic snarls of Somerville.

His one summer camp experience had been at a paramilitary operation in the Adirondacks, and it seemed to young Lenny that the camp was run by neo-Nazis. He'd begged to go home and was not convinced, then or since, that he was a better, stronger person for toughing it out. He became a compulsive nail-biter, that's what summer camp did for him. But he was more mature now, and it was cool to be getting a second chance to sleep in a bunk, to eat in a mess hall, to roam through the woods. The barely legible notes he scribbled into the pocket-size flip pad could constitute a form of whittling. Biding time was sort of what he was good at.

The second morning a vigorous discussion about coffee erupted. It took place in the dining hall. As best as Beibel could tell, there were two distinct factions when it came to java. On the one hand, coffee was a product of nature, if you stuck with whole beans absent any artificial flavoring. On the other hand, it had clearly become the drug of choice for the rat race of Western capitalism and a primary enabler, if not the outright cause, of a range of insidious syndromes.

Rachel, Beibel noted, did little more than smile attentively, despite being repeatedly encouraged, via beseeching glances, to weigh in. He wondered if she was secretly less dogmatic than her hard-core followers. For all he knew, her views just might overlap with his own: Namely, it made little difference what any one person ultimately believed when it came to the gruesome problems of our troubled world. Right now, that was not an opinion Rachel could openly express. He could, of course. But then nobody around EarthKare would speak to him again.

Sunday afternoon Beibel was allowed to tag along for a meeting of the subcommittee on entertainment. It was another indicator that he'd gained a measure of trust.

The meeting was held out by the apple orchard on a grassy slope that had a superior view of the mountains to the north. Exactly why it was called a subcommittee, or any kind of committee, was not clear. Beibel refrained from asking. He'd come to understand that his curiosity was indulged, even welcomed, when it came to questions concerning what was wrong with the world and how they intended to fix it, and much less so when the questions smacked of petty snooping.

The subcommittee consisted of Dorothy, Danielle, who was presumed to know something about the entertainment industry because she enjoyed Zumba and liked to sing in the shower, and an elfin intern named Humphrey Bork, who had experience in student activities at Syracuse University. The subcommittee lacked a budget yet nonetheless needed to fill at least four lengthy gaps in the conference agenda. The fact that EarthKare still had no estimated head count and no hard data about the age, gender, or cultural preferences of the prospective attendees made entertaining them a particularly daunting assignment. Movies were out for tech reasons. Relay races gave unfair advantage to the young and adept. Treasure hunt? Too centrally controlled, too contrived, too mercenary.

Beibel took careful notes and said nothing. It was a lovely afternoon. Earthers stretched out on the grass, basking in the warming sun. If Beibel were a subcommittee member, he knew what suggestion he'd make. The best way to fill empty slots in the conference agenda would be for everyone to gather on this lovely hillside and get blissfully stoned. That's what he'd like to do.

Others had practical suggestions. Humphrey the intern recounted the success that his campus had with a professional outfit called Play Date that provided participatory sessions designed to get everyone interacting and bonding, starting with standard stuff like hugging the person seated next to you, then breaking out into smaller cocktail party-like clusters, and culminating in controlled—but not overly controlled—dancing, singing, kazoo tooting, and primal screaming.

"They charged something like five thousand bucks," Humphrey recalled, "but really, I think I could pretty much, you know, recreate it myself. I might need a whistle. That's about it. And a microphone, depending, you know, on how many . . ."

Dorothy and Danielle were initially speechless. Sure, their base of operations was a former children's summer camp. But their campaign was hardly child's play.

"What's your major, Humphrey?" Danielle asked, breaking the silence. "At school."

"Business administration."

"And remind us: How'd you find your way to EarthKare?"

"My professor thought it would be a good idea for my resume. Going forward, that is."

"That's interesting. Forward, like to where?"

"One of the big energy companies is what I'm hoping. Professor Denby thinks having worked for EarthKare would help me stand out."

"That it would, Humphrey."

The four of them, Beibel included, were lounging on the north-facing slope of the apple orchard. The orchard flowed out of and into a swath of undulating ravines that seemed indistinguishable from wilderness. Knobby and misshapen apples, mostly green but some verging on red, dangled on branches and littered the ground below.

"One thought," announced Danielle with a sarcastic snap, "would be . . ."

A heavy thump, loud as a tree limb crashing to the ground, startled them. Not ten yards away, flat on his back like a prizefighter whose night has unceremoniously ended, lay a rotund fellow with ruddy cheeks dressed in olive-and-brown camo pants and jacket. One hand clutched a bolt-action rifle with polished walnut stock and a menacingly thick barrel. Just beyond the reach of his other hand was a pewter flask, unscrewed, the likely culprit. Evidently, the fellow had been perched in a nearby tree, waiting for deer. Waiting and drinking, it seemed.

Should they approach? The fellow did have a gun. Beibel was keenly aware that, partnered with two women and a feckless undergrad named Humphrey, the role of male protector, and all that entailed, might fall to him. If the guy should wake up. If he wasn't dead.

Thankfully, Danielle beat him to it. In a flash, she was on her feet and looming over the guy like a ring referee administering the decisive ten-count.

Danielle spent a few seconds surveying the vital signs, the heaving of his chest, the quivering of his smartly trimmed chevron moustache, the vivid pink of his fleshy cheeks. Then she kicked at his L.L. Bean-booted foot like it was empty can of Budweiser on the roadside.

"You alive, mister?"

He had to arch his neck to see who was asking. And the site of Danielle in her tight purple jeans and snug lavender fleece—Beibel had wondered why she'd chosen to dress with such flair for the subcommittee meeting and could only conclude it was for his benefit—lured the fallen hunter to sit upright for a better look.

"Yes, miss," he declared with an eager smile. "I am most definitively quite alive."

"Then get your ass out of here."

Maybe participatory journalism was not Beibel's thing, but participatory self-preservation was. He hopped up beside Danielle. Extending a hand to help the lunk onto his feet, Beibel explained in the sweetest and most reassuring tone he could summon, "What she really means is . . ."

"Get. The. Fuck. Out of here!" Danielle commanded.

The hunter managed to scramble to his feet, bracing himself with his free hand while still gripping the rifle. He no longer seemed interested in the pewter flask. He flipped the rifle across his shoulder, perhaps to show he meant no harm. But it also suggested that he'd regained his faculties and knew where the trigger was.

"Hey, sweetheart," he slurred lasciviously. "What say I join the party?"

Danielle'd had it. Grabbing a low-hanging apple, she cocked her arm, and not in a girlish way, shoulder back, forearm raised.

David vs. Goliath. Beibel thought of jotting a note. It was the sort of observation that could make the final cut. But an inner voice, spoken in the language of survival, told him this situation would not be improved if the drunken, humiliated, gun-toting hunter believed the interchange was being documented. Instead, Beibel offered a line he'd heard employed in cowboy movies, always to good effect.

"You heard the lady," Beibel snarled. Or tried to snarl.

The hunter, for whatever reason, reacted appropriately, shuffling meekly backward, stumbling on a rock, then striding back into the forest at a leisurely pace to prove he was in no special hurry.

A congratulatory back slap from Danielle, far too hard, nearly knocked Beibel on his face. Appearances aside, she was one tough lady.

Eight

THE IDEA FOR EarthKare's First International Environmental Conference came from Chas Fullerton, senior partner at McKinsey and an ex officio EarthKare advisory board member. Why this dapper, patrician management consultant had cozied up to EarthKare in the first place and why he was so readily embraced by a collective of counterculture fanatics was puzzling. The short explanation was that Fullerton was an ardent backpacker and kayaker who wished nothing more than to lend his talents to the cause and EarthKare was an environmental group in dire need of strategic advice.

Rachel was aware of the rumors that Fullerton, despite being twenty years older and married, was secretly sweet on her. He'd once commented—to Wolfram, of all people!—that a traditional romantic relationship could help sustain and possibly inspire her for the arduous struggle ahead. That sort of strategic advice Rachel could do without. Even if there was some merit to it.

It was Fullerton who, last April at the tail end of a dispiriting long-range planning session, made the observation that EarthKare's predicament had characteristics in common with other formerly viable enterprises that were presently extinct. Compaq, Blockbuster, and Toys 'R' Us were some of the examples he cited. EarthKare, Fullerton explained, was at a classic fork in the road faced by many organizations: make a commitment to growth or suffer an ugly, painful, humiliating death.

This pronouncement had been made around the Walmart folding table on the second floor of EarthKare's rented office in a DuPont Circle brownstone that was scheduled for demolition. Board members Reggie Takada of Reynolds Porsche LLC and Jacqueline Ott of Kenyon College had attended the meeting, along with Rachel, Wolfram, Celeste Hutchins, their outreach director, and Danielle McDermott, their dimple-chinned all-purpose administrative overseer. Dorothy and Mitchell Wickersham, EarthKare's development team, were slated to be there and eventually did arrive, but only as the meeting was breaking up. The Wickershams apologized that their gig at a Rockville senior center (in their spare time they were a performing duo, modeled on Astaire and Rogers) had engendered one too many encores.

Fullerton seemed so cocksure of his analysis and the case studies he cited—Sears, Sylvania, Wang—were so persuasive that Rachel had to look away, as if from a gruesome scene in a horror movie. Despite the absurdity of analogizing EarthKare and its perpetually depleted bank account to imperiled corporate dinosaurs, Rachel did not doubt for a second that Fullerton's basic formulation was accurate: grow or die.

Fullerton's expert advice: time to let fly with a Hail Mary!

Rachel had learned not to show impatience with the self-important fulminations of her advisory board. They all meant well, these affluent lawyers and doctors and investment professionals, volunteering their time and expertise. They came to meetings when they could. They signed their names to hopeless grant proposals and fundraising letters. They had their secretaries perform emergency administrative chores on the company dime, no questions asked. Don't look a gift horse is what Rachel always told herself.

Near the conclusion of Fullerton's dispiriting overview of their situation, Rachel had sighed audibly. "Got it. So?"

"A conference. Big. Bold. Boffo. Like a product launch."

"We've been around six years."

"Hardly anybody knows it."

"We do."

Fullerton, she recalled, rose to his feet. It was a cheap trick he no doubt employed in the bare-knuckle skirmishes of megabucks corporate consulting. At his full height, with his gray-blond hair swept back and cold blue eyes staring down from his sun-bronzed face, he had the regal authority of an admiral helming a yacht. "Poor choice of words," he acknowledged. "My bad. Not a launch. A rebranding is what I meant. Like Apple after the NeXT tanked. Given up for dead. Gone the way of, I don't know, Polaroid. A rebranding on a grand scale. One big, bold, neon event that says: We are here, and we mean business! That's what donors want to see. That's what policymakers pay attention to. That's what our volunteers and, if I may say so, the paid staff, who are paid so poorly they may just as well be volunteers, want to see. Grow or die. Soar or sink. When Steve Jobs . . ."

It was lunacy, given EarthKare's shoddy infrastructure, yet it also made perfect sense. Something definitely had to change. "Like when do you have in mind?" Sondra Wilensky, another board member and public relations executive, had asked.

"Yesterday," Fullerton stated.

"Ha."

"Fall, at the very latest. In the Isaacson biography, Jobs is quoted as . . ."

"This fall?"

"Is there another?" Touché. The questionable future of mankind's joyride on planet Earth was a recurring theme in environmental circles, and Fullerton knew he'd scored a point.

Easy for Chas Fullerton, Rachel had thought, to conjure such a gambit so long as he would not be the one to have to endure the countless headaches involved. And yet, it occurred to her *that* was the very benefit of having an outside consultant like McKinsey, the special insight achieved by complete detachment from the real-world rigors of implementation. Why not a Hail Mary?

However, there were good reasons, not all of them pertaining to environmental politics, to quicken the pace. Rachel had reasons of her own to want to see EarthKare, metaphorically speaking, shit or get off the pot. As EarthKare's founder, director, chief fundraiser, primary spokesperson, and guiding spirit, she was indispensable. And being indispensable, day in and day out, with no prospect of relief, was unsustainable.

Her resources were dwindling. Her patience was waning. Her spirits were flagging. Her battery needed recharging. Her clock was ticking. Fullerton was right about her in that respect.

Rachel had resolved to take a sabbatical starting this coming winter. She'd told no one of her intention. The pushback from Wolfram, who'd grown dependent on her in unhealthy ways, and from the rest of the staff, who would rightfully fear that Wolfram might step into the breech, would be fierce. She didn't have the strength for that battle just yet. But she'd promised herself it would happen. She'd been at this grinding task for over six years, organizing, strategizing, administering, meeting, schmoozing, soliciting, speaking. She needed a breather. Otherwise, her better self would shrivel and fade. It would drift away like a beautiful red balloon whose string had slipped her grasp. It would vanish into the ether, never to be seen again.

Rachel wanted to be out by the start of the New Year. By "out," she meant not thinking about EarthKare nearly every waking hour, not obligated to respond to the ceaseless torrent of emergencies, big and small, real and imagined, that flooded her consciousness. No emails. No texts. No phone calls. No meetings. Please, God, no more meetings!

And after a few months of yoga and meditation and leisure travel and perhaps a few lively nights tripping the light fantastic with friends (if any could be drummed up), then, with her psychic metabolism restored, she would address the big one: whether or not to have a child.

When exactly did that almighty clock finally announce that time's up? Rachel guessed she had a year or two remaining. Unless, of course, that game had already ended.

55

Nine

LENNY BEIBEL WAS relaxing on the front porch, seated on an unpainted rocker, catching rays. Rachel had folded herself into one of the white Adirondacks chairs, hair in wet ringlets from her morning shower. Steam rose from the ceramic mug she clasped in both hands. The conference would begin in five days.

The temperature was in the low sixties. It was the kind of sparkling September day that began in burnished gold and only grew more polished. The mood around EarthKare, however, was anything but glistening. A grim kind of D-Day foreboding hung like a low gray cloud.

Beibel asked, "Anything yet from Gore?"

Rachel did not flinch. Silence was her reply.

"Maybe he'll decide last minute, show up unannounced."

She rolled her eyes.

"Like those famous rock stars, you know, who get it in their heads to drop in on the Tuesday night jam session at some neighborhood blues bar." Beibel wasn't sure if he was trying to improve her spirits or prove something to himself. "If I was Gore, that's how I'd do it. Just slip into town and do my thing. No fanfare. No big media hype. No security, no caravan. I was him, that's what I might do."

She gave a patronizing smile. "You're sweet."

A ripple of satisfaction washed over Beibel. He truly was starting to enjoy this place. "So he doesn't show. Not the end of the world. Plenty of things get accomplished without the intervention of Al Gore. Like the internet, for instance," he added, hoping she'd get the joke. And look fondly on him for coming up with it.

"Ha."

"So what's Plan B?"

Rachel took a slow sip of the steaming coffee. Her lips lingered at the mug's glazed brim.

"I mean, really, how crucial is he?"

"Nobody's crucial. If time wasn't a factor, if we could just muddle through as we've been doing, bit by bit, if our movement could grow at its own pace, you know, gather momentum until some tipping point where human behavior is transformed, sure, who needs Al Gore?"

"How 'bout George Clooney? Or some Hollywood star. Lots of 'em care."

"On short notice?"

She had him there. What Beibel was most curious to know about was her romantic life. That was, after all, the most telling facet about anyone, including, though it pained him to admit, himself. But he could see no smooth transition to that topic. "So you hold the conference without him. I mean, EarthKare'll keep on keepin' on, as the song goes."

"Sorry, don't know that song."

Beibel had an urge to lean over and pinch her on the cheek, like a kindly uncle bucking up the spirits of a sulking young niece. Good thing he didn't, as Wolfram came clomping onto the porch. He wore a gray-green T-shirt emblazoned with a faded image of Che Guevara in a jaunty beret. Now there was a dude with one helluva faraway look.

Rachel slid deeper in her chair, as if hiding from Wolfram was even an option.

Not to be ignored, Wolfram loomed before her on the step, effectively blocking her view of everything but him. "Can we talk about where things are at?"

Rachel stretched her arms, limbering her torso in a languid corkscrew gyration. "We can only do our best. Just keep on keepin' on. You know that song?"

Wolfram shook his head. Beibel would later learn that the only song Wolfram admitted to knowing was "This Land is Your Land," including all the forbidden verses.

A screeching yelp, shrill as a siren, all noise, no words, erupted from the direction of the footpath. Beibel took it to be another routine EarthKare oddity—ecstatic yoga, getting in touch with your inner coyote, that sort of thing. Initially, he spotted nothing unusual. Just the line of maples enclosing the compound and, far above, a red-tailed hawk gliding in lazy loops.

The shout came again, a long, sharp yelp. A man trotted into view. He was dressed in mustard slacks and a luminescent turquoise golf shirt. Legs churning, cheeks puffed, torso angled forward as if driving toward a finish line, the fellow was either woefully lost or engaged in some inscrutable prank. He clutched a cone-shaped megaphone, bright red, the kind used by the coxswain in an eight-person scull.

Beibel wanted to crack a joke, just to test the waters. Nothing came to mind fast enough.

Midway across the meadow, the runner halted. He sported a hefty backpack topped by a camper's bedroll, which he shucked off his shoulder. Breathing hard, the fellow stood over the fallen pack, hunter with prey. It was an arresting sight, this preening peacock of a man sucking wind amid the pasture's tall grasses.

"This," Rachel muttered grimly, her eyes bulging with disbelief, "is not happening."

Beibel did not have a clue. Rachel's knowing scowl suggested that she definitely did. The newcomer was Henry "On Your" Marks.

Wolfram bared his incisors, girding for danger.

"Down, boy," is what Beibel wanted to say. But it wasn't his place.

You wouldn't call Henry Marks handsome. His nose was pointy, his lips thin, his facial features noteworthy only for a sweetness implied by a softness in the tuck of flesh around his eyes and the hint of a smile. He could pass for a small-market TV anchorperson, not so handsome that he'd climb any higher without an excess of talent. He had razor-cut silver hair, not too short, and pink cheeks, at least when exercised. His body language, in contrast, announced a brash self-assurance, verging on swagger.

Beibel's best guess was this fellow was yet another innocent victim of a badly malfunctioning GPS—the stories were legion—and had blindly followed the commands of an ill-informed electronic device to this mistaken locale. Either that, or he was a lunatic.

The man lifted the red megaphone. "Campers," he bellowed, using a sports radio announcer's voice, "Campers, start your engines!"

With that, the fellow picked up his backpack and strode purposively toward the front porch as though he'd been invited. That was another characteristic that leapt out about Henry "On Your" Marks. Either he was unable to correctly interpret such elementary cues as skepticism and scorn, or he willfully disregarded them. Could be a strength, could be a serious weakness.

Curious EarthKarers migrated onto the veranda, awaiting an explanation.

Henry Marks lowered the megaphone. "A splendid day, ladies and gentleman, for a JogThink. Could not be better."

On the sun-drenched porch, nobody budged.

"Conditions are ripe. So I say to you, friends and neighbors, who's coming along? The moment is here. Miles to go before we sleep."

Beibel had found EarthKare to be as far from bureaucratized as any aggregation united by common purpose could possibly be. Yet it was clear that there was an undeclared pecking order when it came to interactions with outside entities, from sister environmental organizations to news media to foundations and funding sources. In that pecking order, Rachel was indisputably first. Tellingly, she said nothing.

"I know I know I know." Henry hung his head in mock distress. "You've got other things to do, better things to do. You're not wearing the right clothes, the right shoes. You're not in good shape, you already exercised today, you're saving your energy. You don't know who I am or why I'm here. You certainly don't know why the heck you should go anywhere in my company. All good points. All valid as far as they go. But how far, my friends, do they go? Have you stopped to consider that?"

He paused. To catch his breath? To assess the response?

Rachel continued to gawk, saying nothing.

Interestingly, Henry did not quiver or flinch. "Inertia," he brayed. "Yes, the enemy is inertia. And inertia breeds inertia. And I hope I don't have to tell you *that* cannot be allowed. With all you strive to do, with all you yearn to accomplish, for the sake of all who depend on your efforts, energy is exactly what you need. Inertia must be slayed!"

His gaze raked across the group with the mechanical steadiness of a lighthouse beacon, left to right in measured intervals, eyes briefly resting on each individual EarthKarer before moving on to the next. Last was Beibel, and here Henry's stare came to rest.

"You, sir." Henry moved uncomfortably close. "You look like someone up for a challenge."

Later that evening, there was much speculation as to precisely how it came to pass that Henry Marks, a complete stranger to their world and presumably lacking any advance intelligence, possessed the shrewdness to pinpoint the one other outsider in their midst, and a member of the news media to boot. It was, in retrospect, a stroke of brilliance. Whether accidental or not was a moot consideration, albeit one that would come up a lot regarding the actions of Mr. On Your Marks.

"Yes, you," Henry snapped. "Please step forward."

It seemed to Beibel best to play along rather than turn himself into a hero of the resistance. Either way, compliant or defiant, he was already ensnared. First person, here we come! Beibel pulled himself to his tallest, shoulders squared, chest puffed, right elbow out to a perfect perpendicular, and snapped a crisp military salute. "Sir, reporting for duty, sir," he quipped.

Wolfram could no longer sit back and idly watch. "This guy," Wolfram jerked his meaty thumb toward Beibel, "he's not one of us."

Henry shot back. "So?"

Rachel now pushed forward, stepping directly in front of Wolfram. To Henry, "What's this all about? If you don't mind me asking."

"Simple. My agent apprised me of your predicament."

"Did she say that we actually wanted you?"

"Not in so many words. But the message was clear."

"What message exactly?"

"You have a problem. I can help."

"Simple as that?"

"No, no, ma'am. Nothing simple. If Eva implied that it would be simple, I apologize. Sometimes she gets carried away. Take her with a grain of salt, if you get my drift. No, no. This will take effort. It's doable, mind you, very doable. But it won't be a snap of the old fingers, and presto. No way."

"Do you," Wolfram blurted, "even know who we are? Do you know what we're doing?"

"Saving planet Earth?"

Wolfram slumped with palpable disappointment. Beibel was actually moved to slip a reassuring hand onto the big guy's shoulder.

Ten

HENRY, SATISFIED, RESUMED the methodical review, left to right, across the assembled EarthKarers. He'd survived the first round.

"I'll be brief. Before getting into details about what I do, why it works, why it's important at this crucial juncture, before we address any of that, it's very important, critical actually, to make one thing perfectly clear. I need your trust. Not forever. Just for now. And here's my reasoning. I don't have the time, and frankly neither do you, to devote a mountain of psychological capital to convince you to take the first step with me. Maybe if we had a month or two or three. But time, my friends, is a luxury we do not have. We're all on the same clock, you and me and planet Earth, and it's ticking. You're dedicated to making a difference. I'm dedicated to helping you. I need you to put your doubts aside."

Beibel craned his neck for a better view of Rachel. Whatever perspicacity (or insider information) had led Henry to initially pick on Beibel had now settled onto Rachel as key to his general acceptance. Rachel's stone-faced frown, Beibel was surprised to see, had noticeably softened.

"Sure, you have doubts. Who wouldn't? But if you can, flip that switch, and instead of skepticism, focus on the possibility I can really contribute to your campaign. That's all I'm asking. Do yourself the favor, do planet Earth the favor. Join me."

Like the well-oiled gears of a high-performance racecar, Henry's voice seamlessly shifted from that of a pastor presiding at a graveside service to a drive-time disc jockey spinning the Top 40.

"Join me, ladies and gentlemen, and most importantly, join each other. An introductory session, all yours, free except for the price of just a wee bit of faith. What d'ya say? Everybody In?"

If ten minutes earlier Beibel had been asked, hypothetically, how the EarthKare cadre might respond to a bombastic stranger dressed in enemy garb insisting they drop everything and go tripping off on a pointless outing, genial compliance would not have been one of his guesses.

The alacrity with which EarthKarers signed on forced Beibel to consider that JogThink might be more than sheer bunk. At a minimum, it was bunk that slyly managed a real-world impact, and not exclusively with ass-kissing middle managers predisposed to find merit in anything that C-level higher-ups paid money to foist on them. No, something was happening here, and it occurred to Beibel that he might want to add that inquiry to his checklist.

One after another, first Danielle, then Slim, then the spacey woman with the nose ring Beibel'd not yet been introduced to, then the swarthy fellow with the shaved head they called "Chunk," and finally Rachel herself, gathered 'round Mr. On-Your-Marks, awaiting further instruction. Beibel kept his astonishment to himself.

"Don't have running shoes," said Danielle, glancing down at her Birkenstocks.

Henry sized up her footwear. "You won't be left behind," he assured her.

Celeste, tightening her drawstring sweats, asked, "Can I wear these?"

"Anything goes," Henry answered. "The goal line is all we need to have in common. Which," he noted after a brief pause to make certain everyone was listening, "I will discuss a bit later."

"My Achilles is pretty tender." Dorothy glanced around, as if waiting for someone to second the motion. "Both of them."

Mitchell, her partner in song and dance and life, spoke up. "I'm in cycling shape, sort of. But running? Not so sure."

"I had bronchitis last spring," Chunk reported.

"Might do you good," Slim suggested. "Or it might kill you. Either way."

These comments, Beibel observed, were like confetti, fluttering harmlessly. He believed he was in a position, by dint of his reporter's objectivity and overview, to intuit what EarthKarers mired in the thick of it could not. All their niggling quibbles and petty queries amounted to a de facto vote of confidence. They were unwittingly placing their initials onto Henry Marks' signup sheet. Beibel detected an absurdity. Henry was like some fifteenth-century conquistador landing on the Peruvian coast, armed to the teeth and braced for battle, only to be welcomed by the guileless natives as a savior, a god.

"How long you think this'll take?"

"I need a better pair of socks."

Henry cleared his throat. Everyone, he declared, should report back to the main cabin by—he checked his watch—11:15 hours sharp. Thirty minutes from now.

"You," Henry indicated Rachel in her loose black slacks and yellow pullover, "look fine the way you are." To Beibel, it looked like Henry was leering at her in a way that might be construed as sexual. "I, on the other hand . . ." Henry swept his arm from top to bottom. "I need to change. I brought my own tent. Just show me where to set up."

Wolfram waved his arm, indicating out there, across the meadow, past the cabins, preferably far away.

Henry hoisted his backpack, working his arms through the straps. "Back in a jiffy."

As soon as Henry was out of earshot, Wolfram spat, "A jiffy?"

"It's a phrase," said Rachel.

"That's all this guy is. Words. Empty phrases."

Rachel bristled. "I didn't invite him. I'm not going to defend him. Just take it down a notch."

"Promise me one thing."

Rachel groaned.

"Promise me we'll get this guy out of here. Soon."

"Define 'soon.'"

"Before the conference."

Rachel raked her fingers through her thicket of mangle of hair, then buried her face in her hands.

Wolfram soldiered up and wrapped her in his massive arms. "There, there," he cooed, gruffly patting her skull. "There, there. You just need some rest."

"Or," she jerked from his grasp, "some exercise!"

Eleven

LIMBERING UP ON the veranda and not shy about showing off, Henry Marks wore an eye-popping periwinkle polyester shirt with "On Your Marks" stenciled on the back, skimpy running shorts of a matching hue, and a short-brimmed Italian biker's cap, basic white. No megaphone this time.

"One lap of the meadow to start," Henry declared. "From there, we'll play it by ear. Not a race. Everyone stays together. For now, that's all you need to know."

With that, Henry lit out, prancing on the balls of his feet like the Sugar Plum Fairy in *The Nutcracker*. He was followed closely by a clump that included Rachel, Dorothy, Mitchell, and Celeste. The others bunched in a second clump ten yards back.

At the last second, Beibel had found himself in need of a minor equipment adjustment. The crotch of his underpants misfit in a way that might cause chafing, and he'd elected to hang back a minute to discreetly fix the problem. He'd considered asking Henry to hold up, but it had crossed his mind that Henry Marks might like nothing better than to seize on this little inconvenience to pontificate about some alleged analogy. No thanks. Better to catch up on his own steam.

Starting out a full minute behind forced Beibel to hustle to make up the gap. He was not in great shape. Slow-pitch softball, which he'd been playing two nights a week in a coed league in Brookline, did little to build endurance. Unless it was for chugging beer.

By the time Beibel managed to catch up, a surprising camaraderie had taken hold of the group. Joggers were laughing and bantering, seemingly energized. The mood was jocular, joyful.

"Glad you could make it," Celeste greeted him.

Beibel wanted to respond with a quip but was panting too hard to get it out.

Henry jogged backward to intercept him, literally running in reverse while facing forward. "Don't kill yourself," he cautioned.

"Goo . . . good . . . ad . . . advice," Beibel gasped.

Henry stayed in the lead, but only by a step. The pack, two and three abreast, kept close behind. They came to the end of the flattened grass parking area.

Henry hesitated. "This way?"

The question had to be rhetorical. There was only a continuation onto a rutted dirt road. The other option was straight into the woods.

"I get it," chirped Celeste. "Two roads diverged?"

Beibel couldn't resist. "But what if one's not even a road?"

The EarthKare group turned in unison to Beibel with newfound regard. Breathing hard, Beibel had nothing to add.

"Every step we take, in any direction," Henry declared, "becomes a road. All roads have beginnings. All roads have ends. Some, as Celeste here points out, are less traveled. Some, as I point out, have never once been traveled. And some," Henry swept his hand with magisterial grace, a maître d' showing a favored patron the coveted corner table, ". . . are simply the easiest to follow."

With that, Henry's Herd was on the move again. Indian summer, mysterious, delicious, fragile, fleeting. Golden light glazed the valley's west-facing slopes. Nobody spoke. Henry set the pace. There was barely a breeze. The only sound was the heavy huffing of humans.

This long stretch was all downhill. Soon the snaking descent began to plateau. They came aside a frothing river, narrow as a bike path.

Henry broke the silence. "It won't always be this easy."

The herd tightened around him.

"You mean," asked Chunk, mimicking the put-upon whine of a sullen teenager assigned to clean out the family garage, "we're gonna have to, you know, run back up that sucker?"

Henry replied in the same easy, confident tone he used when dispensing other platitudes. "Well, we could see if we can find ourselves a route back to base camp without having to go back uphill. Never been done before but could be worth a shot. Every downhill has its uphill," Henry proclaimed, "unless you've no plans to return."

Earthers awaited elucidation. But that enigmatic aphorism, whatever it meant, was all the pronouncement Henry was making for now. He resumed his jog. Rachel was the first to follow. Beibel again took up his position at the rear of the herd. It was the superior perspective, journalistically speaking.

Lagging a few yards back, without wholly losing contact, allowed Beibel an enhanced view of the enterprise. He could accept that the act of jogging, even at this languid pace, provided benefits. It improved the mood of anyone doing it, and that, to his surprise, included him. Was he starting to succumb to the chicanery? Hard to tell. Yet he did admit that it made him feel pretty damn good, this stretching of his limbs, this engagement of flaccid quadriceps and balky calves, traversing step by hobbling step this gilded expanse of God's green earth.

Such cogitations slowed Beibel further. He was now a good fifty yards behind the last person in the herd, Dorothy with her varicose veins and balky Achilles tendons. Catching up was going to be a chore. Yet the alternative, yelling out for them to wait, would entail a bit more humble pie than he was prepared just now to eat.

The solution was to quicken his pace. A determined double time was really all he needed. In his mind, it seemed doable. The mind was a wonderful thing.

The road leveled out as it neared the river. A phalanx of bobbing bodies fanned out along the dirt road, framed by a canopy of dazzling red and gold leaves. The postcard serenity brought a loopy smile to Beibel's haggard face, but his pleasure was short-lived. He needed to catch up.

The river was high for this time of year. Less than a few feet of bank separated the rushing river from the pastures abutting it. The harvested fields were stubbled with wilted corn stalks. Struggling to make up ground, Beibel found the beauty of the valley, the rounded hills, the shimmering river, the bursts of color amid pockets of primal green, almost a taunt, a subterfuge. Stop in his tracks to soak up nature's glory? Hah! Two roads did indeed diverge: One led to a fuller enjoyment of Earth's bounty; the other led to falling farther behind. Beibel wondered if Henry On-Your-Marks had ever thought of that!

Less than two miles, and Beibel'd become a regular Socrates! A poster child for the benefits of the JogThink experience. He dearly did hope that Henry Marks might illuminate some of the fragmentary concepts now zigging like punch-drunk bees through his brain. But first Beibel had to catch up.

This stretch of the river road was predominantly flat, but Beibel, as he hurried along, was finding it to be riddled with hostile inclines, some lasting forty yards or more without any relief. This was not the precipitous Pyrenees of the Tour de France, but that was no fucking consolation. Of course there were steeper challenges in life. But those tragedies might as well have been ghost stories, bad shit that befell others. Beibel despaired of being able to make it back to the EarthKare base camp without the assistance of a motorized vehicle, say, an ambulance.

Why did it seem that Henry's Herd had pulled even farther ahead? Hadn't Beibel been steadily accelerating? Was it an optical illusion caused by sunlight slanting off the sparkling river? Did such a principle of optics in fact exist? It would be nice to think so. It would, come to think of it, be nice to know as much about the principles of physics and light and electromagnetics and visual perception as, say, the average fifth-grader. How's that for a JogThink concept to chew on? It annoyed Beibel to contemplate how ignorant and ill-suited he was for a world that responded, if it responded to anything, to the man who grasped the hard physical properties of the tangible universe. A journalist was but a sorry handmaid to the real-world machinations that mattered. And a journalist who fell so far behind the action that he was barely near enough to know what was taking place was even less than that.

Sweat stung his eyes. Maybe that, and not the hocus-pocus of refracting light, was the cause of this misperception—for what else could it be?—that for all his straining to catch up, he'd fallen farther behind.

The EarthKare pack was spread out along the dirt shoulder between a cornfield and the river. It occurred to Beibel to apply an auditory test, not that his understanding of acoustical properties was any better than his understanding of light. If he were to shout, and if they could hear him above the gurgling of water and the swish of wind through the fields, then how far away could they be?

But what to yell? "Help!" would send the wrong message. Or rather, it would send an accurate message but not one that served his immediate aims. Which, simply put, were: 1) avoid humiliation; 2) reconnect with the group.

A bright idea flashed like a comet across his sweat-stung eyes. All the literature on genius made the point that it often came on unexpectedly, just like this, a flash of brilliant light yielding as it fades a striking clarity. Damn if this frigging JogThink wasn't somehow working its magic!

Beibel swiped the sweat from his eyes. It flashed again, a blurred streak of gold and cobalt blue. It was a bird. It was *the* bird.

"Look!" he screamed. Or believed he screamed. His lungs were on fire. His heart was pounding. His head was woozy.

"Look!" he shouted with all the force he had left. "It's the . . ."

The next thing Beibel knew, he was surrounded by what appeared from his vantage point, flat on his back, to be an early Christian prayer vigil bidding farewell to a departing soul, wishing it well in the sweet hereafter. The first definitive evidence that he might still be alive was the cool sensation of a human hand on his moist brow. Henry On-Your-Marks was kneeling beside him. Henry's face implied grave concern; whether for Beibel or the endangered JogThink outing, he was in no position to assess.

Earthers huddled over him for a better look. It grew dark and claustrophobic, this suffocating huddle. Beibel lay like a toppled limb among the tall trees as perspiration trickled upon him. One fat drop landed on his lips. He spat it away with disgust, an encouraging sign. "I'm . . . I'm . . . okay," Beibel finally puffed.

"Give him space." It was Rachel speaking. She knelt by his skull, opposite Henry. Her voice was calm. Beibel liked that in a woman.

"Let him breathe," she insisted. "Let the man breathe."

The others swiftly recoiled, in unison, like a synchronized water ballet troupe.

"Overexertion," was Henry Marks' pat diagnosis. "It happens."

"Will he?"

"Survive? I think so." A playful twinkle came across Henry's face. "The more pressing question now is: Will he overexert again? Journalists are tough cases. They don't always learn from their mistakes."

Beibel knew he should chuckle, just to prove he was on the rebound. But he really did not find it funny.

"His face," Rachel gasped, "it's so flushed. You sure he's okay?"

"Possibly embarrassment," opined Henry.

"You think?"

"Wouldn't you be?"

"I don't blush. So I'm told."

"But you do get embarrassed, I hope."

"I suppose I do. More when I was younger."

"Probably took more chances then. Socially. That's where embarrassment really kicks in."

"And you know that because?"

"I was like that once. Then I stopped. Taking chances, that is. Socially. I'm thinking of starting again."

"Any particular reason?"

Another kind of embarrassment crept uncomfortably over Beibel, that of the inadvertent eavesdropper. He wondered if he needed to remind them he was still present, pathetic yet sentient.

"Let's not forget," Henry pointed out, "embarrassment is healthy. It's the quality that distinguishes us from animals."

"We don't know that!" complained a male voice from the rear of the huddle.

Henry ignored the challenge. Still kneeling, still eyeing Rachel, he again slid his hand onto Beibel's pink-purple forehead. "Feel," he urged.

Rachel's outstretched fingers were long and slender, and soothingly cool.

"Hot," she confirmed.

"Yep."

Their intertwined fingers wriggling over his brow felt to Beibel like earthworms mating.

"What do you think?"

Henry chewed his lower lip, the physician pondering the precise diagnosis. "Yellow fever."

Beibel jerked. Henry applied pressure, holding him down.

"Yellow fever in Vermont?" The skepticism in Rachel's tone made Beibel think she was on his side, pulling for him not to be so afflicted.

"Just a hunch. World is shrinking. Case of Ebola last year in Pennsylvania."

Beibel bolted upright.

Henry thrust his arms gallantly outward, a magician displaying for his astonished audience the rabbit yanked from the top hat. "He lives!"

Twelve

STAGGERING TO HIS feet and still wobbly, Beibel permitted Henry, acting as doting parent, to brush away the dust and roadside debris that clung to the back of his sweat-moistened legs. It was more than a little humiliating, but Beibel had to admit he'd earned it. He supposed he should eat more crow and thank Henry. Luckily, Henry stepped back and prepared to address the group.

Beibel appreciated how different this group was from what he imagined Henry's typical audience to be. For starters, there was the matter of money: Earning ever more of it, or any of it, was not EarthKare's goal. Nor was improving organizational efficiency or solidifying innovative approaches to teamwork or upgrading employee satisfaction and retention. Nor was getting in touch with their inner leader or transitioning from good to great to greatest. Nor was creating an optimal environment for meeting the challenges of a turbulent future. Although on this last point, there might be some relevance. EarthKare was concerned with the "environment."

"So . . . what did we learn?" Henry clasped his hands at his chest, the patient maestro. "What, most importantly, shall we learn?"

The facts were straightforward enough. Beibel had fallen behind, he'd clamored to catch up and in so doing exceeded the limits of his limited physical capacity. The gaggle of Earthers had been forced to wait and were now itching to move on. The significance of what had been learned was probably not, Beibel guessed, a question gnawing at anyone.

The semicircle of onlookers that had formed around the fallen Beibel was now respectfully silent, encircling Henry. He had their full attention. Quite an accomplishment in less than two miles, and much of it downhill. It brought Beibel no pleasure to note the contribution his bumbling had made to Henry's early success.

"For starters, we've learned that downhill stretches, so easy on the muscles, nonetheless contain bumps and challenges. Downhill appears easier, and yet . . ." Henry nodded toward Exhibit A, "easy can be a trap. The feeling you get from cruising downhill—of pleasure, of confidence, of promise—that's a nice feeling. A case can be made that it's better to begin by heading downhill. Better than the dispiriting conditions of chugging uphill. Bummer. Not so fun. Instead of getting in touch with boundless hope, you instantly confront your imitations. The aching knees, the complaining muscles, the grunt and grind. Starting off uphill can discourage us from undertaking . . ."

"The quest," Beibel blurted, his first coherent words since collapsing. "The quest to be all we can be!"

Jaws dropped. Including Beibel's own.

Had those words actually sprang from his lips? "Be all you can be" was a trope Beibel deplored, as much for its overuse as for its banality. He'd like to think he'd said it with sarcasm, but the evidence was lacking. Perhaps he had suffered a concussion. He did hope Henry would hurry up and say something. Otherwise, he might have to collapse again to duck the attention.

"Well said, very well said," Henry declared with a crispness tinged by annoyance. "Yes, be all you can be, be all *we* can be. In many ways, that's the goal. Shall we?"

Without further ado, Henry turned and began loping with his pigeon-toed stride up the dirt shoulder of the river road. One by one, Earthers fell in behind. Beibel was careful to position himself nearer the middle of the pack, deeply appreciative that the pace was now markedly slower. As

Exhibit A, he was having an impact on the process. First-person was proving hard to avoid.

They were trundling uphill, hardly faster than a stroll. Henry took the lead. The herd trailed. It struck Beibel that if you didn't know better, Henry, fashion-wise, would appear to be their leader. There was a honed efficiency to his gait, no obvious hitch, no stiffness, seamless with the foot roll, heel to ball to toe. With his periwinkle polyester jersey billowing like a flotation device, with the reflective heels on his Asics kicking back with machine-like regularity, elbows tucked and hands dangling low and loose, chin lifted as though peering across a tall fence, Henry looked, for lack of a better term, like a professional. Even if it was a profession consisting of only one member.

JogThink was a process. That Henry had no idea where he was going, yet continued to lead with unwavering conviction, that his ignorance of local geography—such as where the road led or where incline grew difficult—caused him no indecision or in any way undermined his self-confidence, did not escape Beibel's sweat-fogged eyes.

Beibel tried to recall what situation this quality reminded him of. Little Big Horn came to mind.

Thirteen

LATE IN THE series of extended interviews he conducted with Henry Marks, all of which were recorded on his iPhone and will soon be consolidated into a three-part podcast, Lenny Beibel managed a minor investigative discovery. Not exactly newsworthy, yet still it went a long way to demonstrating that he was a keen reporter with a curious mind. For Lenny Beibel was able to learn that, despite appearances, Henry Marks' arrival at the EarthKare conference was the result of neither misunderstanding nor folly.

As it turned out, there was a reason behind the talent agent's aggressive efforts to slot in Henry Marks as the Al Gore substitute. Henry had actively, deliberately pursued the EarthKare gig, and he did so for reasons that had nothing to do with saving planet Earth. At least not initially.

The Orange Tent Interviews—that was the file name Beibel used for the collection, modest yet memorable—were conducted inside the orange three-person Marmot tent that Henry, a fetishist when it came to his private space, had brought with him to Vermont and in which he resided for the duration of the conference. The sessions had a kind of psychiatrist-patient framework, with Henry stretched flat on his DuraRest air mattress while Beibel as interviewer perched on a tripod trail stool. Beibel's agenda, of course, had nothing to do with anyone's mental health, except insofar as he suspected his own would improve if he could gain traction as a professional journalist. That said, there were many interludes captured on the audio in which Henry came circuitously around to a level of deeper self-awareness that would please many a professional therapist. Which Beibel was not.

The majority of the sessions focused on conventional reportorial inquiries. It was journalism on autopilot, chewing on the usual rote checklist: what mom and dad did for work and pleasure; what sports young Henry played or longed to play; books and movies that left their mark; influential mentors and role models, people he admired and detested; lucky breaks that gave him a boost; defeats that left their mark and made him stronger; etc., etc. It could all be capably accomplished by a smartphone app, which if it did not already exist, would so soon enough.

The Orange Tent Interviews ran for an aggregate of nearly three hours. On several occasions Beibel could be heard in the background of the recording emitting a long, drawn-out, unquenchable yawn. We know it's Beibel doing the yawning because on the audio Henry Marks can be simultaneously heard talking, once about the purse-snatcher incident that made him famous, once about a woman he dated in college who dumped him without warning, another time about some insurance company gig in Ohio. It was clear to Beibel that Henry had trotted out these tales many times before, and for very similar reasons: to shape and polish an image that served his self-evident purpose. Truthfully, Beibel felt it was a triumph of self-restraint to yawn as infrequently as he did. All the while he was itching to pop Henry with the Big One.

The Big One that Beibel dared not ask for fear of getting himself summarily banished from the cozy orange tent was: Do you, Henry Marks, really, truly, honestly believe this JogThink shit?

Beibel understood the unstated ground rules. Cannot Go There. Not now, at any rate. Certainly not until he'd made greater progress. There was much work yet to be done before Henry Marks would consider entrusting Lenny Beibel with his most sensitive, personal, and secret truth. Unless, of course, that tightly guarded truth was merely that Henry

Marks did in fact believe every word of his JogThink shit. That was not out of the realm of possibility.

Henry responded to Beibel's questions with prepackaged answers shrewdly calculated to enable the reporter to assemble precisely the profile that Henry had in mind. This was typical of people who receive hefty doses of fawning media attention. Henry presented himself as a humble Everyman who'd fortuitously stumbled on valuable insights that needed to be shared. As the interviews dragged on, as the riffs and stories that Henry, on autopilot, recounted in nearly verbatim versions of the same riffs and stories Beibel had seen reported in prior accounts of JogThink's road to success, Beibel's audible yawning accelerated. As did his struggle to stifle it.

Except once. A poignant memory of a boyhood incident long ago at summer sleepaway camp in Vermont was not, from what Beibel knew, something Henry had previously disclosed. On the audio recording, as Henry is recounting the tale in loving detail, the only sound emitted by an indulgent Beibel is, "Tell me more."

And so he did. The former summer camp attended by young Henry Marks one fateful July when he was eleven years old had been taken over by a radical environmental group previously based in Washington, DC. Henry learned of this development via a Facebook group organized by one of his summer camp chums, Billy Gillman, or William as he was now called in his capacity as VP for strategic planning at Wells Fargo. Billy had been a wily, curious, hyperactive kid and a lot of fun. Wasn't it LOL that the setting of their boyhood summer romps should become a staging ground for communist crackpots? That carefree, towheaded Billy had managed to rise in the ranks of a highly bureaucratized and scandalously profitable corporation was, to Henry's mind, the real LOL.

The pure serendipity of this brought back cherished memories. The green hills. The granite bluff. The cool running river below with its shallow eddies, the twisting bends where the current slowed and the swimming was easy. He was lured back to this Vermont setting, he explained to Beibel, as ineluctably as salmon returning to its spawning ground. For it was in this portion of the White River valley where his imagination was hatched.

Beibel, no naturalist, felt there was something seriously amiss with Henry's salmon analogy. But all he uttered was an admiring "wow."

It was a summer afternoon at the river's edge, Henry explained. Campers gathered atop the giant granite boulder overlooking the river bend. Gibraltar, they called it, for its lofty prominence and the precipitous drop-off. Kids took turns leaping off, screaming the entire way down. Henry, however, meandered off by himself. It was the kind of camp where solo wandering, within shouting distance, was not discouraged.

He came to a thin, sandy peninsula that jutted into the river bend. Henry wondered—these were days, he confided self-importantly to Beibel, when the act of wondering dominated his inner life—what would happen if he hand-dug a narrow channel across the scruffy peninsula? Would the frothing river choose to take advantage of the shortcut he created? It was less than fifteen yards across.

Kneeling like a field hand, he clawed out a thin trench no wider than a roof gutter. With each dredged handful of moist earth, a trickle of river inched farther in this new direction. A half-hour later, there it was, good to go, a brand-new channel! Entirely of his making! Proud of his creation, young Henry (that's how he referred to himself during this section of the Orange Tent Interviews, in the third person) stood and declared aloud, with nobody around to hear, the official name of this brand-new feature of the ancient landscape: the Henry Marks Canal.

For the remainder of the three-week camp session, Henry regularly returned to the peninsula to check on his engineering feat. The channel was becoming wider, deeper. Silvery minnows were calling it home. He could imagine real fish, bigger fish, fish that knew what they were doing, following suit. Through his own labor, with his own small hands, he'd made a revision, an alteration, an improvement as he saw it, to the natural world.

And that, Henry informed Beibel with a grandiosity he otherwise kept under wraps, was still how he viewed himself. Even if nobody else did. He was a wanderer who once upon a time had followed a whim to its logical conclusion, and lo and behold, "the timeless flow of an ageless river had been changed by the hand of yours truly."

Say what? Beibel wondered if he'd not dozed off and dreamt this juicy little riff. Did Mr. On-Your-Marks, he of *Creating Your Own Finish Line* and similarly vapid homilies, actually view himself as a man capable of profound impact?

Beibel had to ask. "So you're thinking?"

"Yep. Time to step up and be all that I can be."

"Sort of like, what's his name?" Later, on listening to the recording, Beibel was especially proud of having come up with this devious prompt on the spot.

Henry took the bait with a modest chuckle. "If you're comparing me to someone like Al Gore, no, no, no, of course not. But you're getting warm. I guess what I'm saying is that JogThink has always been a work in progress, and in order to reach its fullest potential, in order ascend to the next level, in order to truly flourish, the program needs to expand into new markets with new constituents who are seeking other kinds of add-on benefits. Capisce?"

"So here you are."

"Correct. Here I am."

"But without getting paid."

"Correct."

"That's not a problem?"

"Hey, I've got no plans to quit my day job." Another sly chuckle. "Been damn good to me so far."

84

Fourteen

BEIBEL WAS PLEASED to find Henry so open to discussing the intricacies of the business development strategy behind his career. Dispensing cryptic quips to perspiring followers was, Beibel learned, the essence of Henry's approach. JogThink, in the Henry Marks canon, was the table-setting introductory stage of a half-day workshop that culminated, depending on venue and timing stipulations of the host company or organization, in the program's grand finale, a forty to forty-five minute keynote oration billed as "JogTalk."

Earlier in his career, Henry had been booked by budget-conscious groups to perform only one or the other, either the afternoon outdoor team-building JogThink exercise, suitable for up to thirty participants, or the more formal JogTalk speech, meant for large audiences and frequently scheduled to kick off or conclude a conference. But lately, as his star had risen and his leverage in the marketplace had increased, he'd begun insisting, or rather, his booking agent had, that event sponsors purchase the complete On Your Marks package, both JogThink and JogTalk. That way, it was explained, the full benefits of this unique experience would have their maximum impact. *JogTalk* was where the theory was elucidated. *JogThink* was where the tangible benefits were demonstrated in real time.

JogThink was more or less what the title implied, a leisurely jaunt in the affable company of Henry Marks while prompted along the way to ponder his various insights and sayings. The outings were designed as a primer in Henry's philosophy. JogThink was not billed as a fitness program, but rather as an opportunity for participants to share the insight-enhancing processes that Henry himself utilized used in his famously fertile trots. All his books and the entire package of audio downloads were conjured, so the story went, by Henry while jogging.

One of Henry's shrewder discoveries was that nearly everybody felt pretty darn good about getting out of the office, or out of the convention center, and heading outdoors to grab some exercise. As a consequence, the evaluation sheets afterward uniformly gave him high marks ("high marks for Henry Marks" was, in fact, the summation often written into the notes section of the evaluation form, with many respondents attributing this word-play cleverness to the innovative thinking stimulated by JogThink). Henry's promotional material boasted that he routinely received between four and a perfect five on attendee satisfaction surveys, ratings comparable to those enjoyed by fabled performance guru Tony Robbins and slightly better than those received by football coach Lou Holtz.

On every JogThink outing, Henry insisted on a meandering pace. Corporate clients, particularly financial firms like Wells Fargo or Morgan Stanley, invariably contained one or two ultra-fit triathletes itching to strut their stuff. With these hotshots, Henry felt his job was to rein them in. He liked nothing better than to slyly bring an egomaniacal stud back into egalitarian alignment, and to do so without confrontation. Accomplishing this, he explained to Beibel, was as gratifying as ending an armed hostage crisis without a shot being fired.

First, he'd spring ahead of the field like he was in the hundred-meter dash. Then, when he was in front by ten or fifteen yards, he would turn and run backwards, allowing the hotshot to catch up. Wagging a scolding forefinger, he'd warn, "Being first isn't cool. Staying together is." With no further comment, Henry would then recede to the middle of the pack. Nine times of out ten, the hotshot did likewise.

Interestingly, when he initially developed the program, Henry had been stricken with considerable self-doubt. This was another of the interesting revelations Beibel gleaned from the Orange Tent sessions. In the formative stages, Henry had worried—appropriately, in Beibel's estimation—that JogThink was too theoretical, too untested, too unproven. Jogging as the gateway experience to higher consciousness? Who wouldn't have doubts about espousing something so out there and unprovable?

Yet once he'd made the commitment, it was, to use a phrase Henry was careful to never use in public, full speed ahead. Having signed on (literally, with the prestigious Global Talent Agency) to extoll the metaphysics of jogging, a subject that barely existed prior to the shrewd marketing of his alleged insights into it, there was little point in second-guessing its merit.

At least, Henry was careful to point out, he wasn't peddling anything overtly pernicious like the investment tycoons blathering about risk-free, double-digit returns or those fire-and-brimstone football coaches berating audiences to give 110 percent one hundred percent of the time. The one firm instruction Henry always dispensed at the onset of each outing was that the prevailing ethos would be the opposite of a race; the goal was for everyone to hit the finish line more or less simultaneously. Participation trophies for all was the concept.

JogThink outings were not, as Beibel came to understand, intended as vigorous exercise. Henry himself was not capable of anything overly strenuous. No marathons, triathlons, mountain ascents, or Olympic trials on his resume. Part of his appeal was his essential averageness. A couple inches shy of six feet tall, narrow-shouldered, and a tad pigeon-toed, he lacked the musculature of a true athlete and lacked the overachiever's zeal to compensate through dedicated training. His unruly brown hair, when cropped by unfamiliar stylists, tended to clump like crabgrass and grow just as quickly. His face, once gaunt, was now midway on its inevitable journey to fleshing over. No one mistook him for having that lean and hungry look, which nonetheless remained a self-image he embraced.

He had been a competitive runner once, and fairly decent at the high school level. Beibel was able to verify this. Personal best: twenty-ninth place in the Illinois State cross-country championship. Like any sports-minded youth, he would have greatly preferred being a varsity athlete in basketball, baseball, or football. Or soccer. He'd been as susceptible as any child to conventional fantasies. He'd swung a bat and pretended he was Barry Bonds. He'd dribbled a basketball pretending he was Michael Jordan. Long-distance running was never a consideration until other options dead-ended.

Henry's appetite for running waned as a young adult. As he explained it to Beibel, realization that life was no race and death the only true finish line was the clincher. By sophomore year at Ohio State, he was done. After college, Henry moved to Chicago in search of what was disparagingly referred to, though not by him, as a yuppie lifestyle. It was the only goal he could get a handle on. He had counted among his lucky breaks in life that he did not go into dentistry or insurance or software sales, all professions that were suggested as "promising" based on his career aptitude test results. Advertising and public relations seemed a good fit.

Rawson & Wade was the first place he applied to after college. From day one it was as if the firm, sensing his raw talent, was grooming him for great things. Within two years, his responsibilities expanded to include the scripting of radio spots for Oscar Mayer and penning the quarterly newsletters for Atilla Financial, a surprisingly creative—criminally creative, the SEC would later allege—outfit.

By age twenty-seven, Henry's income was well into six figures. He owned a two-bedroom, $1.2 million Millennium Park condo with a majestic view of Lake Michigan, and he had an option to purchase a half-acre of beachfront on Sanibel Island, Florida. By thirty, he was spending half of his time, professionally, with a fragrance company that threw lavish parties, with or without an excuse, on luxury yachts docked at Navy Pier. For his work on this account, Henry was twice nominated for the Golden Trumpet Award and was invited to appear on a panel at a prestigious public relations conference in Madrid, all expenses paid. He missed his connecting flight in London, long story (Beibel asked, but Henry declined to discuss), and never got there. But "Invited to address the International Public Relations Association convention" appeared prominently on his bio.

Rawson & Wade had an employee locker room, and Henry would occasionally head out for lunch hour runs along Lakeshore Drive. Three or four miles at the most. Working up a sweat in this fashion, he told Beibel, helped restore vitality. The psychological exhilaration created by jogging had an effect similar to that of watching an uplifting movie, minus the artifice of character or plot.

Then one early fall evening, he found himself running hard by the lakefront. This story was well known to Beibel, as it appeared in two of Henry's books and nearly every magazine profile, including the one in *Fast Company* that provided so much of the background information that Beibel found useful.

A gospel choir was rehearsing not far from the Grant Park fountain. Onlookers bunched around to listen. Swerving wide, Henry ran into, literally, a fleeing purse-snatcher. In a burst of temporary machismo (jogging, he would subsequently assert, has a miraculous capacity to bolster courage in unique situations), he tackled the scrawny thief and pinned him to the ground. The incident was captured on video by a DePaul University undergrad who was there in order to film the gospel choir in which his mother was a singer.

Henry's actual feat was nowhere near as heroic as it looked on the interminable TV newscast replays. The perp was an emaciated junky, too wasted to do anything but curl into a ball and wait for the cops to arrive. But the news media had its own agenda. Civilian foot patrols as supplement to neighborhood policing was a topic being hotly debated at the time. Bingo, the "Valiant Jogger." Henry's offhand remark to the *Sun Times* about "staying in shape until your moment comes" landed him on Oprah (she sometimes went jogging on the same stretch of lakefront, accompanied by a security guard, of course) along with an Olympic gold medal gymnast and the author of *Who Moved My Cheese?*

That's how the talent agent Eva Rasmussen discovered Henry and instantly saw opportunities where none had previously existed.

Henry's bread and butter had remained fairly stable since inception. It was a concise, pithy, easy-to-grasp seven-step program (or nine-step or five-step—the number varied depending on customer feedback) that coaxed acolytes in ways to transform the drudgery of recreational jogging into a springboard to personal and professional success. The concept enjoyed the basic characteristics of a fad in the sense that it came out of nowhere, was ridiculously simple in its construction, and might have been invented by anyone. But it was Henry Marks, not just anyone, who'd pulled it off.

And it was Henry Marks, and nobody else, who had the moxie to put JogThink into practice at a fortuitous moment when so many Americans were poised, without knowing it, to open their minds, their arms, their wallets to an articulate proselytizer for the latent merits of leading by following, winning by staying with the pack, visualizing downhill while trudging uphill, how to feel better when you feel like crap, etc. Henry was proud of coming up with all this, and he let Beibel know it.

There was, however, something that Henry did not explicitly reveal, yet Beibel was gradually beginning to deduce.

Namely, Henry had grown so adept at this "act," having developed and honed and nurtured it with such careful attention to detail and had performed it successfully so many times to such a wide array of gatherings—optometrist conventions, software user conferences, mortgage banker offsites, employee reward banquets, and executive retreats for many of Western capitalism's major industries—that it made no practical difference what, if anything, he truly believed. His public persona was so thoroughly rehearsed and so deeply ingrained and had proven over the years to be so immensely profitable, that there was no functional distinction between the *real* Henry Marks, if there was such a thing, and the polished stage version.

Near the end of that first Orange Tent session, Beibel thought to squeeze in a question about Henry's personal life. Journalism 101. "Can't be all work and no play" was how Beibel jokingly introduced the matter, confident that Henry was too self-absorbed to detect the subtle mockery.

After a contemplative pause, Henry slowly spun out a nifty tale of passion and heartbreak that Beibel suspected might have been burnished for promotional purposes, if not outright fabricated. It involved an unnamed lady he'd known early in his days at Rawson & Wade. An amateur poet, a soulful Buddhist, a martial arts athlete, and a beauty, this woman had fallen in love with Henry and in so doing had instilled in him the elevated self-assurance that jump-started his journey. It came as a crushing blow when, without warning, she took up with a Brooklyn-based documentary filmmaker Henry declined to identify except to say the asshole's work aired frequently on Netflix.

Beibel would have been content to let the matter drop, but common courtesy dictated that he ask, "Any chance you'll get back with her?"

His recurring dream, Henry confided, was that this lady would emerge from the throng at one of his JogThink convention gigs and together they'd scamper away, no looking back. The fat tear slipping down Henry's cheek as he wound down this little tale was the surprise. It appeared to Beibel to be the real thing.

Fifteen

WOLFRAM LEANED BACK in the Shaker rocker, right foot serenely hooked over left knee, lips pursed in a cat-ate-the-canary grin. He was doing his best to emulate a person who was genuinely relaxed. The joggers had been gone longer than expected, and that was fine; he'd made quite good use of the time, if he said so himself.

As Henry's Herd came into view between the far cabins, it was not lost on Wolfram that they were bunched closely together rather than spread out, as he would have expected. He suspected they'd waited for each other at the edge of the forest and then slyly reassembled into a cohesive brigade for the homestretch. For what purpose? Ah, that was the question, and Wolfram felt confident it would soon be answered.

Nobody was definitively in the lead. Danielle was four abreast with Slim and Dorothy Wickersham and Chunk trouncing along. There was nothing inherently wrong with that except it seemed so improbable. Slim was an athlete, still capable of leading a fast break and scrambling back to steal a pass on defense. Danielle, a professional personal trainer with a master's degree in exercise physiology from the University of Vermont, was marvelously fit. Dorothy, on the other hand, had heavy legs laced with gnarled veins. Plus she was knock-kneed. The only sport Chunk played was golf. He still snuck off to driving ranges and had come to EarthKare from the movement for slower living. Running, even under duress to the outhouse, was not his thing.

It seemed to Wolfram that the pack of joggers bunching, then elongating, then bunching again as they neared the main cabin was modeling its behavior on a bloom of jellyfish, undulating, fluid, flexible, adaptable. Wolfram scanned the canopy for bird activity, mostly to demonstrate how relaxed and generally chill he was. When he turned his attention back to the oncoming runners, his focus settled on Humphrey, the intern he didn't quite trust. Then Rachel came into view.

Rachel had the buoyant look of a woman at the excursion's starting line rather than coming to its exhausted end. She glowed with a kind of cheerleader *joie de vivre*. Wolfram knew all about that episode in her life because she'd once laughingly told him that she'd had a crush on one of the athletes, football or basketball or maybe both. That was more information than he'd wanted, and he wished she'd never told him that.

Henry was half a stride right behind her, content—*too content*, Wolfram felt—not to pass.

On paper, it was preposterous, a dedicated political activist finding romance with an overpaid court jester to the corporate class. But Wolfram was only too aware of Rachel's checkered history with men, not all of whom had pledged allegiance to sustainable lifestyle practices. That fellow Tony— or Antonio, as he preferred to be called—who drove the yellow Porsche with its paltry seventeen mpg. And may have been a cocaine dealer. The dude certainly used the white powder, irises the size of California olives, chalky particles clinging to his nose hairs, and so persistently tone deaf (or stoned) that he once threw a brotherly arm around Wolfram and urged him to "sample *la vida loca, mi amigo.*"

This was during a Coral Gables eco conference Wolfram and Rachel had attended. Tony was ostensibly attending out of a *muy grande* concern for bird species in his allegedly native Venezuela and was willing to pony up a starter contribution of $10,000 to EarthKare. It was shocking to Wolfram, and more than a little disgusting, that Rachel failed to glean Tony's true intent, which had less to do with wildlife conservation than a non-procreative form of animal mating. Wolfram was not saddened to learn, a few months after the conference, of Antonio's arrest. Wolfram tried to dissuade Rachel from testifying at the deportation hearing but was content in knowing it would be to no avail. Sure enough, Antonio was sentenced to three to five years in federal prison.

Yes, Rachel had issues when it came to men. Unsuitability never got in her way. Judging by her array of romantic interests, you'd think she was a sociologist conducting field research. Henry Marks could not be ruled out. Neither, come to think of it, could that nosey weasel of a journalist.

Wolfram rose slowly from his rocker. The last of the runners, Beibel among them, circled the porch, He yawned and stretched, the very picture of bemused relaxation. He cleared his throat loudly.

"How'd it go, y'all?" Folksy endearments did not roll easily off Wolfram's tongue. His stabs at camaraderie tended to clang.

The runners were a merry lot, oxygenated and bobbing about like soap bubbles, slapping high fives, beaming with sweat-glistened faces.

"Everyone safe and sound?"

Wolfram waited to be acknowledged. It did not matter to him who chose to answer or what the answer turned out to be. The concept of gratuitous exercise annoyed him, yet he perfectly understood its allure: It imbued people with the psycho-pharmacological sensation of accomplishment without having to actually achieve anything beyond one's own fatigue. It was a kind of sorcery, a kind of voodoo. It was also, to his mind, a nefarious subterfuge.

The group's effervescent upbeat vibe only sweetened what Wolfram had in store.

Danielle, flushed and invigorated, took it upon herself to respond. "Really great. Next time you should definitely come along."

"Don't have to be in shape," chimed in Celeste.

"But it helps," clucked Mitchell, sucking wind.

Wolfram fought back the urge to lay into them with a scathing cross-examination as to how their experience was any different than that routinely enjoyed by millions of thoughtless citizens at the members-only health clubs that were as ubiquitous as McDonald's franchises. But he had to be careful. He was aware that his personality lent itself to cheap forms of mockery. And he perfectly understood that these misfits whom he was compelled in the spirit of solidarity to accept as comrades would not, with the possible exception of Rachel, dare do it directly to his face.

Instead, he worked his meaty face into what he believed was a beatific smile. "Swell, that's just swell," he cooed. "You might be interested to know, not just you, Danielle, but everyone . . ."

He tried to make eye contact with Rachel, for she was the primary target of what he had to say. They went back a long way through many convoluted episodes. It was bizarre to be so unfailingly understood on such a deep level by someone who did not even like him. Well, that was his cross to bear.

Rachel avoided looking him in the eye. Henry, the conniving opportunist, had maneuvered next to her. That was excellent. Having them side by side for his pronouncement was perfect. Wolfram could not have staged it better if he were playwright *and* director.

Wolfram cleared his throat again, although there was nothing in it, no phlegm or gunk to generate the guttural snort he sought. He would have to snap everyone to attention the old-fashioned way, by raising the alert level.

"While you'all were away, I was able to do some research."

The Earthers, flushed and mellow, paid no attention.

Wolfram stretched to his full height to deliver his report.

"I Googled our friend here, Mr. Marks."

He waited for this to sink in. Whereas Rachel was his primary target, it now occurred to him that he'd perhaps given too little thought to how Henry himself might react. Wolfram's objective in undertaking the research—he'd only scratched the surface and was certain there was more dirt to be found—was to quash this flirtation with frippery and keep the EarthKare agenda focused on no-frills, Saul Alinsky-inspired fundamentals. These were the only reliable tools they possessed or were likely to ever possess. Al Gore, though a jet-setting aristocrat of Eastern prep school privilege, at least projected allegiance with these values. This JogThink charlatan represented a detour straight into the ditch. That's the point Wolfram was driving at, the need to put the EarthKare train back on track. A modest proposal, really.

What he failed to anticipate was that Henry Marks, instead of lurking in the rear to make a swift getaway, would strut to the very front of the porch like some eager Cub Scout at an awards ceremony. Could Henry possibly be under the misimpression that Wolfram's research would burnish his reputation?

"I'll be brief, and to the point. Facts matter, as we often argue. People are free to draw their own conclusions, so long as they're based on facts. Fact . . ."

Henry was agape and expectant.

Wolfram's impulse was to haul off and swat him away. He would have to do it with words.

"Fact: Henry Marks is not, I repeat, is not who he claims to be.

"Fact: Before becoming this guru, this wise man, he was in advertising working for, among others, Frito Lay and the Holiday Inn motel chain.

"Fact: His competitive running career, if you want to call it that, never went further than high school, and even then there's no record he ever actually won a race.

"Fact: Many of his gigs—and incidentally, that's precisely the term he uses for these appearances; you can look it up: gigs!—are on Caribbean cruise ships. First they have singer who does chart-topping tunes from the '60s and '70s, then an impressionist doing celebrities like Whoopi Goldberg and Donald Trump, then Henry Marks.

"Fact: He sometimes gets his audience, the entire audience, to play along in a game of Simon Says. And guess what? Supposedly, they love it! If you can believe the reviews."

As he recited each article of impeachment, Wolfram swept his gaze across the pink and perspiring faces. With this last bill of particulars, he settled on Rachel. Her response was ultimately the only one that counted. His dependence on her was, alas, Wolfram's curse and his blessing. He understood only too well that, absent that attachment, he was little more than an overeducated white dude crank. She was his bridge to the community of man.

There were several more facts he was prepared to reveal. But Rachel raised her hand, the signal to halt. Wolfram had no choice. He shut up.

"Did your research," Rachel challenged, "indicate anything about audience response? That could be interesting."

Wolfram aimed for a blissful Buddhist smirk. He wanted to believe it was convincing. "You mean, if I understand the question, how have the corporate convention attendees and pampered cruise ship passengers responded to the, ah, performances?"

"Correct."

"Like, you know, how many stars? Thumbs up, thumbs down?"

"Exactly."

Wolfram tried to project several moves ahead. The coast, he believed, looked clear. "For the most part, generally speaking, if you believe the comments, Marks seems to have been well received."

Rachel came closer. "That says something, don't you think?"

"Says," Wolfram chortled, "that they're fools!" It was not often that he made a joke. He waited for the snickering.

"Fools," Rachel parried, "are people too."

It killed him. A rebuke from Rachel was like getting a harsh slap across the face from his stern, disapproving mother—for what? For the crime of being the insolent child he had no way of *not* being! And he was just as helpless now to counterattack. His mother was formidable (Wolfram's strength and size were inherited from her, not his father, an actuary for the United Auto Workers), and his valiant struggle to accommodate her hurricane mood swings left a mark on his personality, a permanent tattoo that could be hidden but never removed. There was no telling how messed up he might be had his mother ever made good on her recurring threat to banish Little Woolie from her heart. Until leaving home to attend college at Wisconsin, nearly everything he did was done under the threatening storm cloud of his mother's harsh judgment. His life was one long, frantic escape from her. Mom wanted him to join a fraternity; he would campaign to have them banned from campus. Mom wanted him to major in business management; he would sneer at the dollar bill and all it signified. Mom insisted he stay away from needy girlfriends; he'd seek out only those who'd never want to be alone in his presence.

His relationship to Rachel had become the sturdy, indestructible cornerstone that kept the House of Wolfram from toppling. Getting chastised by her made him feel like an eight-year-old again, rebuked for being merely who he was and always would be.

And she wouldn't let up. "Fools," Rachel coolly reminded him, "are voters. Fools are citizens. I hate to say it, but fools quite likely outnumber the non-fools. And if that's the case— bear with me here—if that's the case, wouldn't it make sense to have them on our side?"

"I was simply sharing some things I learned."

"Sounds to me like you're sharing something you *failed* to learn."

He should probably have just shut up, taken his lumps, and crept back to the yurt. But that sort of improvisational good sense, the wisdom to deftly reroute when the path was blocked, had never been his strength.

"Back, if I may, to the facts. This stranger who is about to play a big role in our conference . . ." Wolfram tilted his head to avoid looking directly at Henry. "This guy might be—I want to emphasize *might be*, as my research is still preliminary and I intend to do more—this guy just might be, and there's frankly no other word for it, a fraud!"

Until now, Henry had been as mute as a criminal defendant counseled against taking the stand in his own defense. With the invocation of the "F" word, indifference was no longer an option.

Rachel tugged at Henry's shoulder. "Don't."

Henry swiped her hand away. He marched up the porch stairs and stood before Wolfram. His face the very picture of puppy dog innocence, Henry inquired, "You're saying you don't believe in me?"

Wolfram was incredulous. "Believe in you?"

Henry nodded. Yes, that was his question.

"Me? Believe in you?"

"You don't think I can help?"

"Well, sure, help. Everyone can help."

"Well, that's all I'm saying."

Wolfram took a moment to process the potential reasonableness of this. Clarity quickly returned. "Whoa, whoa there, my friend. Let's be clear. You didn't come to us as an activist willing to do whatever's needed to assist our cause."

"Correct."

"We counted on Al Gore. Needlessly, in my humble opinion. Then we get you. That's what we're talking about. Big shoes to fill. The point of my research . . ."

A high-pitched squeal shot from deep in the forest. Nobody showed the slightest interest.

"Be honest, my friend," Henry challenged. "Your so-called research shows that I might be able to pull it off. Doesn't it? Am I right? Doesn't it?"

"Gimme a frigging break."

"Did your research show that I can't do it? Did it?"

"That's like disproving a negative."

Henry smiled. "You know, Wolfram, I've heard that phrase my entire life. And I have no goddam idea what it means."

"It means—"

"Enough!" Rachel snapped. "Back off, both of you. You've made your point."

Wolfram was not so sure he had made his point, but he was not unhappy to retreat. He felt confident that seeds of doubt had been planted in fertile soil. His strategy was to lead his comrades to cast aside this rubber chicken–circuit charlatan. Satisfied that he'd taken a most-promising first step in the right direction, Wolfram strode the length of the porch, clomped down the steps, and lumbered proudly away.

Sixteen

EVERY DAY RACHEL emailed the agent in New York, and every day, promptly, she received a curt reply: "Cannot confirm. Will apprise when know more."

Rachel interpreted this response to be little more than a polite, but not *that* polite, kiss-off. The only question was whether Al Gore himself was behaving so insensitively toward some of his most ardent followers or whether he'd been kept in the dark all along by his conniving agent who had more lucrative opportunities to dangle and seemed to find perverse pleasure in proffering the JogThinker as a replacement. For the time being, Henry Marks would have to suffice. For the time being, EarthKare had other worries.

The big-top tent that would be used for the workshops and breakout sessions needed to be imported from Acme Circus Supplies of Manchester, New Hampshire, and arrangements for erecting the behemoth had to be pinned down with the goofballs who ran Acme. From Green Mountain Appliance in Burlington they'd been able, in theory, to secure three solar-powered refrigerators for storing quantities of food. The entire matter of supplying meals was enormously complicated by the fact that establishing a precise headcount was impossible and, due to rampant paranoia about personal privacy, far more trouble than it was worth. And the complex decisions concerning *what* to feed and *where* to purchase it, topics that had been painstakingly investigated and discussed in more detail than a constitutional amendment in a polarized Congress, needed to be definitively settled, pronto!

Water for the anticipated horde was a concern. Commercially bottled was verboten. The valley was laced with sylvan streams abundantly flowing with cool, clear water that was, alas, often contaminated from coliform bacteria seeping down from the fields of local farmers too unenlightened to abstain from unsafe practices. When EarthKare initially relocated to Vermont, they'd established two 700-gallon rainwater tanks directly behind the main cabin. But recent weeks had been exceptionally dry (great for the leaf-peepers!), and the rate of evaporation had nearly eclipsed the rate of accumulation. The same might be said of EarthKare's collective *esprit de corps*.

Rachel threw herself into this shifting patchwork of administrative conundrums. Concrete problems, even when unsolvable, were preferable to cantankerous policy debates, particularly those involving Wolfram. He was smart. He was dedicated. He was capable of ingenuity. He saw the big picture and understood it in strategic terms. He was indefatigable. He was mercilessly persistent. Yet his presence nearly always gave her a splitting headache. Literally. Protracted discussions with Wolfram left her with a dull throbbing in the bones of her skull as though she'd spent the past hour in the dentist chair and the Novocain was wearing off.

Updating email blasts prepared by Celeste and tweaking the subject line, reviewing foul weather contingency plans (a mud-caked Woodstockian hippie pigsty is just what the Fox News types wanted to see and just what EarthKare needed to avoid), authorizing credit card payments to an assortment of vendors, meeting with the Vermont state police to once more reassure them the gathering would be peaceful, overseeing preparations for traffic coordination (regrettably, many attendees had no means of transport except by reliance on fossil fuel–guzzling automobiles), all kept Rachel preoccupied in a way that provided a strange kind of solace. There were better means of finding solace, but those mostly involved some version of packing up and winging away.

Unlike Wolfram, who thought in terms of pitched assaults against the armies of Satan, Rachel harbored no fantasies of ultimate triumph. The struggle, as she viewed it, would be attenuated and perpetual. Victories, if they could be achieved, would be minor and hard to quantify. It was her belief that EarthKare began from a position of nearly certain defeat, and the only viable strategy was to chip away at the mountain of obstacles opposing them. Itsy-bitsy steps, painstakingly progressing along an endless road, was how Rachel understood the process. That was the nature of activist organizing. She refused to endorse the idea that the upcoming conference represented the potential for a dramatic game-changer. The only true game-changer would be if the petroleum industry suddenly switched sides and threw in with EarthKare. Short of that, all initiatives, including the conference, were little more than "do the right thing" gestures, righteous acts performed for righteous reasons.

It was in this spirit, she liked to think, that EarthKare's International Conference might, fingers crossed, make sense. It would be a gathering of the tribes (such as they were), a supercollider of synergistic activist grassroots politics (Wolfram's concept), a call to action (yet to be identified), a great leap forward (Wolfram again). Indulging these fantasies seemed to energize the EarthKare coalition. Any non-fossil fuel energy was welcome.

From their initial overture to Al Gore, back in early April, and the Nobel Prize winner's mildly encouraging response, as relayed secondhand by his unctuous agent, that "it looked interesting," there'd been a guarded hope that magic might be lurking just around the corner. It had happened before in human history, and not just in the Bible. Santa Claus was pure fiction, yet was it not the case that fantastic gift-wrapped presents often materialized under the tree, right on cue?

Rachel recognized that a good argument could be made to chuck it all while she still had energy, still had her health. If it proved correct that EarthKare's efforts were doomed to failure, was this how best to spend her remaining time? There was more to life, of course. She could shut her eyes, click her heels, flip a switch, and there she would be, the same Rachel yet appearing in a very different movie, fingering the slender stem of her chilled wine glass, face tilted to savor the last lavender hues of the harborside sunset, lazily chuckling at her own joke or her companion's. It would require only a slight refocusing. Not an easy task. Or maybe it was.

Since graduate school, preserving planet Earth had been her focus, her preoccupation, her passion. Yet she was ever mindful of the inherent tension between her activism on behalf of Mother Nature and her desire to have more fun more often. Virgin martyr to a Great Cause was not how she viewed herself, even if fellow travelers were inclined to view her in just that way.

If only they knew. In high school she'd been a cheerleader, for God's sake! Go, team, go. Dee-fense, dee-fense. Cavorting on the sidelines, thighs bared to the salacious delight of boys hungry to know her. She was no Joan of Arc, no Mother Teresa, no Rachel Carson. Water-skiing on Diamond Lake in her purple bikini, sleepover gabfests in Marcy's family's finished basement, long minutes at the bathroom mirror studiously applying eyeliner. That was as much the real Rachel Seagrave as the severe face with the mirthless stare in the black-and-white headshot on that one book jacket. She was sexual. She could enjoy flirtation. She liked surprises. She liked surprising herself.

Of her current cohorts, only Wolfram knew this about her, although she was never quite certain exactly what cues he picked up on when it came to social matters in general and sexuality in particular. Her guess was that he was too befogged by his own cataracts to see her with any kind of clarity.

Wolfram probably did harbor some twisted fantasy. But Rachel was fairly certain it was more theoretical than flesh-and-blood. If he saw her in any way as a romantic partner, it was in the tradition of eminent thinkers like Sartre and de Beauvoir presiding over a hearthside salon of engaged intellectuals. That vision actually did hold some appeal. But not with Wolfram.

She was concerned that Wolfram's recent spate of weirdness grew from a paranoid perception that she was drawn to Henry Marks. Was it remotely possible that Wolfram's bizarre barometer functioned as a better gauge of her true inclinations than her own? Technically, Henry did qualify as an "eligible male." But the task for which he might—fingers crossed—prove eligible was the conference keynote. Anything else was frosting on a cake. A cake yet to be baked.

Seventeen

RACHEL DECIDED AGAINST telling anyone she would be meeting Lenny Beibel for a private interview. If Wolfram questioned why she'd not shared this information or why she'd not invited him along, she'd lay the blame on Beibel's aggressive persistence. Zealous reporters, she'd point out, were a notoriously hard lot to deny.

Beibel had in fact been pestering her to grant him some "time alone." He'd raised the matter his first night at the compound while helping her clear the dinner table and again after the JogThink outing while he was still the color purple. She understood he was angling for a private interview, although she wondered why he could not have simply stated it as such. In truth, Beibel sort of weirded her out.

To begin with, Rachel was not at all clear what kind of journalist he was. Or aspired to be. His lack of prestigious credentials was not a particular demerit in her mind. She'd had enough interactions over the years with the likes of *The New York Times* and *The Wall Street Journal* to know better than to assume that a reporter flaunting such highfalutin' bylines was necessarily talented. Or savvy. Or honest. Or interested.

What most concerned her about Beibel wasn't his lack of all-star credentials. It was the wobbly ambiguities of the ones he did purport to have. Blogs on climate change? Tweets on EPA policies? A short-lived column in *Mother Earth News*? White papers for a UN-affiliated nonprofit? Assigned by who? Read by who? How could she be sure the guy wasn't just making stuff up? Yes, he was supposedly considering writing a book, and depending on how this week played out, the EarthKare conference could factor into it. But Beibel's evasive response when she'd asked him point-blank about the outline of this alleged book made her think it existed only as a talking point contrived to beef up his stature and that he'd put it out there primarily to impress her.

Which linked to another worry. Beibel seemed rather too eager to impress her in a particular way that made her wonder if journalistic access was the only access he had in mind. It had happened to her before. That fellow who profiled her for the Minneapolis *Star Tribune* invited her to spend the weekend ice fishing with him up by the Boundary Waters. It's possible the Minneapolis fellow got the wrong idea; inadvertently sending mixed signals had been a problem in her younger years. These days she was more careful. And with Beibel, there seemed little need to even be careful. He was too wormy, too cagey, and probably too needy.

Still, because Beibel was the only media representative to show any interest in covering their conference, it made sense to grant the one-on-one he sought. Maybe he'd leave her alone after that.

She was pleased with herself for suggesting Beibel tag along on an outing to hunt for Japanese knotweed. It would provide the kind of dynamic setting she knew canny journalists crave, affording readers—God, she hoped Beibel had some—a privileged glimpse of the interviewee in her natural habitat, so to speak. Plus, instead of getting saddled with a stultifying sit-down, this would allow her to actually get something done while spending time talking with him.

The Japanese knotweed was high on the region's most-wanted list. First introduced to the region more than a century ago, it was rapidly crowding out plant species that were native to the region, endangering a variety of insects that were themselves a principal food source for various birds, fish, and mammals. Vermonters were encouraged to kill it on sight, and there was plenty to see. It was Rachel who proposed that the EarthKare cadre make regular search-and-destroy missions for this purpose. Her idea was that it would be a sort of team-building exercise, one with a real-world purpose.

Initially, everyone at EarthKare readily joined in. Once a week, roughly, an hour or two at a time. They often went out as a group. With Dorothy and Mitchell taking the lead, folks would fall into robust choral singing like some Alabama chain gang. The green hills came alive with the raucous crooning of perspiring Earthers belting out "We Shall Overcome." But the labor grew tedious, and it could be tough on the legs and lower back, all the clipping and lopping and yanking by the roots. July was hot, hotter than usual. Mounting tasks related to the upcoming convention encroached. Celeste contracted a virulent case of poison ivy on one outing. Wolfram, initially a dutiful if grumpy participant, developed ethical qualms about ending the life of a living entity, noxious or not. Dorothy and Mitchell decided they needed every spare hour to polish their act. By late August, Rachel was the only one who remained interested in hunting knotweed. Which was fine by her.

Late Tuesday morning, as scheduled, Beibel joined her on Outhouse Path. The reporter looked pink-cheeked and fresh in khakis and a dull blue fleece. On seeing him, Rachel smiled. It was her first smile of the day.

"You seem kind of agitated," Beibel observed.

Really? She wouldn't have thought he was that perceptive. In gray sweats and a fraying copper fleece, she felt as drab as she believed she looked.

"I am agitated," she replied.

"Anything I can do?"

"How about we walk without talking. For a while. That'd help."

Beibel complied with her request for silence. A short hike along Outhouse Path and they entered the forest. An overnight windstorm had dropped a new carpet of leaves as brilliantly colored as the illustrations in a Dr. Seuss book. She was feeling better already. A children's book, bouncy text and dreamy illustrations, would be a lovely way for this whole business to be memorialized.

She sensed the reporter's itch to start talking. He had his notepad in hand and kept clicking and unclicking the ballpoint, no doubt to remind her that he was a serious man on assignment, not just another day-hike companion.

The forest was a sanctuary this morning with the high sun streaming through golden leaves. Rachel dropped to her knees and began thrashing through a thicket of ferns beside the path.

"Gotcha! You little scoundrels can't hide from me."

Straightening, Rachel came up with a fistful of limp, pale green plants. Lifting the bunch for Beibel's inspection, she explained, "They're killers. Japanese knotweed." She particularly wanted Beibel to observe the telltale bamboo-like stem and delicate white flowers. "See this?"

As Beibel leaned forward for a closer look, his eyes veered leeringly toward the open neckline of her fleece. Rachel deftly intercepted his glance in a way that let him know she'd noticed, then quickly slipped into a smile to let him know she didn't hold it against him. Beibel, she realized, might be fun to toy with. She liked that in a man.

Handing over the cuttings, Rachel dove back into the fern bed and extracted another handful of knotweed. She was, she realized, performing for Beibel's benefit. Pure improv, the performance would rely on prompts.

"Damn thing spreads like a virus. Soon it's gonna be everywhere."

It was amusing to watch Beibel mull this over, his mouth working as if a chaw of tobacco was tucked in his cheek. No doubt he was calculating how to bring this around to journalistic relevance. A few pithy quotes from her were what he needed.

Beibel tried sounding casual, not nosey. "You're aiming to get rid of all of them? Kind of a big assignment."

"Too big, I'm afraid."

"And that doesn't, you know, discourage you?"

"Absolutely! Wouldn't it discourage you?"

Beibel was flummoxed. For some reason, she felt sympathy for him. She felt sympathy for anyone who couldn't fathom the pure gratification that comes from worthy labor done solely for the sake of it.

The trick with knotweed plants was to dispose of them in a way that precluded proliferation. Even tiny fragments left behind threatened regeneration. Transporting the plants back to the compound to be properly destroyed without spilling seeds or remnants was the challenge. Rachel went prowling through the undergrowth looking for strips of bark or lengths of vine with which to wrap the bundle.

"You're wondering," she said, "why do this if it won't make any difference?"

Beibel bristled. "Did I say that?"

She had him on the defensive, easier than expected. And more fun.

"Not so much with words. Your body language."

Beibel sheepishly dropped his gaze. The word "body" must have triggered something squirmy. His gullibility, she decided, was a pleasing quality. Although it wouldn't serve him very well as a journalist.

She'd plucked far too many plants. Finding nothing along the forest floor suitable for harnessing the sprawling load, she had no option but to squeeze her arms around the bundle. Standing there holding the plants, Rachel was uncomfortably aware that what she most resembled was a protective mother swaddling a newborn baby. Hopefully that cutesy comparison would not find its way into Beibel's notes.

"Give me a hand?"

Here was Beibel's chance to score a contrarian point, to argue that it wasn't worth the effort, that the pernicious spread had gone too far, could not be reversed, and that it was foolish to think so and even more foolish to spend one's precious time waging a battle that was doomed to be lost. Rachel fully expected Beibel to hit her with this. They all did, the haughty oh-so-cool news analysts and commentators who never could see anything but naïve futility in the quest to make the world better. But Beibel surprised her.

Wedging notepad and pen into his back trouser pocket, he held out his arms, offering to give her a hand. Rachel loaded him up.

They tramped in tandem upon the crunching carpet, back to home base, each clutching a bulging armful of damp knotweed to their chests.

"You know, EarthKare could use a man of your skills," she chided. "If, that is, journalism doesn't work out."

Beibel gave it thought before answering. She worried he might be treating her remark as though it was a serious offer to join their ranks. Could he be that gullible?

"Journalism's working out fine," he finally said. "Finer every day, actually."

Eighteen

DIRECTLY BEHIND THE main cabin was a squat plywood bin lined with black plastic garbage bags for storing the severed knotweed stalks until they could be incinerated to death. After plunging their bundles into the bin and politely thanking each other—him for carrying an armload, she for speaking so freely—Rachel bid Beibel adieu. He was a curious fellow.

With a tug, Rachel yanked open the warped back door into the sunlit kitchen. Nobody there, nothing cooking. Fine by her. She cut through the dining hall and made her way upstairs to the office. Also empty, also fine by her. She flopped into her padded swivel chair, sweetly content from having vanquished a small squadron of knotweed. Now it was time to really drill down.

A page of yellow legal paper listing to-do tasks was taped to the largely empty bookshelf. It was a long list. Two items were crossed off so emphatically with a thick black line that it seemed to shine a spotlight on the far longer list of untouched items. At least that's how it appeared to Rachel.

She'd been trying with scant success to convince herself that it was preferable, psychologically, to throw herself fully into the administrative tasks rather than endure the agitation and distress of a more hands-off approach. Better to roll up her sleeves and tackle them all like they were knotweed. That was the theory.

Chief among her failures at EarthKare was the failure to develop a support team that could be trusted, really trusted, to get stuff done. Her colleagues could be trusted to care. They could be trusted to want the best. They could be trusted to do their best. They could be trusted to show up when the bugle sounded. But none of that was the same as getting stuff done. What she needed was a second-in-command who possessed drill-sergeant management capabilities along with the diplomatic skills to coax maximum effort from activists and volunteers. Wolfram would have loved the assignment. He often scolded Rachel, when she complained of weariness, that the micromanaging should be left to him. "Definitely something to consider," was her stock reply, "after the conference."

The conference couldn't come soon enough. The conference was coming far too soon. Both were true.

Attendance was estimated to be . . . well, there were actually no good estimates. Slim was in charge of constituent outreach. Danielle was his assistant. Neither was particularly strong when it came to research skills or rudimentary statistical analysis. Their much-anticipated report was to be delivered at tomorrow morning's organizational showdown. Even as she hoped for the best, Rachel realized she had no clear idea what that figure should be.

"Transportation," and its several subcategories, was second from the top on the yellow sheet. The physical delivery of attendees to the remote conference site was unavoidably connected to the problematic matter of gas-guzzling vehicles. Joking references to Woodstock hippie hordes stuck for days on the New York State Thruway without ever making it to the fabled rock concert were mostly good fun since the analogy, attendance-wise, was so outlandish. All this was the inevitable consequence of the contentious decision, which Rachel prayed would not be revisited at tomorrow's showdown, to stage the event so far from a mass transit hub.

That debate, rural vs. urban, had raged for months and was not really settled until late spring, and even then more by default than consensus. EarthKare already occupied the parcel in Vermont that was, save for its remoteness, perfect. Leasing an alternative venue would almost certainly require more funds than they had. Unenthused about the idea of the conference to begin with, Rachel allowed herself to be countermanded regarding its location. She had to pick her battles. Too bad there were so darn many of them.

"Audio-visual" was listed midway down the yellow page. A sound system that could project the spoken word with clarity to the far reaches of the outdoor amphitheater was essential. Ideally this system would be installed and operated by an experienced technician who was not a stoner. Rachel felt strongly that they owed it to everyone, whatever the final head count, to avoid the muddled acoustics of amateur night at the school gymnasium. And should Al Gore himself materialize—sadly, the prospects of the Nobel laureate showing up had been downgraded to the point where "materialize," a concept straight out of vaudeville magic, was the operative term—his battle-hardened advance team would surely insist on the highest caliber state-of-the-art audio. Henry Marks would make no such demands.

Directly below audio-visual was "Cellphones??" The EarthKare tract itself was a cellphone dead zone, which made the nominal ban more palatable. Delinquents choosing to smuggle their smartphones into the conference would soon be disappointed. However, the ban did leave a gap regarding the delivery of conference updates and notices and the like. It was Rachel's view that old-fashioned word-of-mouth would probably suffice. Unless attendance grew impossibly large. In which case, nothing would suffice.

"Media relations" would have been listed nearer the top if any journalist besides Beibel had shown interest. EarthKare's usual approach to handling media was egalitarian, democratic, straightforward: Should someone with microphone or notepad pop a question, whoever was nearest or most readily available was authorized to respond. No designated spokesperson, no pecking order, no official press releases, no comprehensive media strategy, nor, God forbid, any deliberate spin-doctoring.

Egalitarianism aside, Rachel was the EarthKare personality most frequently identified by and known to media outlets, mainstream and otherwise. As such, she was alert to the importance of concealing the group's flakier features. For example, Wolfram being interviewed on Fox News by one of their devious sexpots was a nightmare scenario so alarming it was almost comical. Except to Wolfram, who once confided that he had a recurring dream about the two of them making a joint appearance on *60 Minutes*, strolling the banks of a garbage-strewn river as a multi-camera film crew recorded their commentary on a wide range of environmental degradations.

Ugh.

Perusing again the page-long checklist of the daunting undone, Rachel landed with gratitude on the one item that could be definitively crossed off.

The Wickershams' participation onstage as a warm-up act was a settled matter. In her view, Dorothy and Mitchell were the true soul of EarthKare. Selfless and stalwart, they were the collective's only couple. A decade older than any of the others, the Wickershams were often called on to pitch in as surrogate parents by emotionally unstable comrades, and they reputedly performed quite capably in this role, although Rachel had never sought them out for this reason. The Wickershams were unfailingly supportive, empathic, reassuring, and mostly wise. EarthKare was lucky to have them.

Having met as students at Grinnell College in Iowa where they were co-directors of the campus Environmental Action chapter, they'd been together, with the exception of one mind-boggling episode, ever since.

After college, they decamped for El Salvador to work on a rural agricultural cooperative. Next was South Africa, streamlining the medical services at healthcare clinics in the Transkei. Then on to Quito, where they performed similar services on behalf of a Rockefeller-funded NGO.

Peace Corp workers without the portfolio were essentially what they'd become. After Quito, they returned stateside. It seemed like the right time for a stint in the United

States, where pockets of inequality and deprivation rivaled anything to be found in the underdeveloped world. Old friends from the Transkei who'd moved back to DC to work for the World Health Organization took Mitchell and Dorothy to a symposium about climate change and species extinction at the All Souls Unitarian Church off Sixteenth Street. Rachel was the speaker. The Wickershams were sold.

Dorothy was gangly and pale with hair the texture of dried lawn. She had blotchy skin and a myopic squint even when wearing rectangular granny glasses. She was the kind of woman who struck people as middle-aged even when she was in her early twenties. She therefore seemed never to have aged.

Mitchell, tall and sandy-haired, sported a massive beard that curled over his lips, greatly enlarging the surface area of his narrow face. He enjoyed raking the beard with his fingernails as he talked. Like Dorothy, his wardrobe emphasized bargain-basement aesthetics. There was something of the Amish about the two of them, diligent and devout in their renunciation of capitalist superficialities.

The Wickershams' staunch disavowal of capitalist frivolity fell short in only one respect, but it was a doozy. In their spare time, they tap-danced and sang Broadway show tunes. They enjoyed rewriting the lyrics of American songbook chestnuts, with a special fondness for scripting witty repartee introductions to each number. Every chance they got, they rehearsed with the determination of young prodigies lusting after that one big break.

Rachel alone understood what lay behind the Wickershams' strange hobby, and that was only because she'd become, quite reluctantly, Dorothy's confidante. Early one winter evening, they'd found themselves alone in the DuPont Circle headquarters. Sheepishly, Dorothy had asked Rachel if she could speak with her about a deeply personal matter.

"As long as it's not about your marriage," Rachel had joked.

That's exactly what it was about. Dorothy had met another man.

He was younger, Puerto Rican, and, of all things, an aspiring song-and-dance man with dreams of a career on Broadway. They'd met on Amtrak.

"He's just so beautiful," Dorothy had gushed in a schoolgirl tremolo that seemed to come from a different person. "His skin, his eyes, his lips. I want to have him stuffed and put him on my sofa so I can just sit there and stare at him."

Rachel was speechless. Dorothy continued. Of course she'd told Mitchell about the dalliance. How could she not? They'd been soulmates at the most intimate levels of sharing and trust for more than fifteen years. Together they'd witnessed unspeakable horrors, flies swarming the naked corpses of infants, crippled beggars thrashed by *Guardia Civil*. She told Rachel she'd never seen Mitchell so upset.

"You disgust me!" he'd roared.

The confrontation had taken place in the third-floor bedroom of the Adams Morgan row house they shared with several other activists, one from Oxfam, two from the Service Employees Union. Dorothy worried that the outburst would be overheard. Yet it'd pleased her to see Mitchell so passionate, even if the emotion was rage. "He wants," she confided to Rachel with a girlish titter, "to win me back. By taking singing and dancing lessons."

"That's ridiculous," Rachel had blurted. For it was ridiculous.

"He wants us to be—his term—an act."

"Do you love him?" Rachel had asked, not even sure which man she meant.

They'd started out by imitating sequences from *Singing in the Rain* and *Shall We Dance?* They took tap dance lessons with a private tutor. As for singing, they practiced in the shower.

Their marriage saved, a low-budget, ever-ready, all-purpose opening act was born. Adaptable to any liberal-leftist cause, any type of venue, indoors or out, from church basements to blankets on the lawn, in sickness and in health, rain or shine, the Wickershams were willing at the drop of a hat ("Cheek to Cheek" from the movie *Top Hat* was one of their favorites) to enthusiastically report for duty. All Mitchell and Dorothy asked in return was the opportunity to strut their stuff at any activist gathering of fifteen or more. They'd done it outdoors in the rain for a United Farm workers local in Merced, California, and braved a blizzard in Marquette, Michigan, to perform at a Save the Canadian Lynx fundraiser held at an eight-lane bowling alley. They saw themselves in the artist/activist tradition of Woody Guthrie, and one could not help but admire their passion to follow, however modestly, in the great troubadour's footsteps.

There was never a doubt they would be called on to strut their stuff at EarthKare's International Convention. Where exactly in the program they should appear and for how long were the only considerations. Characteristically, Dorothy and Mitchell insisted that it did not matter to them. Realistically, it was understood that they could not be coldly shunted off, say, to the Saturday morning slot prior to yoga. Opening night, after the modern dance troupe, after the scientific lecture, but prior to the keynote, was decided to be safest.

The good thing about opening night of a two-day event was that there would be ample time afterward to rebound from any mishap. Depending, of course, on the scale of the mishap.

Nineteen

IT WAS AN arresting sight, Wolfram astride a limestone boulder, backdropped by primal green mountains, the early sun a spotlight upon his pumpkin face. That Wolfram came armed with a clipboard to use as a prop was, to Rachel's mind, needless overkill. She had no one but herself to blame.

Wolfram presiding over this, their final organizational meeting, was her idea. The old adage "better to have him inside the tent than pissing out" had influenced her thinking, that and her accumulating fatigue with the whole business. But the presence of the clipboard was scaring her, especially Wolfram's saber-rattling way of waving it as a pointer to indicate where along the cluster of limestone slabs he wished the arriving Earthers to sit. Best case, chairing this session would mute his disruptive impulses, and the clipboard would function as a security blanket. A mellow Wolfram would be most welcome.

Rachel was pleased with her decision to schedule this meeting early and outdoors, away from the ranch. The hilltop orchard setting would serve as reminder to all that it was *this*—the windswept landscape, the long green valley, the clear, crisp air, and the dense forest—that knit them together, that gave them purpose, that cheered them on. Nature was their guru. They were forever her acolytes. For all the hassles, the headaches, the aggravation and discord, it was the glory of the natural world that brought each of them, in their own way, to the bargaining table. They were, for now, teammates.

Bestride the boulder, Wolfram struck a commanding pose. Rachel sat nearest, on the ridged lip of a cold, casket-shaped rock. Dorothy, Slim, Danielle, Mitchell, Celeste, and Chunk situated themselves along neighboring slabs. Beibel was absent by agreement. Rachel had expressly asked him to keep away, amusing herself with the silliness of the phrase "executive session" even as she invoked it. She'd found it curious that Beibel did not protest. Beibel's initial interest in the prosaic intricacies of EarthKare processes seemed to have exhausted itself. It certainly had exhausted her.

The sun had not yet risen above the treetops. The orchard remained in shadow. Only Wolfram, tall atop the pulpit-like boulder, was caught by sunlight.

"Shall we?" he announced, forcing a smile.

Warily, Rachel gave a thumbs-up.

Wolfram cleared his throat too loudly. "First order of business, attendance. Let's start with that. Slim?"

Slim, dressed in a pitch-black hoodie emblazoned with a bright yellow question mark, rose to his feet. Clasping his hands behind his back, he briskly tilted side to side, a final loosening up during the coach's timeout before being sent into the game.

Slim slid nearer Danielle, his constituent outreach colleague, sitting comfortably in a lotus position, despite wearing tight purple jeans, on the flat stone.

Slim said, "We ran some comparables. You know the term? Comparables?"

Wolfram brought the clipboard to his brow, a sun visor. He said nothing.

It took Slim a few seconds to recognize that Wolfram's lack of an answer was his answer. Slim proceeded. They'd identified two comparables, a 2015 convention of life coaches held in Port Townsend, Washington, and a 2018 medical marijuana conference in Santa Fe, New Mexico, and he went on to briefly outline the characteristics that made these events relevant: the nonurban location, the alt-culture personality of the core constituency, the relatively low media profile of the hosts.

As Slim stuttered through his report, Wolfram's face was a study in barely concealed disgust. Still, Rachel took it as a positive sign that Wolfram allowed Slim to conclude without an outburst. He was trying.

"Nice work, Slim. I can tell you and Danielle did your homework. Bringing it back home, can we, like, attach a number to that?"

Slim squirmed. "Like how many?"

Wolfram nodded. His struggle to remain placid was showing.

"We're thinking two hundred," Slim expounded. "Maybe four. Hundred, that is. Weather's a factor. Media coverage, for sure. Right now, shit, I don't have to tell you. But if Gore, Al Gore I mean, well, that would definitely skew the tally."

Had Slim said "skew" or "screw"? Rachel couldn't tell. Probably it made no difference. She waited for Wolfram to explode. He remained chillingly calm.

"Thanks, Slim. Moving on, how about parking? Mitchell?"

No need for Mitchell to summarize the dilemma. It was known to all. EarthKare intended to advocate for stringent carpooling. Nonetheless, it would be necessary to carve out space for parking. There was no way to prettify this loathsome fact; some portion of the fields at the edge of the compound would have to be devoted to accommodating the enemy. Even Wolfram acknowledged that automobile owners had the potential to become effective activists. Their reeducation would have to wait until later.

Mitchell and Dorothy, dressed in matching two-tone Patagonia pullovers, squatted beside an indentation in the stone slab that looked, based on a charred fragment of log, to have once been a firepit. "Parking," Mitchell declared, busy fingers combing through gnarly beard, "is a problem."

"Tell me," Wolfram cackled, "something I don't know."

"You don't know," chirped Mitchell with a class clown snigger, "how big a problem it really is."

Before Wolfram could process the degree of this impertinence, Mitchell continued. Best option was to use the far parcel of the meadow nearest the dirt road. Upside: convenience; no added expense; autos largely out of sight. Downside: damage to native grasses; god-awful karma.

Another option was the cow pasture of a dairy farmer down the road named Owen Brown. Upside: less than a twenty-minute hike from there to EarthKare; the conference site itself would be left a legitimately auto-free zone. Downside: they'd have to pay a yet-to-be-negotiated usage fee; farmer Brown was a MAGA zealot who'd be sorely tempted to engage with tree-hugging visitors.

Wolfram swatted his own head with the clipboard, one swift thunk. It had a bizarre calming effect. "Moving on. Bus transportation." He glanced again at the clipboard, which apparently did contain typed notes. "Slim?"

How had it come to pass that Slim, affable yet ditzy, was assigned to logistics? Rachel tried to recall, going all the way back to early spring, exactly how responsibilities had been divvied up. Was she responsible? Back then the whole idea of an EarthKare International Conference seemed so farfetched and improbable that, in the breezy spirit of the old whatever, she might well have consented—yeah, sure, *whatever*—to assigning Slim to transportation logistics.

Slim stood as if facing the firing squad. In a grim monotone, he explained that their best option was Granite State Bus in Manchester, New Hampshire. The company website, according to Slim, looked "quite professional" and stated the company was a full-scale operation with certified, experienced drivers and vehicles that could hold up to thirty-six passengers. Slim added that there should be no problem fulfilling EarthKare's request: two buses, preferably fuel efficient, plus drivers, preferably eco-friendly, operating out of White River, available on two separate dates, Sept 26 when the conference began, and two days later when it would conclude.

"Soooo . . ." Wolfram dragged out the word like a children's hour storyteller building suspense. "Everything finalized?"

Slim was ready. "You bet."

"Great. Do we pay a deposit?"

"Once we get the price quotes. They're sending 'em later today."

"We've got a contract?"

"Once we get the quotes."

"Nothing signed?"

Any remaining fun drained from Slim's eager face.

"The buses, you've got them reserved, right?"

Slim held his ground. "I mean, they said no problem."

"And drivers?"

Slim's gaze swept down the long valley, then out across the orchard with its expanse of stubby trees and gnarled fruit, anywhere but directly at Wolfram.

Again, Wolfram smacked his forehead with the clipboard, this time with no evidence of a calming effect. "Let me get this straight. You believe we've arranged with a company . . . by the way, where did we find these guys?"

"The internet."

"Oh, great. They aren't by any chance virtual buses, are they?"

Slim managed a strangled chuckle.

"Hell, what say we turn this into a Zoom event?"

Slim's gaze sunk to his dirty white Reeboks.

"That'd solve a lot of problems," Wolfram huffed, "going remote."

Rachel pushed out her open palms. Enough already! Halt! Wolfram refused to look.

"What do you say, Slim? Take the whole shebang virtual? No parking problems. No porta-potty problems."

Slim widened his mouth as if poised to respond. No words came out.

"Like get everyone Zooming in from home? Maybe a bowl of popcorn to munch on. Better attendance that way. That what you're thinking? Don't worry. Be happy."

Rachel wanted to scream. Then she did exactly that, a deep larynx shriek that was high-pitched and shrill and very loud. What joy! It had been a long time since she'd really shrieked with all the force she could muster. She shrieked again.

Rachel understood the effect her little outburst would have. She was EarthKare's solid center, its mainstay. The group depended on her for quite a lot, but most of all for stability. Until this moment, she'd never given them cause to worry about her emotional well-being. Well, it was about time they start to worry. Because she was worried too.

Rachel trudged to the upstairs office. The seconds required for her laptop to spiral awake up here in Vermont seemed to take an eternity. On the upside, the interlude allowed her to linger on the enchanting view of the surrounding woods, the dancing light, the skittering squirrels, the pair of proud white birches, all those dazzling maples.

I wander lonely as a cloud. It was a line from a poem she'd had to memorize in high school English. It'd stuck because the image rang so true. She had that in her, the daydreamer. Her thoughts were often lonely clouds gliding upon unseen currents.

Not this day, however.

Finally her Mac blossomed to life. Squinting at the screen (she should probably get an eye doctor appointment once the conference was over), Rachel clicked onto the Granite State Bus site. What she required was a phone number. Click and scroll, click and scroll. Nada. Not even a mailing address. The operation could be headquartered in Indonesia for all she knew. How had Slim even come up with this outfit?

She needed a concrete arrangement regarding the number of buses and drivers and associated expenses and obligations. And that arrangement had to be stipulated in writing, signed by both parties. It was always dangerous when Wolfram was proved right, for it only encouraged what Rachel had come to fear as his Monster Within. Wolfram's personality was the loaded pistol in every EarthKare episode. The only comfort she took was that his MW was most likely to detonate around enemy forces.

At this stage, phone contact was essential. That meant expanding the search to bus companies that actually listed their phone numbers. Googling produced several options. The nearest was in Waltham, Massachusetts, outside of Boston. Rachel poked in the phone number. Her mind a wandering cloud, she waited.

On the fifth ring, a man picked up with a cheerful "Hello."

"Armstrong Transit?"

"Among other things, yeah. What're you looking for?"

At least this wasn't a call center in Manila. Rachel visualized a windowless alley office with a lewd pinup calendar covering a dent in the plaster.

"I need to arrange private bus transport. For an event in Vermont."

A lapse of ten seconds. Rachel was about to inquire if he was still there, when the fellow—she thought it was a male, although the voice could be that of a woman who'd smoked a lot of unfiltered Camels for a lot of years—snapped to life.

"Sorry. A small distraction. Tell me more."

So she did. Two buses operating from White River Junction, available Friday and again on Sunday for a period of five to seven hours each day to function as a shuttle service, back and forth to our conference.

"Sounds doable, yep."

Her spirits lifted unreasonably.

"How many people we talking about, all told?"

EarthKare's failure to get a handle on the attendance question was a symptom of deeper troubles. Asking confederates and supporters to fill out onerous preregistration forms, a wholly reasonable procedure in much of the civilized world, would have provoked suspicion, if not outright alarm. It ran the risk, so Wolfram had argued, of simplifying the task of rounding them all up when the crackdown arrived.

"We expect quite a few," Rachel glumly replied.

"Oh, I see."

This guy could not possibly "see." "Maybe one-fifty, two hundred. Or more. Or less. Depending."

"I like that, depending. I say that myself a lot. Depending." His voice, now that she heard more, was discernibly male, gruff and edged with boredom. "I'll get back to you with a quote. Depending."

Rachel hesitated. Wolfram would eventually demand the information. "What kind of buses?"

"Old ones, lady. But reliable. Depending . . . ha, ha."

Was that phlegmy gurgle a note of mockery? "I mean, miles per gallon."

"Oh, that. Not too good. Unless you're Exxon."

This line of inquiry, she felt, had run its course. Rachel promised the Armstrong Transit rep she would review his quote as soon as he sent it over. One last thought occurred to her.

"Can you provide some references?"

"References?"

"Groups that used your services. Just a couple names. And phone numbers, of course."

"You speak Chinese?"

"Uh, why's that?"

"They love us. Foxwoods. Atlantic City. Niagara Falls. We take 'em by the . . . by the busload!"

Nobody said it would be easy to reverse mankind's abusive relationship with its home planet. Yet there really was no alternative to soldiering on. She'd come too far, was in too deep.

She leaned back in her chair, propped one leg atop the desk, once again resorting to old reliable, the sylvan view out the window, the wandering cloud.

Then she saw it. A bright oscillation of color in the corner of her eye, like the onset of a migraine, orange flecked with cobalt blue. Rachel sprang to the window. The bird had found a perch on the far tip of the lowest limb of the red maple nearest her window. Transfixed, she had the eerie sensation that the bird, with its beady black eyes, was sizing her up.

Here, at last, was a bona fide use for a smartphone. Too bad the devices were banned from the compound. Whereas she mostly agreed with Wolfram's "more harm than good" contention, she'd always known there could come a time when one would come in handy.

Seconds later, the bird was seized anew by the same mysterious whimsy that had brought it here in the first place.

As swiftly as the Oswald's thrush had come onto the stage, it exited.

Twenty

DASHING OUT TO alert others, Rachel discovered she wasn't the only one to have glimpsed the songbird. Celeste reported that she'd been in the outhouse on the west edge of the compound, the one they dubbed Hogwarts, not for its appearance, which was a shack made of rough pine boards with a tarpaper roof, but for the dog-eared copy of *Harry Potter and the Sorcerer's Stone* stashed beside the toilet paper roller. Exiting, Celeste had spotted the Oswald on a decaying stump, not fifteen yards away. At first she thought it was a carved likeness placed there as a prank. She even wondered which dimwitted loony had the piss-poor taste to play such a trick.

The experience was profoundly mystical, Celeste reported. She'd held her breath, literally. She'd dared not move a muscle. A spirit creature straight out of mythology, Oswald seemed to be contemplating *her*. Was she worthy? Gosh, she hoped so. The creature's small round head, perfect as a minted coin, gave an infinitesimal twitch. A nod of approval? Of kinship and acceptance? Of gratitude for all EarthKare was doing on its behalf?

Scurrying around to alert her comrades, her unfastened jeans slipping down her hips, Celeste nearly collided with Henry Marks, who was himself scurrying about like the town crier to spread the news. In his chartreuse shorts and turquoise jersey, he had the coloration of an exotic tropical bird. Had he been better camouflaged, Celeste might have crashed right into him.

"I saw it."

"Me too."

"Are you sure of it?"

"Pretty sure."

"Me too. Pretty sure."

Earthers gathered in the dining hall, huddled in a semi-circle around Rachel, all talking at once. Sunlight pouring through the south-facing windows lent the knotty pine interior the tranquility of an empty church.

Celeste blurted. "We saw it!"

"It lives!"

"Earth lives!"

"Oswald rocks!"

"EarthKare rocks!"

"Rockin' robin!"

"Tweet, tweet."

Rachel beamed. Her colleagues were kiddies on the playground. Without adult supervision. No need to spoil their fun. Wolfram would show up soon enough.

"Little bird, little bird," Celeste sang, striving for a Calypso lilt.

"Like a bi-rd on the wi-re," crooned Slim, who actually could hit the right notes. "Like a . . ."

"Like a marshmallow," threw in Celeste, "on a campfire."

"Hey, that's not how it goes."

Celeste shook a raised fist in mock confrontation. "Making the material my own. You got a problem with that?"

"Hey," Dorothy broke in, "what's that tune, you know, the hit song? 'Two Birds' or something like that?"

Mitchell pressed his eyes shut with his thumbs, racking his brain for the right answer. Billboard chart-toppers were a foreign territory.

"You know, the one by that cute guy with the cool dreads?"

Wolfram, ambling along, cleared his throat and not quietly. The merriment ceased. "Did I miss something?"

"Oswald's thrush," Dorothy gushed. "Multiple sightings, right here." She made a move to hug Wolfram, but he brusquely backpedaled.

Rachel was keenly aware that Wolfram awaited her response. Just to annoy him, she kept up the façade of being delighted by the frivolity. Which, in truth, she was. She appreciated the pent-up desire for silliness among her colleagues. She tried when she could to share it.

"Couldn't make this up," enthused Slim. "Could not fucking make this up! I mean, what're the odds? Endangered birdy. Activists on a mission. Bird returns from the grave to show its support. Cannot make this shit up."

"Rockin' robin," Celeste crooned. Her gyrations to the imagined musical accompaniment had taken a turn in the direction of belly dance.

Wolfram stepped forward. He'd had enough. "Anyone get a photo?"

Glances passed quickly among them like the hot potato game, Slim to Dorothy to Celeste to Mitchell to Henry. To Rachel. Nobody answered.

"Good," Wolfram snorted. "Anyone get a sound recording?" He waited several seconds just to rub it in.

Wolfram strutted to a position directly beside Rachel. It unnerved her to be framed as his teammate, even among teammates who knew the whole story. She took a step back.

"Okay, this can be finessed," Wolfram harrumphed. "But it means our job just got harder. Nobody breathe a word. Nobody! Got it?"

The Earthers froze as if slapped across their smiling faces. Even if Wolfram was wrong about their struggle becoming harder, he'd all but announced that he was intent on making it so.

Rachel stepped in front to face Wolfram directly, her back turned to the others. "See you in the office."

Rachel turned her chair away from the window. She wanted no distractions. She bid Wolfram to sit. He obeyed.

"Yes," she allowed, "this could cause complications."

"Complications? More like a disaster."

"We don't know that for certain."

"Nothing's for certain. Not even extinction, as it turns out."

Rachel couldn't suppress a smile. Although thoroughly lacking a sense of humor, Wolfram nonetheless managed to occasionally produce ingredients of good jokes. With the right comedy partner . . . She quickly put that thought aside.

"Look," Wolfram continued in a stab at conciliation, "I'm as delighted as the next person that the little guy, or gal, has seemingly returned to the land of the living. But . . ."

"Seemingly? I saw it with my own eyes."

"Bad choice of words. My point is that we shouldn't lose sight of the larger picture and our larger goals. The fact that the Oswald may not be one hundred percent extinct does not exactly signal a great triumph. That's what I'm getting at. The bird's not making a comeback, *if* it's making a comeback, because the conditions that drove it to the very brink of extinction have improved in any measurable way." He paused to take up position at the window, placing his left foot atop the sill. He propped his right elbow on his knee, a deep thinker pose. "Unless, that is, its very survival is trumpeted as a sign that things are improving. Canary in the mineshaft, sort of in reverse. That's what I fear. You know, mission accomplished."

"I don't think that, Wolfram. You don't think that. Nobody we work with thinks that. Who's gonna declare 'mission accomplished'? Tell me."

Rachel beat him to it. "Fox News? Ted Cruz? The US Chamber of Commerce? The Koch brothers? Is that who you mean? Guess what? They're saying it already.

"Every time the thermometer dips below freezing for more than three days in a row, they denounce global warming as propaganda. They don't need actual facts. Evidence?

Evidence is for atheist pinheads. They will say what they want and contend whatever suits their agenda, and there is no court of appeals. All we can do is what we do, to the best of our ability. Tend our own little garden, so to speak. Any ray of hope, we grab it. Because the road is long and hard."

"Henry Marks? He saw it?"

"Henry? Maybe."

"Do we trust him?"

"Trust him? In what way?"

"Is he on our side or . . ."

"Or what?"

"Or, to be frank, a double agent?"

Rachel felt a tug toward the window. She yearned to lose herself in the charms of meadow and forest. "I'll talk to him if you want. Truth is, if it's winging around our neck of the woods, it's winging around elsewhere. That's what birds do. They're not house pets. Who's to say we weren't a way station en route to Central Park and then Capitol Hill? To hold a press conference."

"Ha. Back to Henry. You're being evasive."

"I'm not." She hesitated, but the temptation was irresistible. "Besides, he's kind of cute."

Wolfram's struggle not to explode was amusing to watch. Except for the trembling in his clenched jaw, he appeared to have it under control.

"You've got admit, Henry's got mojo."

Wolfram's eyes bulged with disbelief.

"And a kind of freshness."

Wolfram gripped his own chin, keeping it together manually.

"A certain *je ne sais quoi.*"

Rachel felt a tinge of guilt. Getting cutesy in French was unfair of her.

"Bottom line," Wolfram grumbled, "he's not one of us. Never will be."

"We've been over this, Wolfram."

"And?"

"Henry's a skilled presenter. As for his message, it's adaptable."

"Adaptable?" Wolfram howled. "Hey, I'm all for adaptation. In nature. But not when it comes to our political agenda."

Rachel fixed him with a withering frown. Her partnership with Wolfram, for all its rough edges, had served each of them individually and the cause of environmentalism generally. But it was not, when all was said and done, a relationship of equals. On occasion, Wolfram needed to be reminded which of them was the most irreplaceable.

"We're not," she snapped, "having this discussion again. We both wish we could've landed a star. Get over it. I assure you: The very second Al Gore lets us know he's coming, Mr. Marks will be scratched. Until then . . ."

Chastened, Wolfram hid his hurt by turning away to face the window. Part of her wanted to shove him right out, and part of her wanted to pat his massive shoulder and assure him it would all be okay, somehow.

Reeling him back, she sweetly asked, "See anything interesting?"

Wolfram jerked from the window, leaving Rachel with the impression that just maybe he had.

Twenty-One

IN THE BEGINNING, Lenny Beibel had been unnerved by the pervasive sense there was an in-joke floating about that he was not privy to. Or an in-joke that had something to do with him and his outsider status. But over several days he'd adjusted surprisingly well to life around EarthKare.

The stench of rotting vegetables wafting from the compost heap had grown less noticeable. His constipation had eased as the steady diet of crunchy, high-fiber, meatless cuisine gradually worked its cleansing magic on his delicate digestive system. He'd become accustomed to the fly-infested outhouses. Instead of late-night cable news shows, which in recent years he'd come to rely on as an effective sleep aid, he'd been working his way through a biography of Aldo Leopold he'd grabbed from Rachel's office. Several pages at bedtime and he was snoozing. His middle-of-the-night wakefulness subsided as he slowly came to accept the nighttime noises of vigorous fornication and fevered conversation issuing from nearby cabins and yurts as the timeless noises of the natural world. "Make believe you're in the jungle," the ever helpful Slim had counseled, "and you're hearing howler monkeys."

"Those'd keep me awake, big time," Beibel replied. "Especially if I knew they were fucking."

It was clear to Beibel that he was being treated more respectfully. Not to look the gift horse in the mouth, but he sort of wondered why. Soon he gained an insight.

After the alleged Oswald sighting, the central committee had promptly convened an emergency meeting. Rachel, Wolfram, and Celeste. The meeting was held in the upstairs office. The afternoon had become unaccountably warm. Hot and stuffy were the indoor conditions, and the mood.

It was agreed that the sighting, or alleged sighting, as Wolfram insisted on calling it, should be kept secret until they could get a better handle on its political implications and develop tactics for using the discovery, or alleged discovery, to optimal advantage. Whatever that might be. Ideally they would keep it under their hat until after the conference.

Step one was to keep their mouths shut, and step two was to keep busy fingers away from digital leaks. On these, there was no disagreement. But they worried about Beibel. He may have seen the Oswald, and he most certainly believed that others had. Were reporters, like doctors, under some kind of oath that obligated them to divulge truths once they were known? It was agreed that Celeste should address this matter with Beibel, and she should do so before it was too late.

Beibel was seated on a log in the vegetable garden, notebook open, when Celeste approached. Increasingly he was using this quiet patch behind the lettuce bed as his writing studio. It pleased him to be caught in the act of writing, particularly by Celeste.

"What're you writing? If I may ask."

"Spade work, I guess you'd call it. Of a different sort."

"Cool." Celeste bent down, ostensibly to examine an insect clinging to a leafy plant by Beibel's feet. "Can I ask you something?"

Beibel had no choice but to look down the yawning gap in her V-necked shirt. "Sure. Shoot."

"The sighting, you know, of the bird? It cannot be revealed. Not until, well, I don't exactly know how to say this. So I'll just say it. It cannot be revealed until your article. Or book. Or whatever it is is ready. We've all discussed it, and we want it presented in the right way, by the right person, at the right time. You, sir, have an exclusive. Is that the right term?"

Beibel wanted to bend down and plant a kiss atop her lovely, fragrant, satin-haired head.

"An exclusive," Celeste stressed, "so long as nothing is revealed until *after* our conference. Agreed?"

Beibel was tickled by how this was unfolding. The optimist in him, often buried but always lurking, recognized that Celeste, without coming right out and saying it, was coaxing him to make a move. The signs were impossible to ignore. The gushing welcome he'd received from her that first afternoon, her rose-colored appraisal of his journalistic prospects, and now this, giving him the Chosen One treatment. In her own coy manner, Celeste was green-lighting him. He owed it to her to man up.

Morning fog had cleared from the green valley. The surrounding woods danced with the high chirp of happy birds. Beibel rose to his feet. Celeste's eyes, liquid and large, held him fast in a soothing embrace. It seemed as natural as stroking his chin for Beibel to gently slide his open palm onto the warm flesh of her forearm. He was primed and poised, once permission was granted by whatever means she chose to convey it, to let his hand grope its way like a divining rod across the undulating landscape of her body.

Celeste wasn't having it. She pulled back.

Flustered, Beibel shoved the guilty hand into the front pocket of his jeans where it would cause no further damage.

"It happens," Celeste chuckled. "I get it. Don't worry."

Worried? He hoped she didn't see him as worried. Whereas his lustful thoughts had raced far ahead, his actual hand had never strayed beyond a neutral zone inside her elbow. Deniability was on his side. A little friendliness was all he could be legitimately accused of, and since when was that a crime? And what did she mean by that, *it happens*?

Celeste kept staring with those big liquid eyes. She didn't seem at all ruffled or perturbed. For that he was grateful. If he didn't know better—and by now, he probably did—he would've thought she was preparing to green-light him again. Wrong again. "Lot of fellows make that mistake," she explained with a vexing smile. "Believe me, I'm not your type."

Celeste was absolutely his type. She was every man's type. Yet Beibel understood what she was probably too courteous to spell out explicitly: *He* was not *her* type. It made him wonder who was. Slim seemed a good candidate, but Beibel's guess was they'd already taken it for a spin and moved on. Henry? That would be hard to accept.

"You go on back to your writing." She shot him a puzzling wink, and with that she drifted away.

Watching her saunter past the lettuce bed, each slow stride a seduction, Beibel returned to the possibility that she had not completely dismissed him, and with a lucky break or two, he might still turn it around. The prospect of blissful sex with Celeste gave him something to look forward to, something besides the grand opening of the EarthKare conference.

Twenty-Two

THURSDAY MORNING. LENNY Beibel sauntered from his cabin, fuzzyheaded, mellow. That the sun had risen above the stand of birches to the east meant it was 8 a.m. or later. Earthers were not into clocks or watches. They tended to be overtly scornful of anyone expressing a curiosity, much less a need, to ascertain the hour more precisely than could be gleaned by a thumbnail assessment of the sun's trajectory. (Smartphones, similarly distrusted although for different reasons, were banned as a matter of principle from the EarthKare compound.) Beibel once overheard Wolfram lecturing a college volunteer on why this disavowal of "Western time" constituted a secret advantage; it freed up mental capacities otherwise smothered in the universal obsessive-compulsive disorder fomented by the ticking clock.

So it was morning, not too early and not too late. Several Earthers were lollygagging in the pasture, chatting amiably like farmers come to town for market day.

First stop for Beibel was coffee, which meant crossing the pasture to the dining cabin. Rachel was a coffee drinker. In fact, Beibel was hoping to catch her on the side veranda, basking in the sun. She was most talkative after a cup of java, and most fetching, with her freshly showered thicket of hair glistening in the light. The Japanese knotweed outing had him contemplating additional ways he might highlight her in his reporting.

Crossing the meadow, Beibel encountered Wolfram coming the other way.

"Good morning," Beibel saluted. Such a sunny remark could be misinterpreted, but on this fine day he didn't really care. It was, by any standard, a glorious new morning, and he was prepared to defend his remark if called upon.

Wolfram kept moving, and that was fine.

Beibel strolled onward, sunlight warming his face, a light breeze riffling his hair. He had a sensation, uncommon for him, that he was looking especially handsome today, what with a swarthy stubble and having doubtlessly dropped a few pounds due to the compound's no-frills diet. He didn't know if it was Rachel he most hoped would notice or Celeste. Either would do. First come, first served.

Halfway to the main cabin, he realized he'd forgotten his notepad. Turning back to fetch it, he heard a shout. He halted.

Wolfram yelled, frantically flapping his arms in crazed eggbeater gyrations. An agitated Wolfram was enough to agitate anyone, regardless of what was setting him off.

A maroon minivan, caked in dust, coughing and creaking, bumped across the meadow into the perimeter of the compound. Rattling to a halt within spitting distance of the vegetable garden, the van disgorged a slow-moving stream of disheveled passengers. Beibel's visceral response, he had to admit, was no different than Wolfram's. What the hell was going on?

One by one, they emerged in an assortment of shapes and sizes. There wasn't a youngster in the bunch. Some were profoundly stooped. They lingered listlessly around the van like war refugees who'd finally reached safe harbor but were too worn down to celebrate. Even the two African-Americans evinced a vague sort of pallor. There was a stocky no-neck gentleman sporting a floppy safari hat that gave him the appearance of a toadstool. There was a slender woman with thinning gray hair who wore a dark blue Chicago Bears sweatshirt. Several men had full beards that were strikingly white. Others sported hefty double-barrel field binoculars strapped around their necks.

They were birders—a representative sample from what little Beibel knew of that species.

Earthers spilled into the meadow, funneling together as they emerged from their respective cabins. Rachel, in jeans and fleece, pushed to the fore to be the first to make contact. If she didn't do it, Wolfram would.

One birder separated from the group to greet Rachel, emissary to emissary. He had droopy eyes and prominent Dumbo ears, wore a green flannel shirt, and held a clipboard. He could be the tour director. This seemed to Beibel to be a group that probably would have an official tour director.

"Nine of us," the fellow gushed. "Counting me." The fellow reached around with the clipboard to scratch his upper back. "Soon as we heard."

Rachel gasped. "Heard what?"

The tour director rolled his eyes, the universally understood "well, duh" expression. "Facebook."

Religious fanatics flocking to the site of alleged apparition is how it struck Beibel. Whereas most of these were verging on old age, they also displayed a school's-out giddiness, jostling and jabbering.

"Of course you do know," Rachel scolded them with the firmness of a schoolteacher annoyed at having to repeat herself, "it's not confirmed."

"There was a sighting, correct?"

"Fleeting, not conclusive." American Bird Association guidelines leaned heavily on the term "conclusive."

Beibel stepped in. Seeing Rachel in distress brought out a protective instinct that rarely surfaced. In fact, it never surfaced. "Verification," he sternly cautioned, "will in this case be crucial. More so than usual."

"Because?"

"Because the fate of the goddamn world as we know it, and hope to continue knowing it, could hinge on this. We can't afford to fuck up."

The tour director lifted his hands in cartoon surrender. Behind him, the other birders muttered approvingly. Apparently they got it. Whatever it was.

Beibel surprised himself with his little outburst. He hardly knew what it was he was saying, but in saying it, he realized something. EarthKare's general analysis of eco-politics impressed him as largely correct, not that he was any expert. Yet their organizational eccentricities were more likely to derail progress than assist it, and wasn't that so often the case? The world would be so much better off, he mused, if the process for selecting the leaders of humankind's great struggles were as rigorous, say, as the National Football League's annual draft.

Regardless, the birders were not going away. Beibel empathized with Rachel's dilemma. She had little choice but to allow them to prowl about to their heart's content. The forest did not belong to EarthKare. What she did take pains to point out, although it hardly needed to be said, was that the creature's a frigging bird. With wings. Capable of soaring vast distances for no good reason. Maybe its little four-chambered heart's desire was to stay right here in central Vermont to be gawked at by a flock of rickety, two-legged elders armed with oversized binoculars. Maybe after decades of isolation, the creature had grown so damn lonely it preferred to stay put in these gentle hills precisely to cultivate cross-species kinship. That impulse to reach out and bond could, after all, cut both ways.

The birders marched into the woods, two and three abreast, eyes darting high and low like curious children on a treasure hunt. Beibel stood watching the last of them disappear from view, and maybe it was true that he looked upon them with a hint of longing. The birders seemed a pleasant lot, and surveilling the natural world struck Beibel as a perfectly fine hobby, one he might consider taking up in earnest once his life was a little more together.

"You should go with them," Rachel urged.

She was probably trying to get rid of him, but he saw her point. He scurried to catch up.

Setting off with the birders reminded Beibel of a whale-watching trip off Cape Cod he'd once taken with his parents. There were probably a hundred people on board the eighty-foot double-decker, more than half of them school-age children or younger, most of them bribed with assurances that if they behaved, if they didn't run around the deck too much, if they didn't whine for snacks or tease their little sister, if they were good boys and girls and didn't balk too much at the accumulating hours of nothing to see beyond the churning wake of deep sea fishing boats scurrying past, if they, in effect, bit their lips and switched on their very best behavior, they would be amply rewarded with a firsthand sighting of one (or many!) of the storybook wonders of the natural world, an honest-to-God whale!

An hour passed as the vessel performed various zigzag maneuvers in the royal blue waters off Provincetown. Another hour, and the boat changed its position, moving farther out.

The captain would periodically inform the passengers over the nearly inaudible intercom that if they quickly—quickly!—scooted starboard, they would observe a school of dolphins. By the time the Beibel family (mom, dad, younger brother Doug, now an investment analyst in San Diego) fathomed which flank was starboard and trained their eyes southeast, there was nothing but more blue ocean and a distant three-master. Majestic in full sail, it hardly compensated for the absence of whales.

Kiddies grew cranky. Adults grew cranky and mistrustful of the captain's assurances. Yes, the promotional brochures for the whale-watching expedition explicitly stated, in small-ish print, that they were unable to guarantee a sighting. This was *not* SeaWorld, for God's sake. It was God's actual sea, notorious for ignoring the whims and wants of humankind. The sun was inching down. Sunburn was starting to take its toll. The ship's modest galley had run out of soft drinks, chips, M&M's. There was little choice but to chug back to P-town harbor.

And then, with time running out, with land in sight, the captain barked another announcement. Over the malfunctioning PA system, it sounded like he was being strangled. He was already a figure of scorn. Like the great and terrible Wizard of Oz, nobody had actually seen him. Presumably he was ensconced somewhere in the far reaches of the upper deck.

"Starboard! Starboard. Whales! Right whales!" The captain sounded like a chain smoker fighting off an upper respiratory infection.

Most of the children, including young Lenny Beibel, had lost all faith by this point and needed to be forcibly maneuvered to the railing by their parents.

And there they were, three massive shadows just below the ocean's surface, gliding parallel to the boat, playful and compliant. Kids squealed with delight, forgetting their hankering for M&M's and Cheetos. Parents who'd been slumped in deck chairs sprang to life, pointing out fins and spouts, oohing and aahing. When they finally docked, the group was exuberant, joyfully thanking the deck hands for a fantastic expedition and asking them to extend their eternal gratitude to the captain. The dapper old coot soon emerged, shrewdly stationing himself by the gangplank in his white slacks and starched white shirt with naval epaulets. To each deboarding party he doffed his commodore's cap, holding it out for tips.

"Thank you very much," young Lenny had gushed.

"Aye, aye, mate." the commodore had replied.

Twenty-Three

IT TOOK BEIBEL only a minute to catch up with the brigade of birders. They were a slow-moving bunch, slower than JogThinkers.

Mr. Clipboard acknowledged Beibel with a kindly smirk. "Welcome aboard."

"Aye, aye, mate." Beibel saluted, amusing himself but no one else. He'd not thought of that whale-watching experience in thirty years.

The wooded path appeared to be a dried-up creek. It curved irregularly upward, tracing a crease between undulations in the landscape. The water table must be near the surface; marsh and ostrich fern flourished in the gulley. As they climbed, the ferns gave way to thick undergrowth. Beibel spied a thriving clump of Japanese knotweed, tall plants speckled with tiny white flowers. He nearly pointed it out, but thought better of it. Best to simply tag along. The pecking of an industrious woodpecker started up. In perfect unison, birders lifted their binoculars and their superzoom Nikons. Southbound geese in flight is how their formation appeared to Beibel.

"Pileated woodpecker," called out a large woman with pink cherub cheeks and the sprouting red hair of a circus clown.

"Bingo!" confirmed her companion, a slender man with gray muttonchop sideburns and a brown porkpie hat.

They came to the remnants of an old stone wall. Minutes passed. The breeze kicked up. A phalanx of low clouds swept overhead, darkening the gulley. Beibel felt a raindrop.

He asked of no one in particular, "Where do they go when it rains, the birdies?" He really wanted to know. The habit of pondering questions without taking the trouble to research the answers was another reason why he'd not chosen a career in science.

"Same place they go when it's sunny," answered the lady who'd first spotted the woodpecker.

"And snowing," added her companion.

Were they mocking him? Oddly, it pleased Beibel to think so. The silliness of the birders stood in contrast to the unrelenting intensity of EarthKare. He was trying to come up with a witty retort of his own when a lady in a babushka with a long lens camera that resembled a piece of field artillery stopped dead in her tracks and whispered, "Look! Look!"

She pointed her bony forefinger toward the upper branches of a silver birch.

A rustling of leaves, followed by a moment of pure stillness, and again the brisk stirring of leaves. Binoculars abruptly shifted upward, seeking the target area. The birder aggregation had been in the forest less than thirty minutes. Could they possibly be so lucky as to have struck pay dirt this soon? A jostling of an upper branch, a sudden fluttering of its golden endmost leaves. Binocular dials thumbed frantically, zeroing in.

The autumnal camouflage made it difficult. A shimmer of blue, too quick to be certain. Then a blaze of burnt orange, only for an instant. Everyone froze. A bobbing shape winked between fluttering yellow leaves.

"Ah . . . ah . . . ah . . . CHOO!" Beibel's heroic struggle to subdue his sneeze only amplified it. He'd tried to suck it back into his nasal cavity by marshaling every mind-body technique he'd ever heard of, but it ripped out anyway with the raw force of a shotgun blast, both barrels. "ACHOO!"

Birders, oozing disgust, turned in unison to glower at Beibel. You would have thought he'd farted at a state funeral. "I'm only human" was his only defense, and under other circumstances he would have thought it a darn good one. The birders sneered at him for a few seconds more. When, in grunting exasperation, they re-aimed their binoculars to the upper branches only to observe nothing but a gorgeous display of fluttering leaves, no burnt orange dagger, no cobalt blue, they loathed Beibel even more.

Soon the birders remobilized, trudging deeper into the forest, all the while scanning the treetops like a rescue operation searching for disaster survivors (or victims). Beibel knew enough to lag behind, but not so far that he couldn't listen in on their banter.

"It likes to descend to lower elevations around this time of day," opined Mr. Clipboard.

"Oswald's always adapting," clarified the cherub-cheeked lady with the frizzy clown hair. "It's learning all the time about human society, finding out what to avoid, what to explore, what it enjoys."

"Like birdfeeders."

"And beach volleyball. In the 1980s there were sightings at a Club Med in Jamaica."

"It was the nudity."

"Speak for yourself."

"And the jollity. She's known to enjoy human jollity."

"Don't worry," sang a woman with a lovely voice nearly as pure as a bird's. "Be happy."

They all joined in, a discordant chorus throwing themselves into the simple Calypso refrain. It took Beibel, still smarting from being ostracized, a few seconds to realize what they were up to. They were hoping their choral singing would beckon the bird. Apparently something similar had occurred in Negril in 2004, with as many as seven female Oswald's thrushes descending onto the bamboo roof of a Hedonism II cabana while "Don't Worry, Be Happy" blasted from the beach resort sound system during a clothing-optional happy hour event.

"Maybe we should strip naked," suggested the clown-hair lady.

"This is New England," the tour director pointed out. "Nudity'd only confuse her."

"Good point."

Were they making jokes? Beibel wanted to think so. That could indicate he'd be forgiven. Eventually.

The tour director startled Beibel by sidling over and throwing an around his shoulder, buddy-like. "My mother was one of the last to actually see the Oswald, down in its winter home in St. Lucia. Mom swears it was that very night, December 12, 1957, that I was, you know, conceived. Pretty crazy, huh? I kind of feel this quest was meant for me. A lot of us do."

End of story? Beibel felt he should make a comment that showed solidarity, affirming that he too was fascinated by the bird's extraordinary paranormal properties, although sex in the tropics was mainly what was on his mind.

"Must be cool," Beibel declared, sounding like he meant it, "to be a woman on a mission."

For the remainder of the return hike, the birders struggled among themselves to piece together the scraps of evidence they'd gathered. They'd definitely seen "something." The centerpiece of their reasoning was that at least nine savvy, knowledgeable field experts had experienced a visceral "sensation" that was "highly unlikely" to result in "nothing special."

Beibel couldn't help but notice the heavy reliance on a double negative, which seemed to trouble them not at all. Or not trouble them at all. Whatever. It was their collective opinion that as a group they would not have experienced such a uniform and cohesive reaction in the presence of a creature that was merely ordinary, say, a blue jay or tufted titmouse. The sensation was the same for each birder: the electric surge in their fingertips as they adjusted the serrated focusing mechanism on their binoculars, the tingling apprehension of being in the presence of an emissary from another realm, the creature's eerie, almost electromagnetic impact on its surroundings, tranquilizing even an upright brigade of Homo sapiens into a hypnotic calm. This was not the type of evidence that could be used in filing an official Audubon Society confirmation report, yet it surely signaled that the Oswald was out there, up there, somewhere, wily and wary and awaiting . . . well, what exactly was it awaiting?

It wasn't Beibel's place to ask. Not after that bull snort of a sneeze.

Twenty-Four

WOLFRAM LAUNCHED ANOTHER determined Google search: bird groups, bird clubs, Audubon, bird association, for the birds. He had the upstairs office to himself. Nobody to peer over his shoulder at the screen. So long as he remembered to clear his browsing data, no trace left behind. Regarding his research efforts, there was nothing to be ashamed of. It was the inadvertent links and smutty unsolicited pop-ups, unfortunate byproducts of his zealous investigation, that could, in the hands of enemies, who were basically everywhere, cause problems. It was nice to be alone.

From the blog posts and tweets—no, he found nothing amusing about the affinity so many seemed to have for that imbecilic mode of so-called communication—it was clear that bird lovers were a subculture every bit as compulsive and quirky as his fellow Earthers . . . only there were so many more of them!

Prowling their online representations—Birdseye.net, ForTweetSake.com, AudibleAudubon.org, Feathered-Friends.org, and more—Wolfram grew palpably dizzy. Was this what stamp collectors turned to when forced to finally put on their shoes and go outdoors? The birders' hearts were probably in the right place. But their minds? A hasty scan of their voluminous musings and helpful hints led Wolfram to conclude that the birders were every bit as unsophisticated and obtuse as the mindless creatures they doted on ("I've found that wearing a tricorn hat with a slight indentation at the peak into which I place a few kernels of . . ." "I spent two hours waiting for a juvenile least bittern to pick its way along a rock strand toward me. What was it doing there? No clue, but it walked right up to me and pretty much to the minimum focus distance of my 400/5.6 . . .").

Wolfram recognized that his dilemma was not unlike the one that had vexed radical activists ever since mankind first became aware it was possible to overthrow power-mad oppressors (he'd come across the exact date of that historic occurrence on a German Left Party political blog: 674 BC). Namely, how to organize the shapeless mob of shiftless lumpen into effective foot soldiers? He was a secret admirer of Henry Ford who had famously figured this out, although the downside in referencing such an odious example was obvious. Still, it would be nice to do as the great industrial titans had done: Create a visionary plan of action; recruit a workforce capable of implementing the plan; train the workforce to perform specialized tasks; incentivize them to excel beyond mere obedience; then snap your fingers and let the engines of progress roar!

Wolfram abruptly stood. With a firm foot, he kicked his WorkPro swivel chair aside. He was mad at himself. He'd slipped into daydreaming. The internet was one treacherous friggin' sinkhole. More self-control was needed.

EarthKare's biggest enemies, Wolfram had to remind himself, were not loopy tree-huggers and animal rights fanatics. The true bad guys, the ones with the means, motive, and opportunity, as homicide detectives on TV liked to say, were the rightwing corporate fat cats and lapdog shills (not "laptop" as he was once maliciously misquoted by the Associated Press as saying) in the mainstream media.

In his heart, Wolfram was pure Luddite. Still, he couldn't resist the great convenience of the internet. Sure, he was troubled by its seductive capacity to give the false impression that valuable information, the kind that could make a true difference, was obtainable through mere clicks and scrolls. *Real information*—powerful, explosive, incendiary, transformative, revolutionary—was, Wolfram was convinced, only discoverable through fierce struggle. This other stuff, the stuff that abounded on the 'net, was to real information what Cheetos were to cheese.

Just for fun—although his little daydream of instilling in EarthKare assembly line efficiency had already fulfilled his weekly quota of fun—Wolfram Googled, "EarthKare Vermont conference."

The search results scroll nearly knocked him off his stool. Fox News was reporting—the very words "Fox News reporting" filled him with revulsion—something of relevance. The very urge to click the link seemed to Wolfram as sick and voyeuristic as rubbernecking a grizzly roadside accident. Which was something Wolfram indeed was prone to do, although always quick to explain to whomever he was traveling with that he was only trying to learn if help was needed. And that's what he told himself he was doing now as he clicked an item titled, "Logging Industry Applauds Conservation Efforts."

His own obituary would not have been more disturbing to read.

A PR effort was under way. When it came to divining the anthropomorphized thrush's alleged thoughts and intentions, it turned out that two could play that game. What the fanatical birders assumed to be the vulnerable thrush's Achilles heel, its affinity for human society, the crafty strategists of the logging industry characterized as proof of the creature's faith in their benevolent stewardship.

The facts, as presented by the American Council on Logging and Ecology in press releases and statements from a slew of credentialed ornithologists, were these: A bird, at least the female of the species—the male can never be counted on to know what's in his own best long-term interests—that winters in the Caribbean and displays a decided preference for four-star resorts smelling of coconut-scented tanning oil not only feels unthreatened by civilization but demonstrates a preference for its more delectable fruits. Who, if they had a choice, wouldn't choose to summer in New England and winter in the balmy West Indies?

Radical conservation measures, the ACLE pointed out, had been tried before. In the early 1970s, when the alarms were first being sounded about the thrush's demise, a team of scientists from a consortium of North American research universities embarked on a campaign, funded by a grant from the Rockefeller Foundation and employing a network of eco-tourists as volunteers, to "stabilize" the bird's breeding ground in Vermont and its tropical winter habitats. Logging was curtailed in these regions. Use of numerous pesticides like cadusafos, diazinon, dithianon, fenamiphos, and the like was suspended. Swaths of woodland nesting zones were labeled "Do Not Disturb."

The ACLE disputed the popular conception of Oswald's thrush as an innocent, helpless creature threatened by modernity. The truth, they insisted, was even darker: The bird represented a wanton, self-indulgent, shamelessly hedonistic species. Oswald's thrush was polyandrous, meaning that multiple males participate in fertilizing one female. This unusual biological feature was either fascinating or alarming, depending on one's perspective. It was ACLE's contention that the American public should contemplate this bizarre sexual practice, and its implications, before authorizing further expenditure of government resources. Prior conservation efforts, the ACLE noted, conveniently whitewashed the Oswald's sexual perversity. Why?

Linked to the ACLE press release was a Fox News clip featuring a buxom female reporter in a short, tight skirt standing in a forest.

"In an apparent breakthrough in the often acrimonious struggle between conservationists and the American logging industry . . ."

Wolfram watched with one eye shut to mitigate the video's impact.

". . . shows that conscientious logging is a win-win for all interested parties. And that includes the wildlife itself. What radical activists call 'extinction' can often be just a

matter of birds doing their thing, flying naturally under the radar."

Wolfram waited for the shoe to drop. So far, the only visual was the bubbly reporter in the tight sweater gesturing toward the treetops.

"Our key takeaway: We are all in this together. Trees and birds and people like us who are willing to make tough choices that will allow Mother Nature and all her offspring to thrive."'

He braced himself. He could feel it coming, the Big Reveal.

"'Welcome back, Oswald's thrush," the Fox reporter cheerfully signed off. *"Hope you enjoyed your vacation."*

Whew, dodged a bullet there. Or more to the point, ACLE's arsenal lacked that deadly form of ammo.

Onward, Wolfram pointed and clicked.

The ACLE was running full-page display ads in newspapers across the country, including *The New York Times, Wall Street Journal, Washington Post,* and *USA Today.* "Welcome Back, Tweety Bird!" was the banner headline. The full-color ads, which themselves were fodder for additional reports and commentary, featured a lovingly rendered artist drawing with fine-grain, Audubon-esque detail (a glint in the bird's shiny eye, if you looked closely, reflected an image of the Statue of Liberty). The Oswald's thrush was depicted contentedly perched in the open pink palm of a man's hand. The effect was reminiscent of the hyperrealist style associated with Soviet propaganda of the mid-1950s. Wolfram felt nauseated.

The Oswald's thrush was now fully a part of the news cycle, trending upward. The Associated Press had a mindless dispatch that was little more than a report on ACLE's accelerated campaign—as if that itself were news! This item appeared as one of several in a packet of news filler, along with the approaching hurricane in the Gulf of Mexico and a rural Missouri town's round-the-clock hunt for a missing six-year-old girl last seen eating cotton candy at her cousin's birthday party.

What Wolfram found deeply suspicious was why none of these allegedly scrupulous news organizations—forget Fox, but what about *The Washington Post*, *The New York Times*, and the rest?—bothered to point out, even *sotto voce*, what was unquestionably the most salient fact about the situation: Namely, *nobody had* conclusively seen the damn bird since the Nixon administration. Just allegations and innuendo, ghost stories recounted by impressionable children, eyewitness testimony that wouldn't hold up in a kangaroo court. It was enough to drive a fellow over the edge into full-blown paranoia.

The most infuriating aspect of the debacle was the way the reappearance of the bird was being touted as an inspirational, feel-good pick-me-up, draped in the kind of hoary clichés (third and long, buzzer-beater) popular with sports announcers. And with the very same, none-too-subtle message: Be positive! Get motivated! You can do it, baby! Just like Henry fucking Marks!

Henry, it was now clear, was not simply a wrong fit for their conference in all the ways Wolfram already understood. No, Henry was a wrong fit in a very special way. He was not simply some third-string shlub recruited at the last minute to fill a vacant slot. Henry Marks was different all right, and it was the special quality of that difference that troubled Wolfram the most.

Boosting optimism was a cornerstone of Henry's shtick. He boasted of fortifying his listeners, those hapless JogThinkers, with tools for achieving a fresh approach to work and business and life! "Stay positive" was one of the recurring catchphrases in the On Your Marks canon. Likewise, "Quitters never win." Likewise, "Winners never quit." Sound familiar? Almost the exact happy talk words now being extolled by the ACLE and its factotums. Coincidence? Henry Marks air-dropped out of nowhere into their midst at roughly the same point in time that the craven logging industry mounted a zillion-dollar propaganda campaign touting the alleged—not even close to proven, mind you, but merely alleged, alleged, alleged!—return of the Oswald's thrush?

The world had gone mad. And madness was the remedy.

It was time to learn a bit more about this Henry Marks. Wolfram's prior searches, damning as they were, had not gone deep enough. Wolfram wiped the spittle off the keyboard and Googled anew.

First up was the webpage maintained for Henry by his talent agency. Wolfram had hastily perused this when the asshole's name first surfaced, paying scant attention except to note that there was something about the guy's face—eyes too close together, hair too neatly groomed—that made Wolfram think he was less handsome than the photo suggested. Boy, was he correct on that one! Henry's visage, seen live and in person, was a far cry from the swashbuckling visionary squinting boldly into the distant peaks of the future. A tab labeled "tour schedule" appeared on the webpage. Wolfram clicked.

Except for the heart of the pandemic, the guy had been busy. The dates were listed chronologically top to bottom, necessitating a bothersome backward scroll from 2013. Not exactly user friendly, and possibly a ploy to discourage the casual viewer from finding his way to the most recent events? Well, Frederick Wolfram was not so easily deterred.

Arriving at 2023, Wolfram discovered a minor drop in entries. This summer there'd been only three events: an All-state Insurance "Innovation Retreat," a Midwest regional mortgage industry convention, and a Procter and Gamble sales conference in Orlando. For the dates of the EarthKare conference—September 26–28—there was nothing. Interestingly, there was an entry for the last days of the month.

"9/29–10/3, Happiness Cruise Lines, Fort Lauderdale, FL." Wolfram clicked on the blue hyperlink to Happiness Cruise Lines. Immediately, music shot from his Mac. It was a propulsive steel drum rhythm accompanied by a smooth male alto with a thick Caribbean lilt: "Be hoppy, chin up, be hoppy." Frantically, Wolfram wagged the cursor to locate the sound control. "Ain't got no bread, ain't got no friends to feed me head." Wolfram tried clicking onto other tabs—About Us, Package Destinations, Testimonials, Contact—but nothing stopped the infuriating jingle. Worse, each click-through served to restart the inane ditty from the beginning. Finally, he accessed System Preferences and was blessedly able to mute the sucker.

"At last!" he grunted aloud. "Me fuckin' hoppy."

Of course he wasn't. He scrolled through the slideshow depicting the ship's sumptuous luxuries. The photo montage was as unnerving as the soundtrack. Ladies of a certain age in evening gowns sipping cocktails, men in dinner jackets puffing cigars on the top deck, smoke rising toward the starry night. A bare-chested man and a shirtless woman, their backs to the camera, necking in a hot tub. A coffee-skinned waiter in starched whites placing a boiled lobster dinner before an elderly couple at a candle-lit table. A trio of chorus girls in skimpy outfits of shimmering fabric shuffling off to Buffalo. Wolfram hit the Recreation and Entertainment tab.

He didn't know if he was relieved or disappointed to learn that Henry was not listed as the headliner. Henry was fourth on the bill of nightly "culture and enjoyment" options, behind a comedienne who did Whoopi Goldberg and Kim Kardashian imitations; a mentalist who was formerly a senior executive at Goldman Sachs; and a shapely red-haired marine biologist in a skintight wetsuit who swam with sharks and found deep-sea diving a corrective to the aging process. Henry was touted as a leading expert in using personal exercise to "strengthen not just your body but your career, your business, your relationships, and your mind."

At the bottom of the page, it stated, "Check with the ship's captain each day for the exact time of presentations by our all-star entertainers and experts."

Wolfram had seen enough. Shutting the page and pushing away, it occurred to him that Henry's upcoming itinerary contained a potential snag. To travel from an evening gig in rural Vermont and arrive in Fort Lauderdale in time for a late afternoon departure the following day would seem to require some nifty logistics and tight connections. Probably it could be done. There was little that money could not achieve so long as the basic laws of space and time weren't prohibitive.

At any rate, not his worry (not his hoppy either). Let Henry and his conniving agent fret about that. Wolfram could imagine the Borscht Belt quips Mr. JogThinker would gladly insert into his act—yes, by god, an act!—related to travel complications he might have to endure. "Just flew in from Vermont. Boy, are my arms tired!" It always astonished Wolfram how much of the supercilious junk culture (names like Don Draper and Bree Van de Kamp, the marital status of individual Kardashians, which teams were competing in the Super Bowl and who was the favorite) he actually was aware of despite a conscious determination to ignore every bit of it. It was like secondhand smoke insidiously working its way into his bloodstream.

He stood and stretched, satisfied that progress had been made. Without leaving the attic office, without so much as a glance out the open window, he'd managed to see more of the world that really mattered than a brigade of birders could have glimpsed from a hundred-foot observation tower with their double-barrel Zeiss Victory binoculars.

Let the ACLE air its fraud-filled display ads. No way to stop that, and there never would be. Truth in advertising? Ha! One would have better luck praying to Waheguru Moroni than waiting for a megabucks public relations campaign to get slapped down for untruths. Billionaire reactionaries could sponsor a slew of sixty-second spots during the Super

Bowl touting the "fact" that God created the world in seven days, or was it six? Nobody could stop them, and 58 percent of the American public would believe whatever hogwash they were told so long as the production values were polished.

JogThink? What bunk!

Twenty-Five

HIGH ON LENNY Beibel's list of regrets was the decision to forego sports writing. As a haughty younger man, he'd been of the mind that sports were trivial. This attitude was abetted by his own lack of physical strength, physical coordination, and competitive zeal. If he were a better athlete, would he have found athletics to be more meaningful? Water over the dam, road not taken. Too bad. From a writer's point of view, competitive sports offered so much that was absent with this EarthKare project.

Sports, among its other virtues—indeed foremost among its virtues—unfailingly offered up user-friendly narratives. You had a well-defined contest, and it would begin on time. The mode of keeping score was precise and agreed upon. At some finite point in time, the contest would conclude, and there would be an unambiguous determination of a winner. Case closed. Game over. Shut the book.

Exactly what readers prefer. Writers too.

What Beibel desperately needed, both for the still undefined literary project that might bloom from this folly but also for his fragile peace of mind, was a sports-like framework. Would EarthKare win? Lose? Would anyone ever know the final score? Perhaps that's where he, the journalist, came in. But it was hard to see how.

The Orange Tent Interview sessions remained a hopeful development because they allowed him a sense that Henry Marks, for all his hot air blarney, did have aspirations and viewed himself, however myopically, as embroiled in a contest he wanted to win. Moreover, the ACLE had stepped forward as a suitable nemesis, the kind that every sports fan likes to root against. Well, maybe not every fan but enough of them to fill the bleachers.

The loggers had launched a high-profile PR campaign that was increasingly the buzz of the EarthKare compound. The campaign consisted of display ads and free media placements centered around concocted "studies" funded by contrived front groups endorsing ACLE's contention that everyone everywhere wants the natural world to be cleaner, healthier, and sustainable in its optimal state for generations to come. Therefore, the only prudent policy was to place stewardship for the environment in the capable hands of competent grownups rather than fruitcake paranoids who can't distinguish what's worth saving from what has—sadly, regrettably—vanished forever.

Beibel could only imagine how tickled the ACLE was to have drawn EarthKare as its foe. Earthers had been careful never to mention the Oswald's reappearance as anything but unconfirmed and alleged. Nonetheless, more hallucinatory reports—the Oswald's thrush was now being "sighted" with the frequency of UFOs off the Mississippi Gulf Coast, and one lady in the Finger Lakes region claimed to have *spoken with it* in Spanish—invariably brought EarthKare into the story, if only by citing their habitation in the area of Vermont where sightings had occurred. Guilt by association was a damnable practice and pure gold in the capable hands of ACLE publicists. Until now, EarthKare had escaped the worst kind of derision by staying below the radar. How long could that last?

There were a host of organizational mishaps that Beibel could be spending time digging into if he thought any reader would care. The company that EarthKare had engaged to furnish rain-contingency tents seemed to be staffed by clowns. Two days ago their "advance crew" arrived in a rusted Dodge Ram to scout the scene. The crew consisted of three merry fellows who looked to have been plucked straight from the right field bleachers at Fenway Park around the bottom of the seventh, pot-bellied, sunburned, stupid from beer. The tallest of the trio wore mud-spattered work boots and a black Boston Bruins stocking cap.

When Celeste started to run down instructions for early setup, the Bruins fan had quickly waved her off. "Not my department, ma'am. Settle it with the boss."

"Will you," she had asked, "be the ones coming to erect it?"

"Saying it like that, ma'am, the answer's yes, you bet, whenever."

Beibel personally witnessed that scene and had taken note. Yet it was hard to imagine it finding its way into print. At least not under his byline.

Porta potties, whether to arrange for them and, if so, how many, was a matter still not resolved. Danielle had been in contact with a vendor, Whole Flush. If EarthKare decided against going *au naturel*, there was no shortage of available units, and they could be delivered within twenty-four hours. One toilet for every fifty attendees was Whole Flush's recommendation. Err on which side was the question Danielle confronted. A phalanx of seven-foot-high, blue plastic booths reeking of chemical disinfectant was bound to rankle, and not just the hardcore. Less rankled would be anybody who found him- or herself with an emergency need for a prolonged visit. And that population, over the course of two days of mass dining on vegetable- and grain-based meals prepared with little quality control and questionable hygiene standards (food preparation and service was Mitchell's area of responsibility, not Danielle's), could easily balloon.

It tickled Beibel to learn that Wolfram was sticking his hypersensitive nose into this one. Apparently he'd approached Danielle at dinner with his opinion that there were really only two choices: a) dispense altogether with the porta potties and designate a sector of the forest, nearby but not too nearby; or b) rent a few but camouflage them with tree branches to blend in with the landscape.

Danielle ordered four. Was this a matter that anyone without a psychiatric condition would want to read about? Beibel doubted it.

Projected turnout remained a black hole. Numbers tossed around now ranged from as low as fifty to as high as five hundred, but there remained absolutely no rational means of making a reasonable estimate. Advance signups (twenty-six and counting) continued to mean nothing because there was no advantage, logistical or financial, in anybody doing so. EarthKare, promulgating the come one, come all spirit, let it be known that the grounds were spacious (and scenic) and nobody would be turned away. Indeed, the handful who did sign up in advance (an organic farmer from Pittsfield, a Lima, Ohio, labor organizer, a nano chemistry grad student from Reno, of all places) were considered suspect. Early registration seemed to be something only an undercover agent would bother with.

All Beibel could do was persist with the Orange Tent Interviews, loiter in the vicinity of promising conversations among the EarthKare cadre, keep his mouth shut, and try to appeal to everyone's preconceptions of a shrewd reporter: notepad open, mind open, Uniball pen at the ready.

There'd been no more talk on Henry's part about additional JogThink outings. Let sleeping dogs lie seemed to be the prevailing attitude. Which was fine with the participatory journalist, who'd participated quite enough already. Time was piddling on. Never had it been so evident why a superstar personality was needed at these kinds of affairs. Someone famous, and it hardly mattered for what, was the single best antidote to ennui.

Earlier Beibel had spotted Wolfram stomping toward the outhouse and scooted to intercept him.

"Any news yet from Vice President Gore?"

"Fuck you," Wolfram snapped. "And you can quote me."

Twenty-Six

IT WAS, ALL in all, a drab stretch for the action/tension/confrontation type of reportage Beibel wished were unfolding. Henry Marks, his best hope for viable copy, was spending an inordinate amount of time alone in his tent. Writing and rewriting his grand keynote speech was the cover story. Beibel was skeptical. The fellow could be doing just that, or he could be planning his getaway. Both made sense.

Henry Marks' deepest thoughts about JogThink remained a mystery, certainly to Beibel, and possibly to Marks himself. Beibel had poked and prodded around the edges of that million-dollar question, knowing full well that bluntly confronting Henry with it would be a waste of time. Either Henry would dodge it and turn hostile, a reasonable response. Or he might break down and confess like a remorseful perpetrator of a violent crime, blubbering repentance. The former would probably terminate Beibel's Orange Tent access, and the latter would be downright pathetic. An introspective, vacillating, deflated Henry Marks was of no use to anyone.

Beibel was able to coax from Henry one unequivocal declaration concerning his thoughts about JogThink. First and foremost, Henry thought it worked. "Worked" in the sense that it had proven bookable at fees that easily eclipsed the monthly salary of most American workers. The demand for his services had increased by an average rate of 13 percent per year, and repeat business was running close to 19 percent. JogThink Inc. was a product, and it was productive. That's what he thought of it.

Still, Henry admitted some concern that his message might not entirely hold up to scrutiny. It was not lost on Beibel that Henry carefully avoided making any claims so definitive as to be specifically refutable. You could check his video or audio collection or scour any of his three illustrated books, and there was always an embedded out clause, a subtle disclaimer or a mushy use of quisling verb forms: should, would, could, might've. Nearly every statement was, on close inspection, laced with qualifiers: "likely," "usually," "often." Might Henry have enjoyed even greater success by dispensing with these wimpy vacillations and going all-in? Others who did so—Bear Grylls, Malcolm Gladwell, Suze Orman—did not seem to suffer from accusations of bombast.

Self-restraint and pacing were fundamental to the JogThink program. Resist the urge to deviate from a measured stride. Keep highs and lows in check. Keep pace with your own true self. Uphill as downhill, only from a different POV. Steady as she goes, eyes fixed on a distant prize. Where exactly is that all-important prize? Eye of the beholder.

Obviously there were drawbacks to positioning oneself as the contrarian alternative to the ranting motivational maniacs, the fiery football coaches, and the flimflam technocrat tycoons. Life could present instances when a person had no choice but to pick up the pace. There might come a day when Henry would be wise to shift his emphasis and adjust to evolving conditions. His career was necessarily a work-in-progress. For now, however, he saw no reason to deviate. "Play your hits," was how he explained this canny career philosophy to Beibel, "until a better idea comes along."

Beibel had downloaded several YouTube videos of Henry's presentation. He found himself mildly amused by the good-natured, mind-candy palatability of the genre. JogThink was heavy on cutesy anecdotes and light on certifiable data. The anecdotes Henry employed varied from gig to gig, but the core trove seemingly did not fluctuate. In this respect, he reminded Beibel of other professional performers, comedians, and singer-songwriters who rely on a basic set list that can be amended on the spot depending on audience responsiveness or the artist's mood on a given night.

One anecdote Henry enjoyed repeating had him out jogging and suddenly pausing to bend down to tie his shoelace so as not be embarrassed by an overweight woman in Bermuda shorts and clunky Keds who was gaining on him fast. In these videos, Henry displayed considerable skill as a mime, pantomiming the act of running, then appearing alarmed at the clomping footsteps rapidly coming up from behind, louder, louder, closer, closer, then glancing back in bug-eyed disbelief to see not a rail-thin Kenyan marathoner but a chubby lady who was not even young. This portion of the shtick, Beibel learned, was the intro to a protracted riff about the subjectivity of competitive superiority. Or something like that.

Henry took pride in his physicality on stage. He liked to tell the tale of how he'd toughed out a 10k while suffering a tweaked right hamstring. He managed it by mentally engaging in a manufactured competition, his sound left leg vs. the diminished right. Here too he'd mastered a range of actor-like movements, simulating running by running in place, talking all the while, parodying a leather-lunged Kentucky Derby announcer, left vs. right, heading into the home stretch, neck and neck.

He had a litany of stories under the general heading of "selecting the optimal jogging companion." These allowed him to role play, grab a few laughs, flaunt his insight into human nature. Fast runners who pushed the pace yet exhausted themselves through incessant jabbering. Annoying colleagues whose irritating habits provided impetus to leave them in the dust. Potential romantic partners who inspired you to achieve peak performance.

"Speaking of," Henry segued, "have you seen the way Rachel sometimes stares at me? Little weird, don't you think?"

"Not that I've noticed." Beibel swallowed hard. It had been his impression Rachel was warming up him. Could

Henry already have the inside track? "What do you have in mind?"

"Not *my* mind, pal. It's hers. I think she's got the hots for me. Just hope it doesn't become a problem."

The dude was delusional. Beibel had to remind himself that his role was to report it, not refute it. "I don't think you have to worry. Least not 'til after the conference."

Later in that same Orange Tent session, Henry straightened up on his air mattress and dropped his voice to a somber, confessional tone. He'd recently encountered a perplexing situation that he was having difficulty processing.

Beibel perked up, hoping this wouldn't be another warmed-over rehash. "Anything you can share?"

Henry hesitated, a further hint this one might be special. "Okay," plunging ahead, "it was this past July."

The Allstate Insurance retreat in Geneva, Ohio, involved a group that had signed on for a special session 5K run. Henry's keynote the night before had seemingly hit the right notes. His message that jogging was an essential instruction in how to set one's own course, define one's goals, and cultivate habits that would reliably lead, if not to perfection ("Perfection," he'd asserted, "is not my goal; my condolences if it's yours.") to improvement was well received. As was his contention that there's nothing wrong with an activity that returned you healthier, happier, and better prepared to the very same spot where you'd begun.

The group was cruising the groomed woodchip path through an idyllic section of state forest. It was the sort of outing Henry could maneuver in his sleep. Sleep-jogging was, in fact, a theme he'd considered elaborating on.

The woods were cool and hushed. The early sun dancing through the summer leaves lent a semblance of vigor to the executives' labored shuffle. The grinding machinery of another business day had yet to snuff the tranquility. They circled a small lagoon. Pillows of fog hovered above the water. Suddenly a horde of shapes came slogging through the fog. It was a platoon, literally. A unit of the Ohio National Guard dressed in khaki-and-olive camo, nearly a hundred men and women in total.

The Middle East was a hot mess again, and there'd been noise from Washington about potential call-ups. Whether that grim prospect lay behind the cheerlessness of the perspiring faces trouncing past or the early hour and the nuisance of obligatory training caused their sour looks was impossible to determine.

Huffing, limping, wheezing, eyeglasses befogged and caps askew, these soldiers were nobody's lean, mean fighting machine. They resembled a work-release chain gang on a ditch-digging assignment. Henry's cadre of insurance professionals was in better physical condition. And far more enthusiastic.

The two brigades, Henry's and Uncle Sam's, squeezed around each other as they crossed the isthmus between lagoons. At the bottleneck, both groups slowed.

Henry had been about to launch his "creating a finish line that serves your needs" riff, but the presence of the guardsmen creeped him out, made him self-conscious. And nothing undermined his ability to do his thing, he explained to Beibel, like a bout of self-consciousness. *Un*-self-consciousness was the key to his art.

It wasn't simply that these young men and women drearily passing by lacked the proper context for understanding his remarks, should they chance to overhear them. Misinterpretation came with the territory. And it wasn't like Henry was worried that his message would fail to resonate. In fact, he was confident that nearly every statement in his standard JogThink could stand on its own.

No, what truly chilled Henry, he disclosed to Beibel, was the apprehension that his Allstate Insurance charges might recognize in the contrast between their privileged situation and the beleaguered guardsmen a facet of JogThink that he'd just as soon get overlooked. Namely, JogThink, for all its promise, was at its most effective in situations where the stakes were not all that high.

Men and women heading off to a war zone? Where angry bullets sprayed from hidden bunkers? Where madmen lurked in treacherous shadows? Running, for this bunch, could soon become quite important, the faster, the better. Finding your own pace, at your own pace, might not be an option.

Without warning, Henry broke into a flat-out sprint, knees pumping, heels flying, clawing the air. He did not look back.

He'd never done that before, never deserted his followers.

"I'm not even sure why I'm telling you this," he confided to Beibel.

Beibel took it as a challenge: Why the hell was Henry telling him this?

Twenty-Seven

"THE WOODS ARE lovely, dark and deep." Since sixth grade, when Rachel had been required to memorize the Robert Frost poem and stand before the class to recite it, her pleated green skirt revealing just enough of her pink knees to make her self-conscious about boys who might be staring, Timmy LeCompte in particular, she'd not been able to stroll any tree-lined street or path, let alone an actual forest, without that phrase singing in her head.

She was not a loner. But there were many who believed she was, and she knew why. She'd never married. This wrong-headed conclusion was augmented by habits that many thought were consistent with a woman who preferred singlehood. At the occasional dinner, despite friends' best efforts to seat her beside theoretically promising prospects, her attention drifted and her conversation dwindled to brief responses to direct questions. She'd been known to excuse herself early from meetings where an eligible man still lingered. Too often she dressed in drab colors better suited to camouflage in a drought-stricken wheat field than attracting a mate. She was, by all appearances, the opposite of a woman on the make.

In sixth grade, during a spell of staring out the window, Mr. Livingston, the teacher who'd assigned "Stopping by Woods on a Snowy Evening," sidled up and gently asked, "Rachel, where do you go to in your thoughts? When you go away?" Embarrassed, she'd snapped to attention, pretending not to know what he was referring to. But she knew exactly what he meant, and she knew the answer. She'd transported herself into those lovely make-believe woods and the winding path overgrown with hyssop and columbine that led to a rock-strewn creek. Clear water gushing over smooth stones was the only sound. In such woods, lovely and deep, she'd waited for the prince to come and kiss her. The prince could take his sweet time. She had plenty to occupy her thoughts. Why do bees choose a particular flower? Do ants ever grow weary and nap? Do blue jays speak the same language as wrens?

"Nowhere special," she'd told Mr. Livingston. "I'll try not to do it again, sir."

He smiled his kindly, approving smile. "It's okay if you do. Just don't make it so obvious."

"Thank you, Mr. Livingston."

One day until the conference. She needed to get outdoors, early and alone. Rachel wore shorts, sweat socks pulled mid-calf, ankle-high Merrell waterproof boots, and a tan fleece vest she'd probably remove once she got moving. The overnight temperature had dipped to the upper forties. A fog had settled in.

The outhouse path was the least traveled of the several that branched from the compound mainly because it eventually crossed the property of a local farmer who, along with several very large grownup sons, liked to get drunk and practice target shooting. Nobody trusted their definition of what constituted a plausible target, nor their ability to shoot accurately in the right direction. Early morning, Rachel reasoned, was probably safe. She'd take her chances.

Ten minutes in and her mood substantially unknotted. Wolfram, Beibel, ACLE, the big-top clowns—all of them, all of it—began to recede. The forest was a balm. She loosened her fleece and began to hum. ". . . even the wind's whistling at me." Now how did that tune go, and why did it pop to mind?

A few years ago at an EarthKare strategy retreat in the White Mountains, not far from here, one of EarthKare's idealistic college interns—this one was from Brown University, a particularly active feeder campus—had gone for a solo day hike and disappeared. Lindsay had last been seen strolling a well-blazed and not especially challenging trail. It was day one of their three-day confab. The girl had been working with them for just a few weeks. They'd allowed her to participate in the session only because she'd expressed interest in moving on to an unpaid internship during the fall semester. How exactly they intended to utilize use a flaky, myopic linguistics major was a puzzle to be solved later. Slim was the one who'd recommended her, and his motives with women were often suspect.

EarthKare's coordinator of summer interns, also a volunteer, was Dr. Gerald Hutchings, a retired botanist from Syracuse. Scientific advisors, usually faculty trying to "make a difference," orbited around EarthKare. It was Dr. Hutchings' mission, which he performed admirably, to conjure research projects that kept interns busy within a framework that conformed, at least nominally, to standards of academic relevance. When they were not busy, Dr. Hutchings, who had a pretty sharp eye for indolence, would tell them to wander off for a while and be sure to return with at least one good idea.

EarthKare's ragtag staffing situation was a constant problem. Lacking a budget to hire qualified personnel, they had to rely on the dubious talents of feckless volunteers. Rachel knew Lindsay only as another sweet misfit who'd somehow found her way to them. For a certain kind of aimless undergraduate, EarthKare functioned almost like a homeless shelter. In a perfect world, EarthKare would field an army of well-trained activists with specialized skills. It would be a mercenary army.

By midevening, concern over Lindsay's absence had grown from casual quips ("maybe she thinks she can't come back *until* she has one good idea") to genuine worry. Around the campfire, Wolfram tried to summarize the situation in the manner of the no-nonsense homicide detectives on the TV crime shows he claimed to never watch. He ran down the facts: her last known whereabouts, the clothes she was wearing, the possible wrong turns she might have taken, estimates of her survival skills or lack thereof. At the end of his crisp summation, he let slip a concept that had clearly been on his mind but not on anyone else's until then: liability.

A pall more chilling than any ghost story descended onto the group.

"They set out in pairs with flashlights. Wolfram directed the operation. His methodological approach came from manhunt movies. He directed the flashlight teams to move out from points along a compass and stay in voice contact with each other as they fanned outward. Soon the forest was alive with erratically crisscrossing beams of light and shouted announcements of "nothing yet!" After sunset, the forest bears no resemblance to its daytime self. Sounds are magnified. No paths are discernible. Or rather, every gap between trees implies a path. Rocks, rotting stumps, and protruding roots create peril at every step. Noises that would be assuring in the light of day, like the harmless hoot of a far-away owl, become creepy. They assault your ears from all directions, from high, low, ahead, and behind. Each creaking limb becomes a taunt, a mockery of your total ignorance of all the invisible scuttling, seething, churning, and cavorting that's out there and closing in."

The above paragraph is lifted verbatim from the memoir that Lindsay Ahearn eventually published about her ordeal, titled *Old Growth Freak-Out: Confronting Inner Demons on the Road Less Traveled*. Only after its publication and the notoriety it achieved did it become apparent to EarthKare that Lindsay had been drawn to them not out of commitment to environmentalism but because she'd so greatly admired Rachel's largely forgotten second book, *Alone in the Wild*. Who knew?

Lindsay wrote of having been forced to spend two full nights and a harrowing day lost and starving and fearful. It was Slim who found her, butt naked, draped across a moss-covered rock, bathed by the morning sun. At first he thought she was dead. He called her name, and she did not budge. He came closer and, filled with terror himself, touched her hand to gauge the clamminess of her skin. In her memoir, Lindsay compared the sensation of Slim's touch to "God's fingertip in the Sistine chapel." She sat up abruptly and seemed no worse for the wear. Except for severe sunburn on her breasts and private parts, which Slim assured her could be remedied by a botanical salve he kept in his tent.

Why, during the long daylight interlude between nighttime freak-outs, did Lindsay not simply find a running brook and meander along with it downhill to civilization? These were, after all, domesticated hills of gentle farmland and forest, not rugged Denali or the impenetrable Himalayas. In her memoir, Lindsay never addressed the question directly but did assert that throughout the ordeal, she was beset by a bewildering disorientation not unlike that de-scribed by men and women who claimed to have been ab-ducted by aliens. Her rational mind, Lindsay wrote, devolved into something more like a demon state, fuzzy and unreliable, while her subconscious emerged as the dominant navigational tool, guiding her through the nightmare. A con-templation of this vital duality comprised chapters four, five, and six of *Old Growth Freak-Out*.

The point that Lindsay wanted to impress upon readers was that getting lost in the woods, and the mental work she was forced to do to accept the "lostness," effectively thrust her into a fable. Having become the heroine of a fable, Lind-say contended, required the fabled clairvoyance of classic mythology to see her through. Stripping off her shorts and shirt and offering her naked self to the gods upon a spongy bed of cool moss was not something her rational mind would ever identify as a solution to her dilemma.

To her readers, she asked the question: What are the crisis moments in your own life where fable should replace reason? (In the sequel, due out next year, she purportedly offers six easy-to-implement exercises for cultivating this aptitude in ninety days or less.)

Although Rachel had not read *Old Growth Freak-Out,* she shared her colleagues' prevailing disgust with its exaggerations and dim-witted clichés. That the book became a modest bestseller and launched the conniving Lindsay onto the New Age workshop circuit, Malibu to Kripalu to Santa Fe, where she shared billing with the likes of Deepak Chopra, only confirmed what needed no confirmation: American culture was awash with hucksters and bald-faced opportunists. The meek, alas, shall inherit nothing but leftover crumbs.

Twenty-Eight

RACHEL'S ROUTE THIS morning, once past the old mossy stone wall, involved a slow ascent following logical sight-lines, slope to slope, crossing a stream, and tramping through tracts of waist-high grasses.

Twenty minutes in and she was nearly restored. Did she have promises to keep? You bet she did. Could they wait? Indeed they could.

Stepping over the decaying hulk of a fallen birch and across a swath of damp forest detritus, she picked her way down a rocky ridge onto an expanse of overgrown pasture. There, in a surge of pure physical exuberance, she burst into a zigzagging dash to avoid . . . to avoid getting tagged. Until sixth grade, nobody, neither boy nor girl, was quicker afoot and more crafty. They'd tried to nab her, to tap her shoulder and tag her "it." She was too quick.

Except one time. Cornered by the chain-link fence that separated the school playground from an abandoned limestone quarry, she'd tripped and fallen. Timmy LeCompte, pigeon-toed and puckish, managed to nick the back of her leg just before she scrambled to her feet. "It!" Timmy squealed with glee.

She'd Googled him recently. Why? He'd never been a boyfriend, never really played a role in her life except that one lucky lunge on the playground. He now had his own insurance agency in Scottsdale. A more-detailed search might have disclosed his marital status, his alma mater, how many kids and possibly what schools they attended. But these facts she did not care to know. Had she not tripped during recess, she would have absolutely no memories of him. None.

Timmy would be effectively disappeared. The way of all flesh.

Rachel accelerated with giddy abandon. Now she was running, her mind racing along. The breeze swept her hair back, and she was transported to an afternoon in the Rockies listening to a spacey musician with a lion's mane of dark hair, shirtless in the bright sun, improvising on a silver flute. All memories were cousins, connected. Timmy LeCompte was after her, and this time she'd better not stumble.

The tall grass gave way to dense woods that dipped downhill. The forest floor was a bed of fallen leaves. She slowed.

Not fifty yards away, spotlighted by a brilliant shaft of sunlight pouring through the canopy, was Henry Marks, fly unzipped, penis dangling, enjoying a languorous piss. His eyes combed the treetops as his stream pattered softly on the mat of dead leaves. He looked serene, a man at peace.

Rachel had time to slink away unseen. Henry had not spotted her.

It tickled her to be an inconspicuous fly on this colorful forest wall. That tickle, she would later acknowledge, might have another dimension.

She waited a minute. "Henry?" she called out softly, not wanting to startle him.

If he was startled, he did not show it. He made no sudden effort to cover his privates or turn away. Calmly he shook off the last drops.

Rachel gave him time to properly zip up. Stepping cautiously down the slope, she flashed a cartoon truce sign, hands raised, palms open, sheepishly admitting her guilt. For what, she was not sure.

"I was out hiking, you know, to clear my head, and coming up that rise, I . . ." She stood facing him now, perspiring.

"You followed me."

"I did not."

"You followed hoping to catch me with my . . ."

"I most definitely did not."

"And you were getting frustrated 'cause it was taking so long, wondering, what is this guy, a camel? Doesn't he ever need to . . .?"

"It's drinking that camels don't need to do often. They pee all the time."

He looked her over. "You sure of that?"

"Well, actually, no."

"Ha! As I thought!"

"What's *as you thought*?"

"You're no expert on camels. And you have no business using your alleged expertise to squirm away from what you've been caught in the act of."

"And that is?"

"Tracking me."

She wasn't sure if she should feel indignant, but it worked as a default gesture. "Are you out of your mind?"

"Good question," he conceded.

She accepted it as a compliment. "Well, here's another good question. How come you're not jogging?"

"I'm off duty. All work and no play . . ."

He had the cheerfully bemused features of the kind of person you wouldn't mind drawing as a seatmate on a cramped airline flight, providing he did not talk too much. And the flight wasn't too long. She wouldn't call him handsome. He was pleasant looking in an affable, good-vibey way. Minus the braggadocio, it might be possible to enjoy him as fine fellow, basically.

"I assumed JogThink was part of your operating system. No on/off switch. Didn't I read that about you somewhere?"

He shifted his eyes, deferentially lowering his gaze as if to agree. "My promo kit. Ugh. The bunk they put in there, not my doing. Don't get me wrong. I do think more clearly when I'm jogging. But when I want to get in touch with my feelings . . ." He patted the spot on his purple jersey that covered his heart and kept his hand in place like a Cub Scout pledging allegiance. "To focus on feelings, a simple hike does the trick."

Without explicitly agreeing to do so, they were strolling. Together.

Henry was in cruising gear. "The steady, insistent forward motion of jogging meshes perfectly with the hard-wired impulses of the rational thought process. Feelings get cultivated and honed by very different methods. Hiking, for instance. In the forest. With nobody . . . or almost nobody . . ."

Henry fixed her with a dreamy stare that begged to be returned.

She could not do it, not yet.

He kept his gaze on her.

"Could rain," she said.

"What's the saying? Not enough sense to come in out of . . .?"

"Something like that." That was about as far as she would go, not knowing where exactly he was going. If he was going anywhere.

Henry picked up his own loose thread. "How about: Not enough sense to *stay in the rain*, to be moistened and refreshed, to be soothed and revived, to be splattered and bathed, even drenched, to spread your arms and lift your face and welcome each and every drop like it was your first kiss. Not enough sense to linger in the rain and love it? That's something you could say about a lot of people. A lot of losers."

A new gust carried a strong whiff of moisture, and a sudden flurry of insect life, grasshoppers and crickets.

"Is that," Rachel asked, bringing the discussion down to earth, "part of your, you know, your normal . . .?"

"Shtick?"

She nodded. "Shtick." It was a good word, and she was fairly sure she'd used it correctly.

"What you just heard me say," Henry allowed, "came to me just now, spur of the. Not bad, huh?"

Was he asking her opinion? His soliloquy had whizzed by so quickly she did not know what she thought except it sounded smooth, his cadence and choice of words. It pleased her to walk alongside as he spewed. That was another good word, spew. Whatever it was that Henry'd just said, about rain and good sense and values, if indeed that was a correct summation of the themes he was riffing on, it had held her attention. That and the loose sway of his hands brushing her hip without apologizing.

"Interesting," she said after some delay.

"Interesting? Interesting is what people say when they're afraid to say what they think."

"Interesting is what they say when they're conflicted. Can we leave it at that?"

"Conflicted? Over what?"

The rain came, thrumming the leaves like nervous fingers on a tabletop. Neither of them had hats.

"Make a run for it?" Why she asked, she wasn't sure. Henry was neither an expert on weather forecasting nor on running to get somewhere fast.

"No point," he replied, and he was right. Unless it stopped immediately, they were bound to get soaked.

They reversed course up the slope. Where the path was wide enough, they remained side by side. Where it narrowed, he encouraged Rachel, in a small bit of gallantry, to take the lead. She felt compelled to do so, but not without unease. Having Henry watch her backside, literally, brought her no comfort.

For many minutes, they hiked without speaking. The gathering mist enveloped them.

Henry was right; there was no hurry. They would surely get soaked but were likely to make it back before serious chill set in. She recalled that time, at least ten years ago, cross-country skiing in the Adirondacks with Russell, now a senior attorney for the EPA but then a second-year law student. They'd skied further than planned, a storm had kicked up, and they were lucky to make it back to their cabin before dark. The cabin belonged to the family of one his classmates. Russell lit a fire. They warmed themselves with cognac before the dancing flames. That was their high-water mark. She'd hoped Russell would also come to see it that way, without regrets.

Rachel had just about gotten comfortable having Henry behind her in a position to eyeball her backside with impunity. Then he crowed, "You really look nice with your hair wet."

It annoyed her to think he was actually evaluating her in that very specific and sexist way. Annoyed her and incited some tingling. "I'm a mess," she protested.

Swiveling to confront him, she caught him unprepared. There was delight across his face. That's what she noticed, and it came as a surprise. Not that he was beaming at her, but that she *hoped* he meant it.

Henry came close. She could smell his sweat. It was not a turnoff.

"Is it okay," he asked, "to say I think you're beautiful?"

"I'm not."

"But is it okay if I think it?"

Raindrops loudly thrummed the dry leaves. Rachel could pretend not to have heard what he'd said. She could feign obtuseness concerning the distinction he'd just drawn. She could pretend that he'd let it slip simply to be cute, without even comprehending the enormity of what he'd said.

"It's not true," she argued.

"It is true. If I think it."

"You really believe that? Something is true if you think it? Even if nobody else does?"

"Whoa, whoa there! Hey, let's not get ahead of ourselves. I'm only talking about how you look. No need to blow it up into a great big king-size generalization."

Several plump droplets splashed her forehead, and this was the excuse to wipe her hands across her face, hiding it. She did not want Henry to notice what she could no longer conceal, a smile.

"Can we talk about something else?" she asked.

"Sure. But it won't be as interesting. Listen, I have no ulterior motive. I look at you, and the words flew out. I only said it because I feel it. And I only feel it because . . . well, that's always the grand mystery, isn't it?"

They'd arrived at a partial clearing marked by the charred skeletons of twin birches, victims of a lightning strike decades before. The fallen trees lay like supine lovers done in by a suicide pact, limbs crooked and broken, intertwined in death.

"Why," Rachel asked, "should I believe you?"

"About?"

"Let's start with your speech."

"You're not sure Henry Marks can deliver the goods?" He puffed out his chest and gave it a braggart's tap, mocking himself. "Rachel, did you not read all those testimonials on my website? Southwest Michigan Chamber of Commerce? Retail Sporting Goods Association of America? Bank of goddamn America? Have you no faith?"

"Those groups are not EarthKare."

"Who is?"

"Touché."

"Answer me this, Rachel. What makes you so sure the great Al Gore would knock it out of the park? Is there a single thing he'd say that everyone in the audience has not already heard before and thought before and agreed with before? And, I might add, heard almost word for word before? It'd be like watching a rerun on TV. Where's the excitement, the frisson, the thrill, the turn-on, the juice? Where's the risk?"

"The risk, frankly, is what concerns me."

"Hey . . . me too."

"What?"

"Me too. I'm worried too. But guess what? That's the package. Out on a limb and there's no way to know what'll happen. How cool is this?"

Henry leapt directly in front of her. He clapped a firm hand on her shoulder, possibly meant to be reassuring. A raindrop dribbled down her cheek.

"I'll be frank," he said.

Rachel waited, praying this would not be a stock phrase he tossed out automatically, like a political candidate cornered at a rowdy town hall meeting.

"I recognize I'm no scholar on environmental issues. I'm no Al Gore. But I have been hanging around here a few days, and I have been paying attention, and I am a quick study. And you know what I've concluded? Your chances of successfully achieving your mission are, roughly, about the same as my chances of delivering a boffo keynote address. Not exactly a slam dunk, shall we say. On the other hand, a long shot is still a shot. In other words . . . whoa, Rachel, whoa there, I didn't . . ."

With the back of his hand, he reached to dab the moisture from her face.

"Whoa there. Don't cry, please."

"I'm not crying. It's rain, you idiot."

"You sure you're not crying?"

"No. I mean yes."

She feared he might try to kiss her, and she wasn't sure how she would respond. But Henry did a swift about-face and resumed walking.

The rain was steady now. Raindrops, fatter and more frequent, were steadily leaking through the upper canopy. Henry's shirt had taken on a two-tone coloration, deep purple on the shoulders and upper torso, closer to the original lilac lower down. Rachel's hair was the proverbial mop, limp and shapeless. A yellow leaf was plastered like a tattoo on her mud-splattered calf. They could pass for shipwreck victims who'd managed, just barely, to swim ashore.

"You know the cool part?" he asked.

She'd been thinking that it might be a good idea to stagger their arrival back to the compound to deflect any unwanted speculation. She could think of nothing that might constitute the "cool part."

"The cool part," he sang as lightheartedly as if they were skipping through a sunlit meadow, "is that we're in this together."

Twenty-Nine

BEIBEL LAY ATOP his bunk, nearly dozing. There were many interludes during his stint at EarthKare when nothing was going on and he wasn't up to the onerous task of strategizing next steps for his floundering career. This was always a delicious experience, slowly slipping into the sweet nothingness of an afternoon nap. Life was easy. Life was good. Life was a cradle lined in velvet gently rocked by a lovely lady who forgave his flaws. Nothing like a nap.

Ach! The dull thud of a mallet smacking wood, over and over, was accompanied by a jabbering human voice.

He knew that voice. It was a voice that called to him. It was Celeste.

Aroused, Beibel laced up his sneakers—he refused, in silent protest, to think of them as "running" shoes—threw on a clean shirt, swept a hairbrush (property of his bunkmate, Slim) across his scalp, and went to check out the action.

At the far border of the pasture, behind the summer camp cabins, newly sprouted upon the turf, was a two-person tent, yellow on the sides, gray at the peak. Celeste stood with her back to the pasture, hands on shapely hips. The thudding sound was the pounding of tent stakes. The pounding was the work of a large man, bent at the waist, who appeared to be working under Celeste's direct supervision.

Grasshoppers sprang aside as Beibel waded through the tall grass.

"Hey, stranger," Celeste greeted him on arrival.

The fellow pounding tents stakes glanced up only long enough to give a token raised-eyebrow acknowledgment to Beibel before returning to the task.

Beibel's first impression was unsettling. His rival was muscular, fit, tall, handsome, with the gorgeous smooth, dark skin of a Samoan. The big showoff sported a blazing gold tank top—it wasn't nearly that warm out—and a backward ball cap, Beibel's least favorite accouterment on grown men.

"Farther," Celeste demanded, meaning, apparently, the tent's rain flap. "Pull it out farther."

The big lug did as he was told.

"That too. Yep. There. Perfect."

Beibel had not previously witnessed Celeste in bossy-bossy mode. It suited her, he had to admit.

When the tent was staked out to Celeste's satisfaction, including the rain flap, and the aluminum exoskeleton expanded to its optimum dimension, the muscle man assumed his full height, which had to be fully six foot, four inches. After making what to Beibel seemed an exaggerated display of extending his sinewy bare arm to mop sweat from his brow with the back of his hand, the fellow then offered the same sweat-slick hand to greet Beibel.

"Reggie Takada," he announced. "And you must be . . ."

"Lenny Beibel," Celeste chirped. "The writer I've been telling you about."

Reggie, who'd withdrawn his hand after a cursory shake, now thrust out his fist, one bro to another. "If half of what Cee here says is true . . ."

Celeste stepped in. "Lenny, you're probably wondering."

With a curt nod, Beibel confirmed this observation. You bet he was wondering.

As Reggie moved alongside, Celeste explained that the two of them had been "close back in the day." She did not elaborate. Maybe just as well. There'd be time for follow-up questions later. If Beibel so desired. As to what Reggie was doing here at EarthKare Vermont, Celeste explained that Reggie was a longstanding member of their Board of Advisors, a point she punctuated with a baffling wink. More important, he was an influential corporate attorney with extensive connections in publishing, media, and politics. As to the tent, Celeste explained that "back in the day" the two of them had enjoyed a memorable camping expedition in Hawaii as part of a fact-finding mission. They were comfortable sharing a tent, she said, and out here away from the cabins, they wouldn't bother anyone. By staying up late talking, she added.

Reggie flipped the mallet high in the air and caught it on the way down, handle first. "Talking with Cee . . ." Reggie paused to make eye contact with Celeste.

"Lenny's cool," she assured. "Go on."

"Al Gore, don't get me wrong, is a great man. But let's get real. What I'm working on now . . ." Again Reggie paused to wait for affirmation.

Celeste gave the go-ahead in the form a playful nudge, her elbow to Reggie's hip.

"Our firm handles matters for certain high-profile individuals. We're not exactly their managers, but our services often overlap in that direction. Long story short, I've reached out to Bono."

"About pinch-hitting for Mr. Gore," Celeste clarified enthusiastically.

"You mean," Beibel couldn't resist adding, "pinch-hitting for Henry Marks."

"Sure. Him too."

Without disclosing much—attorney-client, Reggie drily noted—he reported that Bono was free this coming weekend, would be in New York City and thus sufficiently nearby for this to be workable, and there were good reasons to think that the globe-trotting Irish rocker-activist would consider a keynote appearance at the EarthKare conference a worthy addition to his expanding portfolio of good deeds.

"One stipulation," Reggie cautioned. "No music. No singing. Just a speech. Bono sings, that's a whole different can of worms."

Beibel's mind was racing. Was this the journalistic break he craved? Bono would be better than Gore. And probably more fun. Damn! And so what if it turned out that Celeste's affections were diverted to another outlet. In the long run, Reggie might be better suited to her needs. And better suited to his, if the guy really did come through in recruiting Bono to make an appearance up here in the woods.

Beibel was happy to leave them alone. He assumed Celeste and Reggie had already moved their bedrolls into the tent. If not, that problem wasn't his. It was possible that, right now, he had no problems whatsoever. And he wasn't even napping.

Thirty

EARLY MORNING, SEVERAL hours before dawn. This had always been the most productive time for Wolfram. When others were asleep, when the forest was asleep, when the world was asleep, when he had the field to himself and was removed from the jostling and crowding and cloying second-guessing that was an invariable byproduct of having to share the stage with others, that's when he was most alert, most energized, most inspired. In that dim, empty non-man's interlude, situations that loomed as hopelessly murky in broad daylight (or evening lamplight) had a way of revealing themselves to Wolfram with crystal clarity. It was the aloneness that produced this special lucidity, aloneness and detachment. Nobody at EarthKare had any idea he was upstairs in the attic office, face pressed into his computer monitor like a bloodhound sniffing the sidewalk, and he was always careful to vacate well before sunrise, before anyone was the wiser.

It was lonely work, and frightening. It was a real struggle to keep from letting loose with a monstrous werewolf howl.

The epic scale of the logging industry media blitz had come as a shock, even to Wolfram. After all, the ACLE had already won the primary battle. The congressional vote on the bill to open hundreds of thousands of acres of national forest to logging and mineral extraction in Montana, Utah, and Texas was certain to go their way, although the final vote would not take place until mid-November. Public opinion polls paid, for by Citizens for Protection of Forests (CPF), the industry-funded nonprofit, showed that a significant majority, over 60 percent, believed 1) humans were more vulnerable than most animal species; 2) death at some point comes to all living creatures; 3) mankind should protect animal species to the same degree that they protect us.

Worse, EarthKare was now being shunned by previously allied groups, like the Sierra Club and Greenpeace, with which they'd been historically compatible in a benign neglect kind of way. These organizations were increasingly inserting an asterisked disclaimer in their fundraising campaigns: "Not all groups espousing concern for the environment are the same, and not all are responsible."

Wolfram could not help but notice how often the word "responsible" was coming up. Under the right circumstances, indeed under most circumstances, it could be considered an accolade. In fact, the word had been a centerpiece of EarthKare rhetoric ever since the organization first filed for a 501(c)3 tax-exempt status. "Who's responsible?" and its sister sentiment, "We're all responsible," were at the very heart of EarthKare's mission statement.

But "responsible" carried another meaning, joined as it was to "irresponsible." Children were irresponsible. Drunks and wackos were irresponsible. To Wolfram's disgust, the logging industry was positioning itself as the dependable, responsible party, the one most concerned about the planet's general welfare and best able to protect it.

The day before the conference, the ACLE ran half-page ads in the front section of both *The New York Times* and *The Wall Street Journal* (page five in *NYT*; page seven in *WSJ*). The ads featured the photo-realist image of a human form overlooking a wasteland denuded of trees. The human appeared to be male (burly shoulders, slouched, unruly hair) and vaguely alt-culture with a corduroy barn jacket and backpack slung over one shoulder. Wolfram couldn't prove it, but he was fairly certain the figure was meant to depict him.

"What, Me Responsible?" appeared in bold type below the image.

The online version of the ad included a link to a bouncy animated video that told the tale of a small boy with a barrel torso and skinny legs (Wolfram believed the image was modeled on how he'd looked as an eight-year-old; again, he couldn't prove it). In the video, the boy wanders from the bright crayon hues of his Edenic backyard into a stark, post-apocalyptic industrial zone. With each hesitant step, the boy grows more disconsolate. Finally he slumps to his knees. An orange-and-blue bird swoops down to alight on his shoulder. "Follow me," tweets the bird. The boy does so, stepping past the burned-out carcasses of autos and soot-coated buildings into a grove of lush shrubs and leafy trees. It's a logging camp. A muscle-bound Paul Bunyan in bushy beard and red plaid shirt hoists the boy atop his massive shoulder. The three of them, Bunyan, the boy, and the bird, ascend to an overlook. Bunyan points, and the image telescopes to the boy's backyard, the swing set, the mowed lawn, the Irish setter patiently waiting.

"Yes, we're responsible," a mellow male voiceover concludes. "Follow us."

Goliath gratuitously piling on a defenseless David. What, Wolfram asked himself, would puny David do if confronted with such a great disparity in firepower? He wouldn't go jogging, that's for damn sure.

Wolfram had heard the rumors about Bono and didn't believe them for a minute. He'd always felt Reggie Takada would say anything to make himself seem a big shot. There was some quality about Celeste that coaxed the worst in egocentric men. It was a lucky thing, Wolfram told himself, that he was immune to her wiles.

Deposing Henry was foremost on Wolfram's mind. Preventing the slick charlatan from doing damage to the cause was now Wolfram's mission. The guy was a menace. His so-called message was in its own modest way downright subversive. His dilemma was that conference-goers would not realize Henry was an enemy plant until they'd had a chance to listen to his blather. A premature intervention ran the risk of precluding the audience from getting fed up and disgusted on its own accord.

But how long to wait for the audience to see the light? Wolfram had no doubt that Henry would bomb, big time. But given the fellow's slippery way with words and refined stagecraft artistry, it could take a while for spectator outrage to reach a tipping point. Five minutes? Ten? Wolfram doubted Henry could ramble on for very long without humiliating himself. Maybe that should be his strategy: give Henry enough rope, as they say, to hang himself until his legs started twitching. Fifteen minutes, at the most, and the crowd would be screaming to have Henry tarred and feathered and ridden out on a rail. Heck, storming the stage and forcibly seizing the microphone from him could actually constitute an act of mercy. Put the dude out of his misery.

Lessons learned from jogging! Why not analogies to badminton? That sport made use of birdies, didn't it?

Wolfram, no slouch when it came to strategy, had a Plan B. Induce Henry, either by persuasion or threat, to skip town before the start of the conference. Problem solved.

Wolfram also had a Plan C. Allow Henry to say his piece in its entirety and be ready, as soon as he was finished, while the audience was too sluggish to move, to launch his own fiery oration. Which he'd been secretly rehearsing, word by word, seemingly forever. The contrast would be dynamite.

Screw JogThink! Those would be the first words out of his mouth and would leave no doubt that a man of passion, of conviction, of vision, of unrelenting commitment had arrived, and not a moment too soon. Finding the pace that works for you as a person? No, sir, not with General Wolfram leading the battle.

He'd never been the main event. But he had all the right stuff. How many times had he sat on his thumbs in the wings listening to Rachel spin out her commendable yet oh-sopredictable disquisition on what ails planet Earth and what we, as human custodians, must do to remedy the illness? He admired her, was fond of her, maybe cared for her in deeper ways that would never be discovered unless she threw herself at him with unabashed longing, and probably not even then. But when push came to shove, and that's what was unquestionably coming, Rachel was a nurse practitioner when an emergency SWAT team was what the situation demanded.

Rachel's stump speech—he'd heard it a hundred times—conveyed meaningful information, as far as that went. But it always made Wolfram yearn to toss a live grenade—just to shake things up, not to cause anyone injury. Of course he possessed no such grenade. Still, that was the feeling that came over him whenever he listened to Rachel or most other like-minded activists deliver lectures about Earth's perils. It rankled him that Rachel could appear so measured and complacent in the face of onrushing calamity. That, with all due respect, would not be his approach.

He was not ungrateful. Without Rachel's blessing and the advantages that came from being her trusted, indispensable sidekick (a phrase she often used, although he never believed she truly meant it), he was just another overeducated crank whose only hope for notoriety was to someday make it onto the FBI's Most Wanted list. Yet he realized that at some point the imperatives of their cause would *compel* him to step out of her shadow. Time was ticking. Lots of things were ticking. Countdown to crunch time wasn't just for football players facing third and long.

Upon seizing the mic, step one would be to trash JogThink and everything it stood for. A minute or two would be all he'd need for that. He would then briefly thank Rachel for her years of service, an olive branch to the former regime. Then he would crank it up, full blast, clenched fist, muscles flexed, teeth bared, no holding back, leave it all on the field.

Creating your own finish line! What crap!

Thirty-One

WOLFRAM STRUTTED INTO the dining lodge flanked by Dorothy and Mitchell. The gray light from outside, what remained of it, had the gloomy quality of fog. Each day darkness was coming earlier to the valley. Late afternoon with low clouds and intermittent drizzle, the indoor visibility was sketchy. This Thursday was the darkest afternoon of the week.

The rattling and clanging of the kitchen crew, a rotating assignment, were the only sounds. A pungent scent of curry hung in the air. Unscented plumber's candles placed in a tidy row along each table lent a druid haunt to the dining hall, cozy but a bit creepy. Like a resource-deprived Mongolian village, EarthKare resorted to electric light only when absolutely necessary.

Squinting, Wolfram identified a human form seated at the table nearest the kitchen. Good timing, as he had planned. The person at the table reached for a candle, then groped the tabletop for the matches that were always kept in a nearby finger bowl. The lit candle flared. Sure enough, the seated figure was Henry Marks.

Wolfram took a seat directly beside him. Dorothy and Mitchell followed, taking seats directly across, looking glum, saying nothing. Wolfram worried the Wickershams were overplaying their role. Or modeling it on a Broadway musical he'd never seen and never would.

Henry acknowledged their presence. "Make yourself comfortable,"

"We need," Wolfram stated, "to talk."

"Hey, talk away."

Henry's cheery nonchalance was, Wolfram supposed, admirable. They guy did have some character strengths. Just nowhere near enough of them.

Wolfram gave a minimalist nod, Godfather-like, in Mitchell's direction. A stage cue. Your turn now. They'd not specifically rehearsed this scene, but they had gone over the script and what it aimed to achieve.

Mitchell cleared his throat, a prelude. "We think it's best, not just us, but the whole planning committee." Mitchell faltered. Dorothy placed a supportive hand on her partner's shoulder.

Henry's face disclosed nothing, and it struck Wolfram that Henry might be taking perverse pleasure in Mitchell's squirming. Wolfram could relate to that. In a perfect world, he and Henry might find they had things in common. Wouldn't that be a wonder?

"We've come to the conclusion, and we feel, with regard to your, ah, presentation, that it's best for all parties . . ."

Henry's eyes bulged with the bright anticipatory glee of a child beholding the presents piled beneath the Christmas tree. He was not going to make this easy. Surely he understood Mitchell was no Santa Claus.

"Content-wise, we feel it would be more appropriate . . ." Dorothy's supportive hand migrated to the back of Mitchell's neck. Like a ventriloquism act, master and dummy, Wolfram thought.

"We just think that what we need, what the event needs, is to hit hard on the facts and the politics, and, given our audience and where they're coming from, and of course where we want to steer them, given all that needs doing, now and in the future."

Henry glowed anew with an even brighter smile.

Reflexively, Mitchell smiled back.

Wolfram had had enough. It had seemed a master stroke to get Mitchell to play the heavy. As it turned out, he'd have to do it himself. "We want you," Wolfram snapped, "to withdraw. Okay?"

Henry calmly pushed back from the table, beaming the same daft smile, good cheer and glad tidings.

Wolfram was undeterred. "We've decided to go in a different direction."

"That's cool. Just tell me where."

"Cut the crap, Henry. You know what we're saying."

Christmas had ended. "You cut the crap. What are *you* saying?"

Wolfram leaned in tighter. It was now one on one, man to man, respective captains facing off on the battlefield. Wolfram spat it out.

"We don't think you can do the job. Okay? That BS maybe works for some. Maybe it works for people who have a big appetite for BS. But that, my friend, is not EarthKare."

Henry stood. This wasn't to be taken sitting down.

"BS you call it?" Henry's voice was calm, but the anger leaked out. His face in the dim light was a study in determination—tight squint, furrowed brow. "That's one way to look at it. But not the only way. What about trust? What about faith? What about trust and faith working together, acting together, moving forward together? And yes, jogging together. BS, my pal, is exactly what people sometimes need to get over the hump and get the job done. You call yourself activists, and you don't know that simple, basic fact?"

Had Henry capitulated? It sure didn't seem like it. In fact, Wolfram had a sinking feeling that this arrogant huckster was finding a second wind. It was becoming increasingly apparent that the only way to keep Henry off the stage was through brute physical force. That time might come. It hadn't come yet.

Wolfram had loathed Henry from the get-go and loathed him even more now that he was refusing to peacefully abdicate. Shoving his trembling fist within inches of Henry's chin, Wolfram snarled, "Listen up, fella. Listen good. This is bigger than you."

"That it is, my friend." With that, Henry Marks strutted away proudly without turning back. Slim, entering the dining hall, held the door open for him.

"Smells good," Slim declared with a hearty gulp of air. "What's for sup?"

Thirty-Two

IN THE GLOOM, Rachel spotted Henry skulking along the path. She had an L.L. Bean Trailblazer flashlight to help navigate the dark and trained it now on Henry. Henry kept coming.

She'd known in advance of Wolfram's plan, and the only reason she'd done nothing to discourage him was because she was fairly certain he would fail. Bulldoze Henry Marks into dropping out? Twenty-four hours before showtime? Only someone with Wolfram's mangled understanding of human nature could believe that a bumptious personality like Henry might be so easily deterred. In point of fact, she'd made her peace with Henry's appearance.

It wasn't as if Henry needed to become Martin Luther King. Or Al Gore, for that matter. No need to immortalize the conference with "I Have a Dream" or a rousing *Inconvenient Truth*. Were Henry to manage to scramble even a few rungs up those lofty ladders, Rachel would happily reconsider all her doubts. Realistically, adequate would be acceptable. As to what might constitute inadequate, Rachel had to believe she'd know it when she heard it.

Aiming the flashlight, she tracked Henry's shuffling approach in the manner of a nature documentarian filming in the wild. She held still; he kept moving. The Green Mountains loomed, behemoths in charcoal gray.

"Done with dinner?" she asked as he neared. Best to play dumb, if possible.

"Do you think that?" Henry snapped. "Do you?"

"Think what?"

"That I'll flop. Do you think that?"

"I don't want to."

"Don't want to? Don't *want* to?" Henry flapped his arms to enunciate his dismay. His movements illuminated in the narrow flashlight beam had the herky-jerkiness of an old-time flip book. Calming down, he resumed. "I have to tell you, Rachel, I'd hoped for a bit more from you."

She switched off the flashlight. This interaction would go better in the dark. "I do want to believe it. I really do, Henry."

A sudden gust swept through the upper branches.

"I need more than that, Rachel."

"I'm not that person."

"What the hell does that mean?"

She was glad for the darkness. If she had to look straight into his face, so wrought with sincerity, she wasn't sure she could handle it.

"That's not me. Sorry."

"How do you know?" he railed. "How do you know, really, who you are? You're a lot of people. Same with me. You think I was destined to be here, doing this? But guess what, here I am. All the many possible lives, all the different roads . . ." He flung out his arms, encompassing the vast world around them. "See what I mean?"

She did, and she did not. She swiped a lank strand from her eyes. The wind swept it right back. She really wanted to take it down a notch.

His voice jabbed at her, taut and insistent, boxing her in. "Has it never happened to you that someone—sure, a man, but it doesn't have to be—gets so turned on by you, your wit, your spirit, your whatever, and suddenly you see it too? Like, behold this dazzling human being! And it turns out the dazzling human being is you!"

Henry reached to draw her close. Rachel pressed her forehead into his shoulder but only as a wedge, a boxer's clench to keep the adversary from throwing another punch. Deep in the forest, a few cicadas whirred, holdovers from a vanished summer.

"Will you," Henry pleaded, "come to my tent?"

His proposition was beyond preposterous, another reason for doubt. Although his words, if he meant them, were lovely, another reason to pray he had the right stuff.

She withdrew from the clench, careful to steady her voice so as not to seem ruffled. "When all this is over, all I can say is, well, who knows?"

With that, Rachel switched on her flashlight, and they parted, each peeling into the night along different paths.

"Watch your step," she called to him, probably too late to be heard.

Her direction before crossing paths with Henry was to the dining hall. She had no appetite now. Returning to the cabin, Rachel spotted a dark figure scampering that way. She followed Celeste through the creaky pine door.

For much of the past week, they'd been roommates. Before Celeste moved out on Slim, Rachel had the stuffy cabin to herself, a lodging perk like officer quarters at a military base, granted her as EarthKare's first-in-command. Rachel found she preferred having a roommate. It harkened back to dormitory life and the spirited, ad hoc, free-flowing intimacies she'd enjoyed with girls she hardly knew until she knew way too much. Celeste would have been fun as a dorm mate. Fun ranked higher back then.

The cabin beds were lumpy Goodwill castoffs set upon crude board platforms. In the months since EarthKare had made its full-time move to Vermont, Rachel had rarely enjoyed a solid night's sleep. Anxiety was certainly a contributing factor. A bumpy mattress and the musty chill didn't help. Celeste, on the other hand, usually slept like a drunken sailor and snored like one also.

Rachel collapsed onto her mattress, flustered from her run-in with Henry. Should she say anything to Celeste? The vexing interchange had been the sort, fraught with murky innuendo, that would've provided fantastic fodder for the off-the-cuff wisdom of the girls of Chadbourne Hall. Does the sight of him make you hot, they'd immediately want to know. A reasonable place to start the discussion. If Rachel were still an undergrad. If EarthKare were but a term paper assignment.

They kept the Coleman on a shelf that jutted between the beds. Celeste went to it now, priming the fuel pump, striking the kitchen match, lighting the wick. The amber flare threw a crazy hand shadow onto the low pinewood ceiling.

"Bono," she groaned, plunking onto the bed. "Not happening."

Rachel had never believed otherwise, although she'd withheld her skepticism rather than overtly support Wolfram in his.

"It was worth a try," she said unconvincingly.

"Yeah, well."

Rachel allowed her to stew in silence. For all her gushing enthusiasms, Celeste had a brooding, contemplative side. Then, "Can I ask you something?"

"Is it about Henry?"

Wow. As shrewd as those feisty gals back in the dorm and quick on the draw. "Yes. But not what you think."

"I know more than you think."

Before Rachel could switch the subject, Celeste leapt right back in. "Sorry. Didn't mean to be snippy. I've been dealing with some stuff."

"Reggie?"

Celeste nodded. "Back to Henry."

Confiding in Celeste was perhaps not a great idea. Warily, Rachel continued. "He's from a different universe, I get that. We couldn't be more different. But . . . "

"Stop. Stop right there."

Rachel stopped.

"The dude's smooth. He's nice looking, sort of. He's got a way with words." Celeste stretched a hand across the gap between beds, a sisterly show of empathy. Her hand didn't quite reach. "Can I be frank?"

Having granted Celeste special stature by reaching out to her, Rachel supposed she had to suffer the humbling that came with it. "Go on."

"You don't want to be part of his act. You want a guy who'll be part of your act."

Rachel considered telling Celeste about encountering Henry pissing alone in the woods. She might tell Celeste how seamlessly the two of them fell into an easy, jokey banter and how comfortable it was hiking alongside him. She might confide her secret titillation at the way Henry praised her while fully recognizing his words were but a cotton candy confection spun by a man who did it for a living. She might even disclose that this openness to a mismatched man from another planet was not as strange or unprecedented as it might seem on the surface. There was a history. Rachel did not question the good intentions behind Celeste's cautionary warning, at least as it applied to Rachel Seagrave, founder and director of EarthKare International. The other Rachel Seagrave? She was unknown to Celeste and to most others.

Celeste broke the lull. "You want to know who I would pay attention to? If I were you?"

Rachel played along. "Who?"

"Lenny. The reporter. He's unpolished. Kind of a fixer-upper. But if things turn out the way we hope? You know, professional success can smooth out a hell of a lot of wrinkles in a dude." Celeste leaned nearer the lantern with a half-cocked wink. "Been known to happen."

Celeste meant well. Rachel gave her credit. It wasn't easy dispensing earnest romantic advice to a mature woman.

"I'll reflect on it," Rachel assured her. "Thanks."

"Want some more advice?"

"No."

Celeste giggled. "Good. Because I've given you all I got."

Thirty-Three

YOUR TIRED, YOUR weary, your huddled masses. The cloying phrase stuck in Beibel's mind like a burr in a hiker's wool sock. Which was weird because what he actually observed about the EarthKare attendees arriving Friday afternoon with their bulging REI backpacks and sagebrush bedrolls were men and women who mostly appeared healthy, vigorous, animated, vibrant. Masses, huddled or otherwise, was an overestimate. Tired and weary, perhaps, but rarin' to go. The persistent echo of the tired-and-weary adage, a dim memory of some obligatory grade school recitation, was, he decided, one of those inexplicable (to him) quirks of neurological circuitry that, like melodious song snippets, cling like lint.

Beibel had staked out a position by the mossy stone wall that divided the lower woods from the clearing. The first bus from White River had chugged in roughly when expected, 3:30 p.m. For all the painful negotiations, Rachel had come through with a pair of groaning Crown Coaches, a bit past their heyday, yet, knock wood, adequate to the job, along with two grizzled drivers who didn't say much.

Beibel's plan was to take note of every detail, large and small, observable and subjective, the potentially poignant along with the manifestly trivial. There was no telling exactly what aspects of this might add resonance, for he was beginning to conceive of this endeavor less as an examination of the concrete challenges facing activist environmental causes (that sort of tome could be written by any number of tenured professors) than a slice-of-time portrait of a quirky citizens brigade, told in soap opera segments.

Beibel stood like a sentry at the narrow gap in the old stone wall where the troops funneled past. On second glance, a few did appear rather tired and a tad weary. Dressed more conventionally than anyone else on the premises (creased khakis, Sta-Press shirt), he might be mistaken for plainclothes security. In fact, a young lady in spandex tights and an electric blue sweater halted directly in front of him and began fishing nervously through her backpack. When she yanked out her driver's license and sullenly displayed it for his inspection, all Beibel could think to do was check her photo ID against the real thing. He waved her through without comment.

The "no cellphone" policy, which EarthKare proudly featured in pre-event communications, nonetheless seemed to catch some by surprise. Beibel watched several new arrivals, upon spotting the policy prominently posted on a yellow octagonal stop sign nailed to the gray trunk of a tall birch, glance around furtively to make sure they were undetected by the authorities, which was itself risible, before deftly shifting the outlawed iPhone from pants pocket to the bowels of a stuffed backpack.

Several attendees came buzzing with informational questions. Where to register? Where to set up their tent? Was there a message board where they could leave a note for Gordon Chan? What was the nearest location to get internet access? Where to defecate if they'd rather not use a porta potty? (A holistic approach to nature's call was not just sanctioned but encouraged; indeed, there would be a panel discussion on Saturday afternoon titled "Why Do Bears Shit in the Woods?")

"Hey!" a chipper male voice yelped. "Isn't that the guy?"

Beibel looked up. A cluster of new arrivals was pointedly giving him the eye. Their attention, he realized, was being directed his way by the outstretched bony finger of the one with droopy eyes and comically protruding ears. Beibel recognized him from the birder brigade. Except this time he held no clipboard.

It was mostly the same crew as a few days ago. There was the burly fellow with the Santa beard, the squat no-neck man wearing the same silly safari hat, the slender gray lady who now wore a beige sweatshirt with a great blue heron stenciled on it.

Beibel was somewhat surprised the birders had chosen to come back for the conference. He would not have assumed that bird buffs would necessarily line up behind EarthKare's alarmist agenda, although he recognized that "canary in the coal mine" was a more potent slogan for birders than it was for most. Beibel did find it heartening that this group's prior visit, marred in the unfortunate way it was, had not totally soured them on involvement with the activist fringe. Perhaps the birders had forgiven him. Clearly they'd not forgotten him.

Acknowledging Mr. Clipboard's shout-out with a dry smile, Beibel quickly resumed note-taking with the hope they'd proceed to stroll right on by. And they nearly did. But the blue heron lady couldn't resist.

"Gesundheit," she cackled. And for good measure, she mimed yanking a handkerchief from the front pocket of her cargo pants and honking her nose.

By late afternoon, the apron of trampled grass surrounding the dining hall was a swarming beehive. With an obvious queen. For all her determination to divest herself of micromanagement burdens, Rachel remained the undisputed go-to person. Slim was in charge of facility logistics and event staging. Celeste was responsible for food and sustenance, as well as recycling. Danielle oversaw the assignment of tent sites and was the backup when it came to transportation and general troubleshooting. Each was fully authorized to make all decisions concerning their assigned spheres of influence. Each, however, preferred to consult Rachel if there was any complexity involved. It was clear to Beibel that Rachel would have to vanish altogether if she really wanted to reduce her role.

Watching her patiently respond to the hurled queries (Had Professor Rautenberg arrived? Would there be Sunday service options for the religious? Where in the woods had the Oswald's thrush been sighted?), Beibel returned to the image of huddled masses. Rachel with her humble peasant attire could be Our Lady of the Harbor. He jotted a short-hand note: "hudd mass, stat lib, R."

A new brigade came trudging by. The second bus must have pulled in. There was a certain Noah's Ark quality to this cluster. Although they shared some characteristics—worn jeans and backpacks crammed with dangling accessories—they were individually distinctive. A tall man with a curly black beard and a shiny gold necklace. A silver-haired woman holding the elbow of a much younger woman with the perfect posture of an Alvin Ailey dancer. There was a squat man in a ratty green Oakland A's sweatshirt who had a Tourette's-like neck twitch. Another man was dressed in what looked to be a NASA flight suit, bright white polymer with red and blue trim, all one piece. Close behind were a pair of younger fellows who could pass for junior faculty in the humanities department at a private college, combed hair, clean shaven, Pendleton shirts with sleeves folded to mid-forearm.

The women fascinated Beibel. Especially the cute ones. Why weren't they back in the metropolitan social whirl where they could have their cake without stress or strain? He liked to think of himself as a connoisseur of women. Beibel's informal—informal but hardly inexpert—studies of the female gender had, to his way of thinking, achieved a PhD level of sophistication (it was a mere GED when it came to guys). His antenna for the nuances and subtleties of women, their latent potential and private yearnings, was more highly developed than it was for men. With men, his radar was primarily attuned to the elemental and obvious: Did they appear to be capable of breaking tackles? Did they know how to fix an internal combustion engine? Were they a threat to bully him?

Beibel wavered in his estimation of the actual significance of his perceptions. On the one hand, he was hopelessly corrupted by centuries of profit-driven sexism and misogyny. The early 21st-century American male, which, no way around it, remained his fundamental cultural identity, was simply incapable of an honest, unsullied appraisal of women. Too much baggage, too much noise. That said, men had eyes, and those eyes, befogged though they may be by cultural impurities, were the most reliable tool available. What was the old canard? If all you possess is a hammer, then every problem looks like a nail.

Since watching her step wearily off the bus in White River, Beibel had had his eye on Rachel. He liked to think of himself as a shrewd scout of undiscovered gems, in feature news and in women. It was this shrewdness that had led him to EarthKare, and how fitting that Rachel should occupy that very field of vision. There was, he was starting to believe, a holistic continuity to his place in the fragmented cosmos. The same perspicacity that guided one avenue of investigation guided the other. Stories that reeked of espionage and skullduggery and murder most foul were the equivalent of buxom blondes flashing cleavage. Big deal. The true challenge, journalistically and romantically, was to discover the hidden gems, the quiet dramas, the unassuming beauties behind the veil.

No aesthetician, he was completely ignorant when it came to the subtleties of makeup, powder blush, lip gloss, eyeliner, foundation, and the like. Yet he recognized that Rachel, with but a few deft touchups, could be recast into the sort of leading lady who . . . who wouldn't give him the time of day.

But in her current incarnation, dressed like an indentured farmhand, her hair a bird's nest snarl, cheerless and unrouged, well, he just might have a shot. She was rapidly approaching the age, biological clock clanging, when her dreamboat fantasies, if they lingered at all, would be giving way to practical calculations about what kind of man would make a suitable father. And Beibel had to believe there was nothing, except possibly his lack of a stable income, that rendered him ineligible.

There was, however, the problem of Henry Marks. Beibel had witnessed a few stolen glances between them that lingered too long. It couldn't be ruled it out. Mr. JogThink had a cocksure charm that could be enchanting to a lass whose defenses were down. For now, he trusted that professional ethics would compel the two of them to keep it under wraps for the duration of the conference. Afterward? Well, afterward, let the best man win. Darwin again.

That Rachel, as far as he could discern, showed zero interest in him was not the last word on the matter. It was possible that she too lagged in deciphering the inner wisdom of the sexual urge. They didn't have much else in common.

She was unflappable; he got flapped over a missed turnpike exit. People trusted her instinctually; he aroused suspicion, even when keeping his mouth shut. She was an avid hiker, swimmer, skater, skier. He was a gym rat by nature, but no longer in condition for any sport, indoor or out. Their contrasting characteristics were so profound and extensive, yin to yang, that it occurred to him that together they might constitute a unified whole, a seamless circle. That she apparently picked up on absolutely none of this while he saw it with increasing clarity was but another fascinating feature of their intriguing duality. It thrilled him that this book-length narrative nonfiction project might include a bona fide first-person romantic quest.

What remained foggy was what would be in it for her. Why Lenny Beibel among the vast universe of eligible sperm donors? Watching Rachel masterfully playing maître d' to the jabbering conference arrivals with the self-composure of Buddha, a pang of doubt crept over Beibel. Would *he* choose *him* if he were her?

It was fascinating to watch her operate with such suave aplomb. Rachel patiently informing a sturdy woman in farmer coveralls that she and her Rasta-haired boyfriend could pitch their tent anywhere in the neighboring woods so long as they did not obstruct the flow of a stream (a joke) or encroach on anyone else's campsite (not a joke). Directing a muscular African-American fellow with creepy forearm tattoos to the kitchen for answers to his peanut allergy question. Telling a bookish fellow with a wispy goatee where he could refrigerate his colitis medication. Follow the dude with the tattoos.

She never grew testy or curt. An older gentleman approached, bracing himself with a walking stick to keep from toppling over. Severely stooped, he was barely able to lift his eyes to meet hers. She bent lower to accommodate him. Instead of a backpack, which would have proved an impossible burden, the man had jerry-rigged saddlebags looped onto his snakeskin belt. He wanted to know if there was a printed program of the conference agenda, as for obvious reasons—he swept his free hand up and down his torso—he'd packed light and did not bring his laptop.

"I printed out a copy," he sheepishly told her, "but left it in Asheville."

"I love Asheville," Rachel said. "In my next life . . ."

Beibel took note: another detail that could come in handy, and not necessarily with his book.

"A great place," the fellow gurgled. It seemed as difficult for him to speak as it was to straighten up.

There was no printed program, Rachel told him, out of paper waste concerns. But there was a message board at the entrance to the dining hall—she pointed in that direction—that listed all events with times.

"Is there something in particular you're looking for?"

"Al Gore."

Rachel did not flinch. With the consummate congeniality of an airline representative announcing to the mob at Gate 12 that the departure was on hold due to air traffic congestion, she explained, "He is not currently scheduled. Our opening speaker tonight is Henry Marks. You can read about him on the message board outside the dining hall. Not as famous, of course, as Al Gore, but . . ."

Rachel fell silent. It was not clear if she'd run dry of things to say or could not bring herself to further tout the credentials of Mr. JogThink. Beibel suspected the latter.

Cinching his saddlebag, the stooped fellow peered up. "What's the name again?"

"Henry Marks."

"Any chance he's related to . . .?"

"Karl? Not a chance."

Thirty-Four

IN THE EARLY 1980s, a rustic natural amphitheater had been carved out of the nearby forest through the efforts of ten- and eleven-year-old summer campers and their teenage counselors. A short walk through the woods from the cabins, the semicircular amphitheater was terraced like an Indonesian rice farm. The ground at the base was flat enough to be stage-like, and the ascending rows of earthen terrace made for perfect bleachers except when damp.

Woodstock—the gathering of tribes, not the colossal mud bath—remained a guiding vision. The bulky big top, reeking of mildew and elephant dung, had been delivered early that morning by the jolly team from Acme Circus who promised they'd return to set her up should the forecast indicate rain. In another foul weather precaution, the entertainment sub-committee had fortified the rutted dirt floor stage with slats of sturdy plywood. The backstage area was similarly crude, a modest cubicle cordoned off with army blankets suspended over clotheslines. In his notes, Beibel referred to the backstage area as "BS," fully aware that this abbreviation could result in the occasional mix-up.

Diligent note-taking was critical at this point. A few hours earlier Beibel had learned that the conference would not be bailed out by rock star Bono, and therefore neither would he. No explanation was given. Reggie Takada had also departed the compound. No explanation there either. These machinations, or non-machinations, were beyond Beibel to interpret. Lemonade out of lemons was the challenge he faced. It was the same challenge confronting the entire conference. Beibel loathed the metaphor.

Regarding the BS set-up, he took particularly diligent notes. There were folding chairs (four), a refreshment table with a goatskin water jug, several cups (plastic!), hand-carved wooden bowls filled with trail mix and assorted glop. A green Coleman lantern affixed to the center pole threw off a sharp, pulsing light. The closest to the sort of inner sanctum luxury typically reserved for entertainment industry headliners was a reclining beach chair of thatched blue and white vinyl strips, perfect for sunbathing. Not until much later, not until the aftermath, did Beibel learn how this anomalous piece of furniture came to occupy the BS area. The beach chair or "some mutually acceptable facsimile" was a stipulation in the Henry Marks performance agreement.

No, EarthKare was not paying Henry Marks a dime. But his wily agent had not relaxed her standard checklist of niggling demands simply because no money would be changing hands. When Beibel first got a look at the document (he promised not to reveal his source; it was Henry himself), he thought it was a parody.

The agreement stipulated that a) Henry could cancel for Act of God reasons or for reasons of "overriding personal or professional responsibility"; b) any public announcement or official notification of Henry's cancellation be handled solely and exclusively by The Agency, as it was termed in the contract, and EarthKare was enjoined, subject to penalty, from making any public statements related to this; c) videotaping of Henry's presentation was precluded; d) the Sponsor, as EarthKare was indelicately termed, was obligated to provide a public address system capable of projecting the Artist's speech throughout the venue; e) the Sponsor would provide a private "dressing room" supplied with "healthy" snack food, orange Gatorade (the specific brand-name drink, not some home-brewed knockoff), and a chaise lounge or some acceptable facsimile suitable for "power-napping."

Contract violations could, technically, provide Henry with an excuse for getting out of this. Yet from all that Beibel gathered, if Henry Marks wanted out, the door was wide open.

Beibel sauntered backstage, mindful that legendary journalists before him had come away with carefully observed gems by means of sneaking behind the scenes. Backstage reporting was hit or miss, like all sideshows. It could be utterly bland and unrevealing, or if luck was on his side, it might offer up something poignant, like the fraught machinations of sycophants and handlers in that classic piece of behind-the-scenes journalism, "Sinatra Has a Cold." Beibel would approach the situation hoping for drama but resigned to the quotidian.

Which reminded him: Where was Henry? Beibel had not seen Mr. JogThink since midmorning when he'd stopped by Henry's tent in hopes of grabbing an advance copy of the keynote speech. He'd never covered Capitol Hill or any major political campaigns, but he was aware that the press corps was routinely handed advance copies of major addresses, State of the Union and the like. This was different, but there was no harm in asking.

Beibel, a patient suitor, had waited outside Henry's tent in the mellow morning ground fog. "Knock, knock," he'd announced himself in what he felt was a cute little joke. He'd augmented the joke by gently rapping his fist against the flimsy polyester tent flap.

"Who's there?"

So far, so good. "Any chance I can have, you know, the advance text?"

"Text?"

"Of your speech."

"Sorry, pal," Henry answered sleepily without bothering to unzip the flap. "Not the way I work."

"Not even an outline?"

"The outline," Henry'd answered from within, "is my entire career."

"Oh, that helps a lot."

"Yes, I thought it would. Anything else?"

"Going for a run?"

"Not today."

Through the orange translucent tent wall, Beibel thought he could see Henry shifting within his sleeping bag.

Beibel tried again. "You know, jogging clears the mind. Stimulates thinking. Gets you up and out the door."

"Thanks for the tip."

"Jogging can be peaceful. And soulful. At the right pace."

"Hey, you're learning."

"Ignoring your own sage advice? Do I detect a contradiction?"

"I have no fucking idea what you detect. Now leave."

Who knew Henry could be such a nervous Nellie? Beibel had no choice but to yield. "Good luck, tonight."

"Tonight, tonight." Henry sang out. He had a bad singing voice, off key and unexpressive, for a man with such a sonorous speaking voice.

Beibel had waited for the next line of the song's refrain. Nothing was forthcoming.

In the shadows to the left of the stage, Lenny Beibel took up a position. It seemed like a good vantage point from which to take in the preliminaries. He planned eventually to retreat to the bleachers, which is where he could best get the pulse of what was happening. Or not happening.

Several performers were slotted as warm-ups. These included a Native American anti-fracking activist who promised to keep it short, a hip-hop dance troupe from New York City, a research botanist, and EarthKare's own singing duo, Dorothy and Mitchell. The dance troupe, performing a piece about climate change set to an atonal composition by John Cage was just about finished.

Entertainment critic was another facet of journalism Beibel had opted not to pursue. The pressure to find merit in self-indulgent nonsense would have driven him nuts, and there were quicker, more enjoyable ways to achieve that state. Of the dance troupe, he might have opined, "Close your eyes, plug your ears, and what's not to like?"

Parting the thick army blanket curtain, Beibel stepped into the lantern-lit enclosure. There was Wolfram, hovering over the snack table, surveying his choices. No sign of Henry.

Wolfram dug in, plunging his bare hand ravenously into the bean salad, pausing only to make a grunted acknowledgment of Beibel's presence. Someone was mighty hungry. And stressed.

From onstage came an overamplified outcry, high pitched and panic inducing, from Dr. Bethany Markakis, an associate professor of botany at NYU. Beibel had been able to secure an advance copy of her scripted remarks. She was out there methodically informing the audience what would become of life on planet Earth, decade by gruesome decade, should mankind fail to enact an abrupt about-face.

"Nervous?" Beibel asked Wolfram. The question was meant as a conversation starter. He did not expect Wolfram to reveal his feelings.

"'Bout what?"

"The main event." Employing show biz terminology was plainly passive-aggressive.

Wolfram scowled, as Beibel hoped he would.

"Have you seen, you know . . ." Wolfram was having a hard time bringing himself to call Henry by name.

"Our headline attraction?"

Wolfram dug his paw into the bean salad and came up with another handful. The dancing light of the Coleman lit his meaty face like a Harlequin mask.

"Probably out for a quick jog. Clears the mind, you know. Puts a person in touch with deeper realms."

"Spare me."

"If it'd help, I'm available to pinch-hit. I still remember the words, most of them anyway, to the Gettysburg Address. I could . . ."

"News media'd fuckin' love that. They say we're a throwback to the '60s. Might as well be the 1860s."

Had Wolfram cracked a joke? The pressure must be getting to him.

Eyeing the vacant beach lounge, Beibel eased himself onto it. A minor adjustment of the backward tilt and there he was, the very picture of a man at peace with his place in the cosmos. What would unfold would unfold.

"Wolfram," he said brightly, "I'm afraid the news media, present company excepted, already have their angle. You're the frivolous kiddies, and corporate America is the responsible parents."

"Yeah, responsible for waste and devastation."

Wolfram's eyes fell shut. His bulbous lips began to tremble. His full moon visage was flushed red, code alert. For an instant, Beibel thought the big guy might be suffering a stroke. A moment later, Wolfram snapped to attention, eyes afire.

"You," he intoned, his voice spooky and grave, "you are here for a reason. You were brought here, to this place, this moment, to tell the world. No matter what happens, our story needs to be told. Situations can bring out the best in a writer."

Beibel understood that he was going to have a hard enough time finding a publisher for whatever it was that he was writing without burdening the project with the need to explain EarthKare to the wider world. To argue sincerely on their behalf would be publishing-career suicide. A book that told the EarthKare story in a manner that would meet Wolfram's exacting standards for accuracy and readability . . . no editor in her right mind would touch it. There wouldn't be more than a few hundred potential readers in the whole of the Western world. And most of them were here for the conference.

Beibel tried shutting his eyes, just for a moment's tranquility, only to be summarily snapped to attention by Wolfram's heavy paw clamping hard onto his shoulder.

"This," Wolfram declared with ghostly seriousness, "is your big chance. This, my friend, is the big game. All the marbles. This time it's time . . ."

Had it come to this? Was he, Lenny Beibel, really the recipient of a pep talk delivered by the most oppressively downer person he'd ever met?

". . . to be all that you can be!"

Satisfied that his message had been effectively conveyed, Wolfram gave a solemn nod and retreated.

Stunned, Beibel rubbed his eyes. And what he saw, ducking under the army blanket into the soft, hissing glow of the lantern, was Henry Marks.

Thirty-Five

HENRY MARKS, SLIPPING through the backstage blankets, was dressed in black slacks, a shiny black suit coat, a light blue denim work shirt, and a tall black satin top hat befitting a carnival magician. Ditching the pastel country club leisurewear indicated to Beibel that Henry just might be catching on to the fact that this crowd was not his typical brigade of corporate managers. Always good to get in touch with one's audience. It occurred to Beibel that he might take a tip from Henry on this point, although as yet he had no real audience to be in touch with.

Wolfram's reaction was less generous. "What's that fucking thing on your head?" he yelped.

Daintily reaching up to be certain the top hat was still neatly perched, Henry replied with straight face. "Once belonged to a bona fide nightclub act."

"No shit."

Henry did a graceful half-turn, like a runway model displaying the goods. "You like?"

"You're scaring me."

Henry reverted to full frontal. "Fear, you know, can be a good thing."

Wolfram feigned a forward lurch. "I'll show you fear."

"Now, now." Beibel wedged between them, thrusting his hands outward like a boxing referee separating the brawling contestants.

Wolfram sneered and went back to the snack table.

"You recording this tonight?" Henry wanted to know.

Beibel pulled his trusty Olympus digital recorder from his pants pocket.

"Good," Henry confirmed. "Just in case . . ."

Wolfram paused his voracious chomping of a sturdy celery stalk. "Just in case what?"

"Just in case I hit it out of the park."

Wolfram coughed up a spray of vegetable matter.

"Both of you!" Henry pointed to the entrance flap like a biblical elder banishing sinners from the Temple. "Out! Thirty minutes quiet time. In private. Check my contract, pal. Mandatory. Now beat it."

The night air held the burnt sugar scent of fallen leaves. Outside the BS, Beibel scribbled a few notes in the darkness, trusting the old muscle memory to guide his penmanship. It proved an interesting exercise to busily write without being able to view what was written. Scribble, scribble. The Uniball pen skittered smoothly across the darkened page. He could have been writing on air. With invisible ink. "druid campfire, backstage glow." That's what he hoped he'd jotted. "forest sound, cracking twig, breeze whoosh waves beach, beach chair!!, ants snack table, nobody notices."

He was interrupted by one of the interns EarthKare had recruited to assist with assorted admin chores. A flock of them had arrived earlier in the day. It was Slim's idea. The flaw, now glaringly evident, was that untrained labor was only truly useful with an efficient management system to direct the effort. The interns, some two dozen of them, had spent the afternoon floating about the compound like milkweed seeds, airheaded and aimless. Beibel had encountered several of them already, fresh faced and enthusiastic with nothing to do and nobody to turn to. EarthKare's heart might be in the right place, but little else was. There was, however, one useful function he could imagine these feckless youngsters fulfilling: They could help fill the seats closest to the stage and be instructed to voice enthusiastic approval at all the appropriate junctures of Henry's keynote. Like a canned laugh track on a tacky TV sitcom. It was not, however, Bebel's place to propose such an assignment.

This intern's name was Melissa. Slim's one successful gesture was to get them to wear bright yellow identifying badges with their first name spelled out in block letters so they could be summoned *by name* . . . if anyone could find anything for them to do. She looked vaguely Malaysian with smooth skin, silken hair, dark eyes that gleamed.

"Anything you'd like me to do?" she asked, assuming Beibel to be a person with official responsibilities.

A persnickety notion popped to mind. Beibel was not proud of it, but there it was. He pointed toward the army blanket entrance to Henry's lair. "The keynote speaker? He's in there."

"Mister Gore?"

Beibel was taken aback. "What in the world makes you think that?"

"'S what people're saying."

"Just a rumor, I'm afraid. No, I'm referring to the gentleman who will actually be speaking tonight, Henry Marks."

Melissa worked her delicate upper lip as though stifling a sneeze. The name did not ring a bell.

"He's in there."

"And?"

"He might need help."

"You mean like with . . .?"

Beibel parted the blankets, showing Melissa the way.

Henry was flat on his back on the beach chair. The stiff brim of his top hat slanted across his eyes. He looked like a Tombstone dandy passed out from rotgut whisky.

"My god," Melissa gasped. "Is he, like . . .?"

Henry wiggled a foot, answering the question.

"Melissa," Beibel explained, "is a student intern, and she wants to know what she can do to help."

Henry re-angled the top hat just enough to permit a squinting view. He sat up for a better look. He smiled. He winked. "Maybe later. Depending."

Melissa pretended not to know what he was talking about. And perhaps she didn't.

Henry lifted the hat brim from his eyes and sat up straight. "How's it look?"

Melissa came forward. Carefully, like a beautician applying the finishing touch, she shifted the hat an inch sideways, a jauntier look.

"Perfect," she beamed, stepping back to assess. "Depending."

With all the vigor of a condemned prisoner finishing his last meal, Henry creakily made his way to his feet. "Time, I guess, to do my thing," he soberly announced. "So I shall."

It was that clunky phrase, "so I shall," laden with Elizabethan self-importance, that crystallized Beibel's conviction that whatever happened tonight out there on the stage, it was going to be good. If not for EarthKare or for the fate of life on the planet, then at least for his nonfiction, yet-to-be-specified, breakout project.

Thirty-Six

CARVED FROM THE surrounding forest, the amphitheater blended with the wooded hillside as seamlessly as if Frederick Law Olmsted himself had designed it. There was a medieval spookiness to the setting, accentuated by the dark, winding, narrow, tunnel-like path leading to it. Back when the compound was a functioning summer camp, impressionable children squirming in the earthen bleachers found it easy to conjure witches and goblins lurking in the wilderness nearby. It made for excellent audience attention.

The evening agenda called for Rachel to begin her formal introduction of the keynote speaker somewhere in the vicinity of 7:30 p.m., not that anyone would be keeping close track of time. Presenters had been given suggested parameters. Compliance was voluntary. Audience attention, to the extent it was discernible, would function as the policing mechanism. The police would be unarmed.

Rachel stood silently at the side of the stage. She was not exactly hiding, although the nearby shrubs did provide potential cover. In the semidarkness, she groped for a small slice of zen-like calm. Eyes closed. Hands dangling. Neck loose. Mind empty. Ommmmm. For the time being, nobody was bombarding her with logistical problems or angling to shake her hand and proclaim how much they appreciated all that she'd done.

On stage, the Wickershams were warbling the last of their three-number set, a rap adaptation of Edgar Allan Poe's "The Raven" with unmistakable relevance to the politics of climate change. The attendees, some 165 of them (at last, a head count!), were assembled along the terraced sod benches. Did people seem engaged, amused, curious, attentive, sympathetic? Rachel tried not to look.

After the Wickershams concluded, it would fall to Rachel to step forward and set the table for Henry Marks. Aware of the mounting buzz that Al Gore might swoop in at the last minute a la Superman, she would need to officially quash that one. Best to get it out of the way immediately.

It seemed only yesterday she was a carefree girl scampering across the schoolyard, swatting down her skirt to keep the boys, always a step slower then, from peeking. Or was yesterday that road trip west after college with Frank, the erstwhile folksinger who was at his best around a campfire doing his Hank Williams imitation, and wouldn't it have been nice if she could have believed the twangy homespun simplicities he sang of and forced herself to believe hapless Frank could deliver them? Or was yesterday that starlit night on the Costa Rica coast, half-naked and free—free from the clock, free from gringo news, free from who she'd been— waiting for the timeless *tortugas* to flop ashore and lay their precious eggs on the same ancient sands?

So many alternate paths, so many diverging choices, any one of which would have veered elsewhere, yielding a very different life. Henry, she recalled, had made a point of pointing this out to her, although his motives were suspect. And she'd heard it before. Rewind the tape of life on Earth and replay our long evolution, she'd heard a famed biologist once profess, and it would never, ever, not in a million years, come out the way it did. That made sense. None of the paths Rachel might otherwise have chosen would have brought her here, to these woods, to this moment. She'd never intended to lead a crusade. It had not been her aim to serve as anything except a volunteer foot soldier. Yet here she was, gritting her teeth.

The Wickershams' rhythmic patter grew louder, more emphatic, harder to ignore. Their foot stomping (or was it tap-dancing?) grew more urgent. Rachel had witnessed this number many times. Their set list did not deviate. They were entering the homestretch of "The Craven," with the famous refrain, "Never more," recast as an ominous punch line brimming with double entendre.

Unlike Wolfram, Rachel believed the Wickershams to be essentially harmless. The little dishonesties involved in pretending to enjoy their performances were, she felt, a small price to pay for their many years of extraordinarily selfless contributions.

Not once had the Wickershams ever refused. They had worked on water purification projects in the Himalayas, referendums against strip mining in West Virginia, and campaigns to secure property rights for indigenous people in Chiapas where they'd also briefly served as translators for the enigmatic Comandante Zero. Nobody, not even Wolfram, disputed the fact that the entire community of social justice progressives was deeply indebted to them for their dogged service.

So what if the actual performance—their puerile stabs at humorous stage banter (endangered species jokes!), their awkward parody of high-strutting Las Vegas dance moves, their lame rewriting of the lyrics to folk song staples like "This Land is Their Land" and "The Big Tar Sands Mountain"—was amateurish? So what if their "message" ditties like "The Craven" were moronic oversimplifications of what every member of the audience already knew and wholeheartedly agreed with? All that really mattered was to honor the basic terms of the transaction: The Wickershams had donated their talents, and it would be a sadistic slap in their good-hearted faces to say no, thanks, maybe next time.

Rachel had made her peace. In addition, there was one indisputable benefit. In the classic vaudeville definition of the term, Dorothy and Mitchell would be anything but a tough act to follow.

Thirty-Seven

"CAN YOU HEAR me?"

Of course they could hear her. The state-of-the-art JBL loudspeakers were arranged for and installed by Champlain Sound, a company out of Burlington that did the Pfish tours and was donating the equipment and its services. The head tech guy was a woman with gray-brown dreads tumbling in thick ropes from a green skullcap. Her name was April, and she had assured Rachel that there was no need to project her voice any louder than she would need to do at a cozy corner table for six.

Rachel cleared her throat and instantly regretted it. The dry rasp boomed forth like the amplified barfing of a nightclub comic doing a riff about binge drinking. Won't make that mistake again.

"So great that you could all make it to this important gathering." This seemed like the right kind of thing to say, and yet it left a rubber chicken staleness in her mouth. She quickly tried to correct. "I am proud to be among so many dedicated activists, and I am excited for what we can accomplish together."

Rachel had done enough public speaking—university lectures and conference panels and fundraising pitches—to understand she could get away with a few minutes of aimless pleasantries, maybe a quip or two. She did have a wry sense of humor. Everyone said that about her. But she understood that what they mostly meant was that she possessed a delightful laugh. Friends enjoyed trying to coax it from her. She gravitated to people who had the knack.

What people did not mean when they said she had a good sense of humor was that she was good at making jokes. Generally, she was bad at it. Had she been better prepared, she might have pulled one off the internet. There were plenty of Al Gore jokes out there, and probably a wealth of jokes about jogging. For all she knew, there were decent jokes that could be made about global warming and ecological Armageddon. Know thy audience was the first rule of speaking. Know thyself was the second.

"I want to remind everyone that the Wickershams will be leading a workshop tomorrow morning on singing with the birds." Mirthful twittering fluttered up from crowd, and for an instant Rachel wondered if maybe she'd arrived at a joke without intending it. "The workshop addresses the way art and nature intersect. It'll be fun and instructive. Check the board outside the main cabin for details. Now, for our next . . ."

She'd decided against scripting her introductory remarks. She had tried, several times, with a yellow legal pad by lamp glow in her cabin. But she'd come up with nothing she liked enough to reread, much less speak aloud. Part of the problem was that her role was simply an introductory one. Henry's resume in highly edited form (i.e., no testimonials from insurance industry associations) had been posted on the bulletin board outside the dining hall. No point in repeating what was already known. And it wasn't as if knowing more about Henry would make the audience more appreciative. Regarding Henry's accomplishments, the less said, the better.

"Our keynote speaker . . ."

Before she could say another word, before she could even get her head around what was happening, before she could shoo him back where he came from, Henry, flaunting the unbridled zest of an overeager starlet auditioning for a Broadway production of *Follies*, pounced onto the stage.

He came to a halt directly in front of her, clicked his heels, and snapped off a crisp West Point-worthy military salute. "Reporting for duty," he proclaimed.

Horrified, Rachel felt dragooned into an improv sketch with no chance of escape. All she could think to say, because she had to say something, was, "Aren't you a few minutes early?"

"Better early than never."

The daft top hat gave Henry the look of a New Year's drunk revving up for the countdown to midnight. It occurred to her that might be his problem. Except at this point, all his problems were also hers.

She needed to buy herself a few seconds with the hope—yes, it had come down to hope—a solution would emerge. She made a show of theatrically stroking her chin, mulling over what next. Her proximity to the ultra-sensitive mic closed off one avenue, whispering harshly for Henry to get the hell back to where he came from. She could only communicate silently, and she did so now, beseeching him with all the urgent pleading she could muster through body language and weary eyes. Please, please, please do not fuck up. Whether in his addled state Henry possessed the cognitive capacity to interpret her meaning and do anything about it, time would tell.

Again, Henry saluted her with an almost comical parade ground precision.

"Good luck, soldier," she blurted, helpless to escape this nightmare improv sketch. "Safe travels."

In the aftermath, many would take this comment as an indication of foreknowledge, which Rachel found beyond ridiculous. If the entire episode proved anything, it was her utter lack of not just foreknowledge but forethought.

Thirty-Eight

"HOW MANY OF you out there are joggers? Show of hands?"

With those words, Henry Marks launched his keynote address at the first International EarthKare Conference.

Lenny Beibel had located himself midway up the terrace. The real story—God, he hoped there was one—had to be out here among the restless rank and file, why they came here, what they hoped for, how they were affected. As one of three members of the media in attendance, along with a hipster lady with purple hair and purple eyeglasses from *Sustainability Times* and a college-age stringer for Al Jazeera, he'd been offered a front-row seat. Which he readily declined. Proximity to the stage meant little to him. He was not some prissy theater critic. It was not his aim to evaluate Henry's performance on a one-to-ten scale or render a moronic thumbs-up, thumbs-down verdict. His mission was to drink it all in, slosh it around, and spit it back out in a riveting narrative. And then sell the sucker to . . . someone.

There was plenty of empty space, the hundred-plus members of the audience having ignored repeated pleas from the Wickershams to relocate to the front rows, in order to be closer together, to better "share the solidarity." Beibel had settled on a grassy shelf toward the rear. He had a clear view of the podium as well as the surrounding audience: men and women and otherwise, svelte and gnarly, old and young, shabby, spruced, weary, huddled, etc. What conclusion might be reliably drawn about them? For starters, they cared enough to have come all this way.

The birder clan was clumped nearby, just below and to his right. They hadn't noticed Beibel, and he was glad for that. Still, it would probably be a smart idea to approach them afterward for a postmortem interview. Getting reactions from the audience was standard reportorial practice. He had to believe Henry's performance, win or lose, would give rise to some colorful quotes.

Actually, most of the attendees seemed like they'd be interesting to interview. Any person who'd go to these lengths, literally, for the purpose of . . . the purpose of what exactly? Beibel still didn't have a clear grasp on why anyone beyond the EarthKare inner circle had chosen to come here. He'd love to be able to get away with pat assumptions about who these people were, the way one might, for example, if reporting on a Make America Great Again rally at a NASCAR track in Georgia. But EarthKare was too quirky and the conference attendees too demographically varied and, he, Beibel, in the final analysis, too journalistically diligent to simply wing it. How to pigeonhole the regal, silver-haired fellow in the black turtleneck who vaguely resembled Mitt Romney? Or the dark-skinned lass in a Persian carpet blazer Beibel had spotted earlier in the day quietly doing yoga by herself in the meadow? Or those three bros, two in baseball caps, one in skullcap, who were so immersed in babbling spiritedly among themselves that they'd nearly collided with Wolfram out by the stone wall. It was fun to watch Wolfram pull back, just barely, from reflexively throwing a punch. Oblivious, the buddies kept right on babbling, slapping five every few yards. They looked like they'd be fun to interview. It would be fun to be one of them.

Beibel felt he had done his spadework, logged the requisite hours. He'd spent enough time with the Orange Tent Interviews that he could, he believed, roughly intuit most of the relevant thoughts running (note: jogging the pathways of Mr. JogThink's thoughts, a riff to exploit) through Henry's nimble mind. Crunch time, here we come! Henry Marks wasn't the only one approaching the starting line.

For an extraordinary realization had seized Beibel, bordering on epiphany. For all their evident folly, EarthKarers just might be onto something. Regardless of the daunting challenges they faced, regardless of the invisibility of progress, regardless of the great likelihood of failure, for the most part they all seemed pretty hopeful. They all seemed spirited. They all seemed jazzed.

The EarthKare cadre appeared to suffer from none of the aimlessness, listlessness, inertia, and uselessness that plagued so many. Their crusade had a name. Their journey had a direction. Their road was far from a lonely one. No wallowing, no floundering, no whining, no treading water, no crying out to be rescued. They were like a self-help cult with a mission. Their mission gave them purpose. A righteous mission, it appeared, could make a person healthy and whole.

Beibel wondered if Henry Marks was possibly picking up on any of this? It would help him out if he could.

Onstage, Henry took a moment. He closed his eyes. He puffed his chest. He inhaled deeply, exhaled slowly. He let his hands dangle. He bent slightly at the waist, forward, then side to side. He shook out his left leg. Then his right. Then, with a frenzied shudder, his eyes popped open. Beibel saw it, even if nobody else did.

A transformation was under way. Before their very eyes. Henry Marks was toeing the starting line. He was anxious. He was focused. He was determined. Did he have it in him? What stuff was he made of? Was he willing to pay the price?

The starter pistol tilted skyward. Calm before the storm. On your marks . . .

Pressing his mouth to the microphone's soft foam sheaf, Henry again thundered, "How many of you out there are joggers?"

Zip. Nothing. No audience response. Beibel spotted Rachel squatting in the wing, not quite hiding. She had both hands cupped over her eyes, as though afraid to look. Her greater worry, Beibel observed, should be audio, not visual.

Rachel hunkered in the shadows, partially concealed by a low boxwood hedge. From here on, she'd be only a spectator, helpless to do anything except cheer on her home team, go, go, go. Even that she could only do silently. And silently was no way to cheer.

"Show of hands?" Henry crowed. In the lull that followed, he made a showy display of scanning the audience, shielding his eyes from the nonexistent glare.

"Come on, folks. Raise 'em high."

Who did Henry think he was addressing? An all-school assembly of Hillcrest Elementary? Eventually several arms did lift, but mostly, it seemed to Rachel, out of politeness.

"Okay. Great to see it. Now how many of you are familiar with my *JogThink*, Parts I and II? Video and audio?"

Nothing. Not a murmur from the crowd. Their passivity stung Rachel. Her helplessness made it worse. What this show needed was a stagehand parading back and forth with a placard that beseeched people to "laugh!" "cheer!" "applaud!"

"Fair enough. No matter. They can be purchased online. Let's start with the basics. We're all faced with dilemmas about where to go. Know what I mean?"

This time Henry did not wait for the audience to flaunt its disinterest. He was learning. Whether fast enough, only time would tell.

"So you've got somewhere to go, and it's a long haul to get there. What goes through your mind? Well, if you start out too fast, even though you might be in a hurry, you run the risk of losing steam before you get there. On the other hand, you start too slow, the basic conditions might shift during the journey. Follow me?"

Henry's furrowed-brow gaze methodically swept the audience right to left, like a prison yard searchlight, then back again. Very polished, very professional. But did he notice the fidgety folk turning to each other in dumbstruck exasperation? How could he not? Unless, and this possibility was even more alarming, Henry was stuck in that danger zone wherein he could only do what he always had done, audience be damned.

"Take two," Henry bellowed. Until now, his rhetorical pace was a jogger's, neither rushed nor lazy. "Let me tell you exactly why I'm here and why it's important. My friends, it has to do with time. My time, your time, but most significantly, the precious time all of us have together on planet Earth. Who's counting? Well, we all are."

Rachel felt guardedly hopeful. Henry really was attempting to draw a meaningful link between the recreational act of jogging and the plight of the global environment. Not a soul, she felt certain, would be able to grasp such a flimsy, contrived connection. But Henry's willingness to try was heartening.

From behind the hedge, Rachel had a clean sightline across the stage into the audience. Taking a break from dwelling on Henry, that's where she gazed, out upon the congregation. A flutter of activity midway up the terrace caught her eye. A man with fluffy poodle hair and pink cheeks swiveled to say something to a young woman in a Persian blazer. Who promptly turned to her left to say something to a hunched fellow . . . it was Beibel. Rachel had wondered where the reporter had decided to situate himself. She envied him his detachment.

"See where I'm going with this?" Henry cupped his hand lookout-style above his eyes, and she was back to watching him. A half-smile broke across his face. "Don't see where I'm going? Well, no matter. What does matter is that we all go there together. That, my friends, is the one inviolable rule of the JogThink Experience."

Henry turned abruptly to peer at Rachel. No hiding now. His gaze lingered only long enough to fill her with dread. What? Did he want help? She tried to summon a supportive smile. Before she could manufacture it, he'd turned back to the crowd.

"Let me add, so you don't get the wrong idea, that I often preside over half-day or full-day or, in special cases, multiple-day programs in which I cover several topics and explore them in far more detail. These sessions are designed for groups with goals far more specific and, dare I say, far more easily achieved than yours. Tonight, due to time constraints—hey, there you go. Time, you old devil! Always showing up to spoil the party . . . where was I? Right. Due to time constraints, tonight I need to narrow my focus. Hey, due to time constraints, don't we all?"

Could it be he was finding his stride? You sly fox, Rachel thought. At the very least, Henry seemed to have bought himself, and her, a bit of time.

"Can everyone," he threw open his arms, a Hollywood Moses before the fake Red Sea, "can everyone please stand?"

A gruff catcall rocketed from somewhere in the audience. "What is this, huh? Simon Says?" The man's tone would be familiar to anyone who'd spent time in the right field bleachers.

"Yes! Correct!" Henry brayed. "You got it! Simon Says. Everybody now, Simon says, stand up!"

There'd been indications buried in some of the testimonials on his website credited to satisfied customers identified solely by their titles—"Human Resource Director, Chevron," "Head of Strategic Planning, Allstate Insurance," "Chief Marketing Officer, Deep Ocean Technologies"—that this childish game, darling of pre-K classrooms, somehow factored into Henry's shtick. Wolfram in his disgust had once urged Rachel to watch a YouTube video of Henry allegedly exhorting a pharmaceutical sales audience to stand up and do stupid things. At the time, Rachel shrugged it off. For all she knew, that stuff worked superbly with sales and marketing groups.

Earlier in the week, however, Henry had dropped another reference. It was Wednesday night, and the three of them, Henry, Rachel, and Wolfram, were outside the main cabin about to disperse to their separate quarters. The night sky was cloudless. The infinite speckling of stars, constellations as vivid and easy as in any astronomy textbook, had them all gazing upward, a shared moment of reverence. Rachel had been trying to pin Henry down on exactly what he intended to say to the EarthKare conference. She'd expressed concern that he keep his remarks to a reasonable length. (Privately, she feared that what he had to say of actual relevance might not consume five minutes.) Out beneath the stars, as they all gawked upward in awe, she'd tried once more.

"Your speech," Rachel had sheepishly prodded. "We should probably know something about what's in it. Content-wise?"

"Hey," Henry'd joked, or Rachel had assumed it was a joke. "In a pinch, there's always old, reliable Simon Says."

"Hah."

"Simon says," he'd cooed to Rachel, in what seemed at the time like self-parody, "give Henry a big old hug."

It was Wolfram who complied, smothering Henry from behind.

"Simon says, back the fuck off, Wolfram!"

Thirty-Nine

HENRY BARKED AGAIN, "Simon says. Stand! Now!"

By Beibel's estimate, 10 percent of the audience rose to its feet. Whether they did so in polite compliance or simply for a welcome stretch of the legs was not clear. Either way, 10 percent did not constitute a vote of confidence.

Still, Henry was sticking with his game plan. From what Beibel could discern based on fragmentary Orange Tent hints, the strategy was to employ core facets of the tried-and-true JogTalk while throwing in a concluding twist or two to meet the needs of a brand-new constituency. Henry did aspire to fill the void left by Al Gore's absence. He really did imagine himself transporting the audience to a better place. Sounds good on paper was Beibel's opinion. Journalistically, it would be preferable if Henry managed to pull it off. A report detailing how a second-rate talent blundered in a mission he should never have undertaken in the first place was hardly headline material.

"Hey, gang, come on." The vehemence in Henry's pleading sounded to Beibel a lot like desperation. "I really need y'all to get with the program. Just this once. I know it might seem kinda silly. But so what? Just between you and me," cupping his hand to his mouth, speaking on the QT, "a little silliness never hurt anyone. Sooo . . . I'll it try again. Everybody. Come on. Everybody, on your feet!"

Half of those who'd been standing promptly sat. Soon, the few who remained upright glanced around, saw what was obvious, and slumped back down, making it unanimous.

"Okay, okay," in the spirit of concession, "you win. Forget it. I was just trying . . . well, what does it matter what I was trying? I was hoping we could all do this together. I mean, that is the point of it."

Henry began shifting his weight foot to foot, at first slowly, then picking up speed, like a person in a big hurry to pee. "Homestretch. Promise. Will be brief. No detours. No metaphors. No parables. No analogies. No fluff." Henry sucked in a long, soulful breath. "No jokes."

This edgy little jig, one foot lifting, then the other, again and again, a bit higher each time, appeared involuntary. Of course it was calculated. Everything the guy was doing and saying was calculated. Or damn well should be. Then it hit Beibel, although it hardly made sense. Henry was running in place, like it was Saturday morning exercise class at the Y and boosting the old heart rate was the way to start things off.

Henry accelerated, feet lifting, thighs rising, up down, up down, knees churning like pistons. Perspiration slithered down his chin, darkening his shirt. Panting, gasping, mouth pushed to the mic, breath thudding, thumping.

"Before I go. Want to clarify. One misunderstanding. Critical feature. Of jogging. Is returning. To same place. Where we began. But. But better prepared. For what lies ahead. However, my friends, that's not all."

His cadence double-timed into a vibrant, finger-snapping rhythm. Jauntier lyrics and Beibel could almost imagine the audience jumping up to dance. Dancing in the streets. Now *that* would make for some kind of Hollywood ending.

"In conclusion. We joggers are average folks. You, me, all of us. We hang back. We bide our time. We stay in shape. That's what we do. We joggers need a good reason. A really good reason. A crucial reason. To pick up the pace."

Henry halted, dead in his tracks. He lengthened his arm as if showing off shiny cufflinks, then drew his hand back to his face, flipped the hand over so he was staring at his own wrist, then made an exaggerated demonstration of closely examining his watch. Or where the watch would have been if he had been wearing one.

"We simply cannot," he declared, "proceed at a jogger's trot. Not anymore. It pains me, Henry Marks, to say this. But I say it all the same. Go fast. Our planet is sick, and it may be dying. No time to spare. Pace ourselves? When the clock's winding down? When crunch time is upon us? Uh-uh. Go fast, my friends. If we want to last!"

His knees again began pumping. His pounding feet slammed into overdrive. He thrust a triumphant fist, Olympic victor crossing the finish line, and without another word he bounded up the earthen incline, heels kicking high, elbows knifing back, hands clawing the air. The audience rose to its feet and in unison turned to follow the action, to see what would happen next. At the top of the terrace, Henry's boxy black top hat caught the wind and flew from his skull like the escaping dove in a nightclub magic act.

Forty

THE ABANDONED MICROPHONE beckoned.

Rachel, hustling, got there first.

"Well," she harrumphed, aiming for the put-upon tone of a TV housewife frustrated at hubby's failure to clean out the garage as promised, "that's not exactly what we were expecting."

Within seconds, Wolfram was elbowing her aside, grabbing the slender steel neck of the mic stand. "May I?"

She'd done her best. The conch was his. There was no point in engaging in a wrestling match she was sure to lose. The evening had not gone as she'd hoped nor, interestingly, quite as she'd feared. All she knew for certain was the one indisputable takeaway she'd gathered from the performance. Henry Marks was not the only one with good reason to flee. And maybe that, by way of example, was his advice for her.

Backpedaling, she scurried onto the forest path that led to the cabins. She knew the route well, even in the darkness. A faint glow of moonlight filtered through. The curving path back through the forest to her cabin was a quarter mile at most and sufficiently trampled to be discernible so long as she was careful about it. There was no hurry. Nobody was chasing her. The show had moved on to another act.

Her backup plan was now her main plan. She'd pack her belongings, several changes of casual clothing, a few T-shirts and shorts, two pairs of sneakers, REI hiking boots, the puffy Patagonia she'd owned since grad school, the long floral skirt, partner blouse, and low heels that comprised her fundraising outfit, plus toiletries. It wouldn't take long. At dawn, she would depart. Depart to where? TBD. She could make it on foot to River Road; the route was almost entirely downhill. From there it might be possible to hitchhike to White River or beg a ride from one of the grizzled locals who regularly gathered for coffee at the shabby diner behind the abandoned depot. And then?

At any rate, it would be fitting, aesthetically and otherwise, to set off at dawn. Dawn of a new day. Dawn of a new life. Dawn of a new era.

It did cross her mind that if for some reason Henry circled back toward the cabins—come to think of it, why did he go storming off in that unlikely direction, uphill and deeper into the forest?—they might yet intersect. And wouldn't that be strange? Encountering him, she was as likely to lash out in fury as she was to rush into his arms. Entertaining such radically contradictory options was not the sign of a balanced mind. Another indication why it was high time to go.

Wolfram's opening volley resounded like a thunderclap. Rachel scurried onward, past the igloo-sized boulder, listening, trying not to listen. It was coming. She'd heard it all before, just never amplified, never so near to being real. Desperate measures for desperate times. Bodies on the gears of the machine. They'd argued about methods. They'd argued about agenda. Now the floor was his. Now the audience was his. Would they listen? Would they agree? Would they follow?

Wolfram hammered away, a martial drumbeat. Boom, boom, boomboomboom. Was the concussive power of rap and hip-hop a major influence? Crazy to think it, but she really had no idea how he spent all those gloomy solitary hours.

"Turn the tide!" Wolfram bellowed. "Fire with fire!" he roared. His stridency chilled but did not surprise her. They rarely disagreed on analysis, only on strategy. "Our dead bodies," she heard him rant and prayed that the word "over" had been swallowed by a sound system defect and not deliberately omitted.

Quickening the pace, Rachel stumbled, nearly fell. A knobby root was the culprit. Slow it down, girl. Nobody's after you.

Wolfram's consonants, popped P's, firecracker T's, ricocheted through the forest like pistol shots. Thankfully the racket was only words, and soon she'd be out of shooting range. She kept marching in the direction of calm. Another hundred yards and Wolfram would be reduced to background noise.

Then the night went quiet. Nothing. No words from the loudspeaker. No thudding, no thumping. No microphone static. Just the soft rustle of settled forest. This was strange. She'd not fled that far that fast.

Wolfram, she was quite certain, had just been getting revved up. There was no way he was done, not with all he had to say. He'd not served all these years as her understudy only to keep it succinct upon finally commandeering the mic. Fidel addressing the throng in Havana's Plaza de la Revolucion was Wolfram's model, not Lincoln at Gettysburg.

The silence jolted her. Rachel couldn't ignore it. Something was happening. Taking her chances, she turned back toward the amphitheater. Once again she stumbled. The wind dropped to a whisper. Catching her breath, she heard only her breath.

A swarm of men and women were spilling down from the terrace as she came into the clearing. Were they scrambling to leave? It didn't seem like it. She tried swerving to bypass the sprawl but was blocked by the oncoming surge. Like the coordinated wave of a stealth military assault, folks clamored silently onto the lip of the stage, nobody talking. It was choreography without a soundtrack. Indeed, people seemed to be taking extra care to keep quiet, gesticulating without speaking, carefully shuffling.

Wolfram stood at the microphone, no change from where Rachel had seen him last. His head was arched back, his face tilted upward. Bug-eyed and gawking, his arms hung limp at his side. Rachel tried to recall if she'd ever seen him like this, so stupefied and helpless. She had not.

Forty-One

ONE NIFTY PIECE of stagecraft. That was Beibel's impression of Henry's abrupt exit, all the more remarkable for having seemingly been improvised on the fly. That Henry managed to finagle core aspects of his hackneyed shtick into a program that had nothing whatsoever to do with the laughably trite message he'd made a career out of promulgating was, by any standard, no small achievement. And slapping an exclamation point on the whole shebang by dashing out of sight and thereby leaving the clueless audience with a sneaking suspicion that what had begun as folly was in fact an organic fulfillment of his life's work . . . what can you say? Give the guy credit, not just for trying but for coming darn close.

Audience response was another matter. Upon Henry's exit, the folks seated nearest to Beibel remained inert, dumbfounded, mute. No applause. On the other hand, to be fair, there was no jeering, no protests. No nada. Nobody, it appeared, even knew what had happened. It was the silence of a suburban living room just after the TV movie had ended, a bit too enigmatically for everyone's taste, and the family, husband, wife, children ranging in age from seven to twelve, lingered on the couch without reason to speak, too tired to switch off the lights and head upstairs to bed.

Beibel jotted in his notepad, "Mr. on your fucking marks back for encore? No way, José."

Beibel had briefly considered clapping to stir things up, just one quick flurry to test the waters. Such a gesture might be a bit too first-person for his journalistic style, but it would provide readers, should any materialize, a chance to learn the final result: Did attendees join in the applause or refuse? Initiating the clapping would be tantamount to polling the audience: thumbs up or down?

In the end, Beibel chose not to clap. This affair was not for him to orchestrate. He was, after all, an impartial observer tasked with dispassionately chronicling whatever came to pass. Best to have someone else to step into the void. And Beibel had a pretty good idea who that someone would be.

After the way Wolfram so brusquely dispatched Rachel, Beibel fully expected Wolfram to plunge straight into the breach, fiery rhetoric-wise. Yet his first words were so whispery and timid, Beibel feared the big fellow was suffering stage fright. Beibel couldn't be certain he'd caught the opening words correctly. A most uncharacteristic "Thank y'all for coming" was what it sounded like to Beibel.

Wolfram quickly got a grip. "Fire with fire!" he snarled, launching an incendiary cascade of brutal facts and figures pertaining to climate change, sea levels, biodiversity, carbon capture, deforestation, acidification. "Turn the tide!" "Do or die!" Everything but "win one for the Gipper" to Beibel ear.

Perspiration broke copiously across Wolfram's broad forehead, and he appeared to revel in what drenching sweat conveyed, a hard-working man proud to be working hard. Wolfram jabbed his fist skyward to illustrate a battle cry that Beibel didn't quite catch. It might have had to do with ozone depletion.

For long seconds, Wolfram held that pose, frozen in place with clenched fist extended, as motionless as a street corner mime emulating the perfect stillness of a statue. Beibel got it. Wolfram was Malcolm. He was Che. He was Mandela.

The audience gasped. Beibel gasped. Nobody moved.

There was the Oswald's thrush, posed atop the green-and-gold EarthKare banner that flanked the stage, fluffing its wing feathers like a preening starlet, fearless, unflapped, nodding left, nodding right, gazing down, gazing out, blithely indifferent to the swarming paparazzi. The reputedly reclusive creature struck Beibel as being as comfortably acclimated to human society as a household parrot. Oswald want a cracker!

The amphitheater was hushed. Folks edged silently forward, like parents wary of waking a sleeping baby. As the center stage area became logjammed, people spilled to the sides, quietly seeking a better view. Beibel stayed put. His vantage point remained excellent for his purposes. He could see the bird. He could see the crowd. He could see Wolfram.

Beibel wondered what thoughts must be churning in the big guy's heated brain. Frustration had to be there, tinged as always with paranoia. Would he attempt something rash? Fling a pebble to scare the Oswald away? Beibel recalled a snippet of that first stilted conversation back in White River, some mix-up regarding birds and stones. For now, Wolfram was checkmated. Couldn't happen to a nicer guy.

Beibel scanned the throng for Rachel. Getting a real-time reaction from her would add spice to his reporting. Journalistically, he was still uncertain exactly how to typecast her. Rachel Carson, the *Silent Spring* Cassandra, held some promise, but the biographical pieces really didn't fit. And truthfully, how many readers had ever heard of Rachel Carson? Erin Brockovich checked a number of boxes. There was Jane Fonda, but Beibel needed to aim for a younger audience. Greta Thunberg was certainly environmentalism's current It Girl. Yet comparisons with a prominent teenager had to be were risky. There was no telling what kind of left turns such youngsters might take tomorrow.

Could Rachel have fled? It wasn't impossible. He was aware that she'd been contemplating an exit strategy, and he'd found it kind of endearing that she believed this was a closely guarded personal secret when, in fact, many were aware of her longing to begin a new life. Dorothy had remarked on it to Beibel. Even Humphrey the intern seemed to know about it. And rumors aside, it was reasonable to assume that Rachel, who was only human, and female human at that, would at some point, and possibly quite soon, experience burnout or take emergency measures to avoid it.

Beibel'd last seen her on stage getting elbowed aside as Wolfram brusquely stepped in to relieve her of her duty. She'd looked stunned and fearful and, in Beibel's opinion, in acute need of some TLC. If he were in her shoes . . . and wasn't that a ridiculous thought? For all the hours Beibel'd spent hanging around Rachel, and the diligent effort he'd made to get to know her better, including in ways she might prefer not to be known, she remained a bafflement.

Beibel continued to scan the crowd. The problem was that from his location stuck on the fringe he could not see faces. Beibel thought he spied Rachel halfway down the incline. The woman was Rachel's height with the same fluffed dark hair and dancer's posture. But when the woman rotated sideways, Beibel saw it wasn't her. This lady had chubby cheeks and a downturned mouth, closer to the dour look on Rachel's original book jacket photo. It was a look Beibel now knew to be at least somewhat misleading.

Atop the EarthKare banner, the Oswald seemed to be enjoying himself, taking little stutter-steps up and back along the crossbar like a runway model at Paris Fashion Week. The mesmerized audience pushed closer in a tightening circle. Beibel felt he should probably wedge forward for a better look. He was, after all, no ordinary patron. He was a vested member of the fourth estate and one who might yet enjoy a bright future. Still, he was gun-shy about causing disruption or making noise. Been there, done that.

Beibel thought he spotted her in the quagmire off to the right. Same thick head of tangled hair, same upright posture. Leaning forward to snatch a clearer view, he saw that the figure was a male with a jutting chin and the deep forehead that comes with balding. It struck Beibel that in his brief time knowing her, he'd encountered such varying visual impressions that he wasn't sure which Rachel he was looking for, which he would find. The austere activist of her first book jacket? The bright-eyed adventurer from the second? The handsome lady of newfound purpose adorning the glossy back cover of a yet-to-be-written work, one for which she might require editorial assistance?

A lull fell over the throng. The Oswald, having ceased its playful skittering along the EarthKare crossbar, peered superciliously down at the reverent onlookers as if daring them, any one of them, to make a move. Simon says, Do not budge! Beibel wondered: Did these folks really believe the bird would linger here forever if everyone remained perfectly well-behaved? Was superstition a feature of their philosophy?

The observations and insights were piling up. Time to resume some serious note-taking. Careful to make no noise or sudden movement, Beibel slid his hand into the rear pocket of his trousers. Slowly he extracted the spiral notepad. As he lifted his pen to jot a note, the formerly endangered Oswald, twenty yards away, pivoted on its perch and, with those beady black eyes, launched a lethal dagger of a stare straight his way. Yes, straight at Lenny Beibel. Why'd it do that? You'd have to ask the damn bird.

Forty-Two

RACHEL MANAGED TO snake her way around the outskirts of the mob and was slithering forward for a better look when she spied Beibel, also trying to wedge closer. Watching the reporter's valiant attempt at jotting notes in his silly notepad while getting jostled from every angle, she had to chuckle. He'd get inadvertently poked and bumped. He give up for a few seconds, then go at it again, gamely scratching away. There was something cartoonish about him and now, finally, she could enjoy it.

What Beibel might really need, journalistically, was a happening so memorable that there'd be no need to rely on notes.

Rachel snuck up from behind, careful not to frighten him.

The winds dropped to a whisper. She stood, becalmed. In place of consternation, a delectable stillness. Gone was the drumbeat to get it right. Her overriding wish was for calm, lightness, serenity, peace.

Gently, she lowered her hands upon Beibel's slumped shoulders. Beibel did not squirm or shift or swivel. It was as if he understood. Posture was another of his features that could stand some improvement. Her hands remained resting upon his shoulders, which seemed already a little less slouched.

She would need fortitude going forward. Beibel could be useful, pending modifications. He was, she'd come to realize, predisposed to positive spin. That was a pleasing trait in a man, if not ideal for a reporter.

Atop the EarthKare banner, the Oswald's thrush remained poised like a pop star preening for awestruck fans. How peculiar, Rachel mused, we must appear from the bird's point of view. Large, predatory, hungry mammals gaping in stupefaction as though voyeurism itself satisfied our hunger. Was that behavior rational? Ridiculous? Neither? Both? Large questions, worthy of exploration. Rachel flashed on the idea of resuming her doctoral studies. That could prove most appealing: a college town, a faculty slot, advisor emeritus to the struggle.

For now, she felt no pressing need for instant escape. In fact, it felt soothing to be bunched among the warm bodies of her fellow activists. Lately, she'd been too stressed out to pay it proper heed: Better or worse, rain or shine, sickness and health, these were her people.

She'd stay through the conference's end. As originally slotted, she would deliver the closing remarks. The capsule wrap-up would be easy enough. She'd done it before at many a conference, from Tucson to Toledo. Go forth and multiply. That theme always did the job. Even when the words were vacuous, the phrase managed to ring the bell, invoking the Bible and biology and grassroots organizing. There'd be no need to go grandiose. No need to knock it out of the park. No need, as Henry Marks might say, to be the one to break the tape. The closing remarks would be her swan song. Her farewell would be without fanfare. Quietly into the night was her preferred mode. EarthKare would go on. The struggle would go on. She would go on.

The prospect made her giddy. Soon she'd be free to fly away.

And with no good explanation, not to herself or to him, Rachel Seagrave pressed her dry lips to the salty nape of the bewildered journalist's neck, just below the hairline.

Lenny Beibel shut his eyes. He dared not move.

Forty-Three

IT WAS SAID that Henry Marks kept right on running, faster and faster, until exhaustion overwhelmed him, and over the ensuing days and weeks, his carcass, decaying and decomposing, became part of the wondrous cycle of life, picked on by bald eagles and broad-winged hawks with the gritty morsels left over for ground-dwelling predators, red fox, black bears, and raccoons. The idea of Henry's flesh nourishing the very creatures that his dubious methodology could not rescue made for a nice little wrap-up to the story.

Beibel did not believe it for a minute.

Nor, however, did he care to investigate. Some accounts cry out to be verified or discredited. Others are best left to stew in hearsay and speculation. Beibel felt he'd gathered enough material already to land a publishing deal, assuming he could wrangle the mess into a coherent proposal. It didn't hurt his prospects that, in addition to the inviting topic of environmental collapse, his book would touch on epic clashes (activists vs. industry), archetypal human drama (Wolfram as mad Ahab, Rachel as Joan of Arc), magic realism (the Oswald's miraculous return), and finally, international celebrity.

For at the last minute, Al Gore decided it was possible to make it to the EarthKare conference's closing session. According to Gore's staff, the Nobel Prize winner had always been enthused about addressing the conference, as EarthKare was precisely the kind of gutsy, innovative startup that Gore in his venture capitalist capacity specialized in identifying for beta-stage support. The complication had always been his prohibitively overstuffed calendar.

What changed was not exactly clear. In the telephone notification Rachel received from Gore's chief of staff early on the morning after Henry's disappearance, no mention was made of the 17 million YouTube hits for the posted video of the Oswald's thrush gracefully swooping down to alight upon the EarthKare banner. The Aspen forum at which Gore had been scheduled was evidently able to secure a substitute, freeing the former VP to take a private jet from Colorado. This put him into Lebanon, New Hampshire, the nearest airfield, by 4 p.m. Saturday, in plenty of time to keynote the closing session.

What Vice President Gore said that day in his speech to the reenergized and suddenly spotlighted conclave would be little noted nor long remembered. The horde of print and broadcast stringers who'd flocked north for this assignment uniformly quoted the Nobel winner as declaring that the situation remained urgent and that mankind could not afford to deceive itself into thinking otherwise.

By then, the mercurial thrush had departed to God knows where. Gore made scant reference to it in his prepared remarks. For Beibel's purposes, it mattered only that the former vice president had come through in a pinch, that Rachel was thrilled and delighted (and not just with Gore!), and that Henry Marks had vanished. Could any ending be any more wonderful?

Actually, yes.

Henry, as it turned out, had not expired in the Vermont woods, lovely, dark, and deep as they were. His cagey agent, demonstrating an extraordinary capacity for can-do problem solving, had covertly arranged for a private security swat team wearing night vision goggles to intercept Henry in the forest a quarter mile east of the amphitheater. It was all preplanned.

From there, Henry was escorted to a black Range Rover parked on an overgrown logging road by the west slope of the apple orchard. He was then driven to the Lebanon airfield. A Cessna paid for by Happiness Cruise Lines, sponsor of his upcoming gigs, delivered him to Fort Lauderdale where he was promptly whisked to the Port Everglades pier. It was there, in his luxury guest suite on the eighth deck, while merrily lathering his jaw for an overdue shave, thirty miles out to sea and heading southeast, that Henry first received the news, via an urgent inquiry from an Associated Press reporter on deadline, that the Oswald's Thrush had officially returned to the verdant land of the nonextinct. Did Henry Marks care to comment on this development?

We know these minor details because Henry very cleverly worked them into his opening monologue that night in the first of his two scheduled shows on the Happiness ballroom main stage before an audience gathered to hear the Elton John imitator. Henry was the warm-up. That was the clever concept the cruise ship entertainment booker had in mind— a warm-up act that actually warms people up. Get it?

The news flash about the Oswald gave Henry an opening to deviate from his standard JogTalk. Instead, he elected to recount, with minor embellishment, the topsy-turvy escapades of recent days, his fish-out-of-water involvement with the EarthKare conference, the surprising affinity he'd discovered with central Vermont folkways, the invaluable self-knowledge that resulted, and the unexpected drama that brought it all to a close. Recounting this took longer than Henry had planned. Some of the Happiness audience drifted deck side to have a look at the exquisitely vivid constellations. One jerk registered his discontent by loudly humming "Crocodile Rock."

Henry, savvy veteran, was not obtuse to audience dissatisfaction. "Almost done," he sang, nipping it in the bud. He was thrilled, he told them, to learn that the once-endangered bird was, for the time being, alive and well. He was lucky to have been associated with this heroic recovery and felt only humility that others more knowledgeable than he were giving him credit for forging an important link between the leisure-time habits of humans and Earth's survival.

He had no immediate plans, he assured the audience, to switch careers or amend his lifestyle. Like a newly minted jackpot billionaire who promises to be unaffected by his wildly upgraded financial circumstance, Henry pledged to simply continue his life's work, to remain the same person he'd always been, doing what he loved to do, enlightening audiences, just like this one here tonight, on the valuable insights to be culled from recreational jogging.

Audience impatience was a ticking time bomb, but Henry had one last piece of information he wanted to confide. His agent had contacted him with promising news: A veteran journalist was interested in collaborating on a book project that would combine the essence of the JogThink philosophy with an ardent call for environmental stewardship. Henry could not yet disclose the identity of this journalist, except to say it was a person of considerable talent who enjoyed special access to a key influencer in the green movement, a woman whose name he must also withhold until the scope of her involvement could be formally confirmed.

For there was also the prospect, suggested by his agent who knew him well and rarely steered him wrong, that Henry and this unnamed environmentalist might forge a partnership that could potentially extend across multiple platforms.

All of this, Henry hinted, could prove extremely appealing. When things slowed down. When at last he wasn't moving so fast.

Acknowledgments

MY THANKS TO Gerald Peary, Ann Bartholomew, and Doug Wilhide (again) for their close reading of earlier drafts and helpful suggestions for making the novel stronger. A special thanks to Bill Burleson who got the joke and then applied his sizable editorial acumen toward helping this book, to grab a catchphrase from a highly-regarded motivational speaker, be all that it can be.

About the Author

BOB KATZ IS the author of several books, including the novel *Third and Long*, winner of the Independent Book Publishers Association Popular Fiction award; *Elaine's Circle*, a nonfiction account of a dramatic episode in the rural Alaska classroom of an heroic teacher; the novel *Hot Air*, about a mystical South America revolutionary on a speaking tour of US college campuses; *The Whistleblower*, a nonfiction exploration of a college basketball referee's struggle to keep the game fair; and *EZ and the Intangibles*, a novel for middle readers.

His journalism and commentary have appeared in *The New York Times*, *Los Angeles Times*, *Boston Globe*, *Chicago Tribune*, *Newsweek*, *Mother Jones*, *Newsday*, *Slate*, *Spy*, and many other outlets.

9 7 9 8 9 8 8 7 2 1 3 2 1